Praise fo

"Great stuff. Touches ... Bayley, David Britton and Steve Ayl... ... the splendid originality of this book. Henry Gee is thoughtful, funny, original. And pretty thoroughly mind-expanding in the tradition of Wells, David Lindsay, Stapledon and Clarke. In fact everything you yearn to find in a good contemporary SF novel. Really enjoyed it!"
—SFWA Grandmaster **Michael Moorcock**

"Siege is compelling, grandiose, and breathtaking in its spacetime and its characters are intriguing, personal, and complex....This book of Henry's is going to be high on the charts."
—Greg Laden, scienceblogs.com

"One of the very best books I've ever read."
—Critique.org

"I got so engrossed in it that I could not put it down. Siege of Stars is a very good Sci-Fi novel, in the tradition of Arthur C. Clarke and Ray Bradbury. It spans space and time on a grand scale, but at the same time delves into the questions of what it means to be human. I recommend this book."
—Lee Gimenez, bestselling author of *The Nanotech Murders*

SIEGE OF STARS

Book One of
THE SIGIL TRILOGY

Books by Henry Gee

Fiction

The Sigil Trilogy
1: Siege of Stars
2: Scourge of Stars
3: Rage of Stars

By The Sea
Futures from *Nature* (editor)

Nonfiction

The Beowulf Effect (forthcoming)
The Science of Middle-earth: revised e-book edition (forthcoming)
The Science of Middle-earth
Jacob's Ladder
In Search of Deep Time
Before The Backbone
A Field Guide to Dinosaurs (with Luis V. Rey)
Shaking the Tree (editor)
Rise of the Dragon (editor)

SIEGE OF STARS

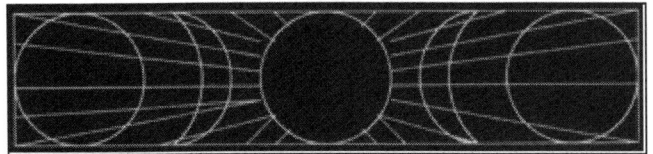

Book One of
THE SIGIL TRILOGY

Henry Gee

ReAnimus Press

Breathing Life into Great Books

ReAnimus Press
1100 Johnson Road #16-143
Golden, CO 80402
www.ReAnimus.com

© 2012 by Henry Gee. All rights reserved.
The rights of Henry Gee to be identified as the author
of this work has been asserted in accordance with the
Copyrights, Designs and Patents Act 1988.
The characters in this novel are not intended to bear
any resemblance to any real persons alive or dead.

Cover art by Clay Hagebusch

ISBN-13: 978-0615691619

First print edition: August, 2012

10 9 8 7 6 5 4 3 2 1

For Karl, who gave his name to a small, destructive and (mercifully) fictional asteroid.

Acknowledgments

The germ of this story—or, rather, two germs—can be found in two SF vignettes I wrote in *Nature*, one pseudonymously. One, called *Et in articulo mortis* (*Nature* **405**, 21; 2000) describes Post-Embryonic Petrosis as an evolutionary response to star-hungry dragons. The other, *Are We Not Men?* (*Nature* **435**, 1286; 2005) reported the emergence of many hitherto-mythical hominids onto the world stage, including Sand Druids and Jive Monkeys. Perhaps ill-advisedly, I thought I'd put the two ideas together in a box and see what came out. The result is as you see.

I offer my thanks to Karl Ziemelis, Andrew Burt, Vonda McIntyre, Ian Watson, Jack Cohen, Brian Clegg, Bruce Goatly, John Gilbey, Richard P. Grant, Heather Corbett Etchevers, Jennifer Rohn, Chris Surridge, Peter Watts and all the residents of the LabLit community forums, and the many others who read various drafts of this book, for their continuing encouragement and comments. David Doughan and Adam Rutherford helped me with my Latin, and Tony Kerstein with my Hebrew.

Chapter 1: Salesman

London, England, Earth, May 1979

Gawan, that sate bi the quene
To the kyng he can enclyne
'I beseche now with sazez sene
This melly mot be mine.'

(Gawain, who sat by the Queen
Towards the King inclined
'I implore you, with a prayer plain
That this fight should be mine.')

Anon. — *Sir Gawain and the Green Knight*

Ruxton Carr knew he'd never forget that rainy Monday when She came into the shop. One reason he remembered (as he later tried to tell himself) was that Mrs T had just got in as Prime Minister. He felt an inner thrill — at just 18, he'd voted for the first time ever, his first general election. Mrs Thatcher supported people like him — young guys who wanted to do things, go places. No way was he going to be a salesman in Khan's Electronics forever. The second, and never mind what happened next, was that She — that's She with a capital 'S' (and not Mrs T, let's make that clear) was not just anyone. She was special. You know that specialness, when you meet someone for the first time and you're convinced you've seen them before? Special, like that.

He was giving this geezer all his Grade-A patter about a Japanese music centre, direct drive turntable, FM like crystal clear, dual auto-reverse decks with Dolby, brushed aluminium fascia, smoked acrylic hood, and a little beyond this punter's financial comfort zone. He had almost succeeded — he was the best salesman in Khan Electronics by far (it was Ruxie's weirdly cat-like yellow eyes against his dark skin, Mr Khan had said) — but that was when She arrived.

Purposeful, she brushed aside the glass door against the heavy weather of Tottenham Court Road, windswept, spattering raindrops all over the shop floor. She was tall, slim, in a tan raincoat with big lapels. Her face was very pale — as pale as he was dark. Her hair was long, intensely black, and completely unkempt. But the main thing was her eyes. Huge, round like an owl's, black as her hair, and looking straight at *him*. She didn't look pleased.

Ruxton panicked at first. Was she a customer storming in with a complaint? He'd served so many people. One after the other, blam blam blam, set and forget. Best salesman in Khan's, remember? But no, if he'd sold *her* something he'd definitely have remembered. Maybe she was complaining for someone else? Husband? Boyfriend? But no, she wasn't carrying anything, a broken radio or whatever, like angry customers usually did. Neither did he feel like he sometimes did when he was caught doing something he shouldn't, like smoking or looking at girlie mags, which was as if they'd found him with his pants down. No—when he looked up and at her the thing that came into his mind was—of all things—skiing. Skiing? He'd never been skiing in his life.

"You've convinced me," said the music-centre man. "I'll take it." Ruxie was brought back to life with a jolt. From behind the oblivious punter the woman's eyes pierced him like lasers.

"Wha…? Oh yes, of course. My colleague will serve you. Rashid? *Rashid*?" Ruxie beckoned at the new boy, who looked as hopeless as he usually did—or was he just stunned that Ruxie would give up a customer for anyone? A sale was a sale. Rashid got the message. He hurried over, all smiles, and led the customer to the till. There was nothing, now, between him and Her. She. Nothing except a display case full of personal stereos. And what she said was…

"What's taking you so long, spaceman?"

"Spaceman…?"

She rolled her eyes and sighed. "Why does this always have to be so difficult? I said, 'what's taking you so long, spaceman?'" And then with one long, pale forefinger she touched his wrist and he felt the world spin.

Chapter 2. Drover

Milky Way Galaxy, Orion Spiral Arm, *c.* 68,700,000 years ago

Mit der Dummheit kämpfen die Götter selbst vergebens
(Against stupidity the Gods themselves struggle in vain.)
Friedrich Schiller — *Jungfrau von Orleans*

"Help me!"

The voice of Roland resounds among the mountainous stars. Merlin stirs from her brooding.

Too slow.

"Wake up, sleepyhead!" comes another cry. "What's the matter with you?" It is Guinever, scintillating past. Merlin can only grunt in answer. She falls in behind.

Roland is a speck of brightness overwhelmed by the Drove. Some have broken loose from the main stream headed for a distant metal-rich nebula, tempted by a distraction closer to hand. It is a red dwarf in the Oort cloud of a nearby yellow sun. The red star is rank with rottenness. No wonder that some of the friskier outliers of the Drove are tempted. No wonder, either, that they drown the bleats of Roland. Pathetic though he is, Merlin thinks, one can hardly blame him.

Space rings with the calls of the Drovers, the gravitic keening of the Drove. Merlin, trying hard to concentrate, ravels space towards the melée. Guinever whips in a few of the more recreant Drove, while trying to console Roland.

"Some of us seem to have to do everything round here," she chides. Merlin broadcasts contrition. She hopes it sounds genuine, given her preoccupation. The problem is bigger than poor Roland. Bigger than all of them.

And it can only get worse.

How can she stop them, forever, and she alone, when, right now, it will take her, and Guinever, and Roland, and whoever else they can rustle up, all their power and concentration to round up a few chancing strays?

Merlin gains on Guinever and Roland and sees that Dante and Elaine have joined the chase. But five of them are too few to corral the swarm now descending on the red dwarf, scattering comet-cloud debris like chaff.

In the end, the five Drovers can only hover, and gather, and wait, as the Drove warps the small star into nothingness, altering the gravitational balance of the space immediately around it.

There is little they can do to alter the flux of debris, now directing itself, slowly at first, towards the G-type dwarf less than two light-years away. The yellow star with that hopeful retinue of silicate-mantled planets, at least one of which has retained warmth and volatiles suitable for the emergence of life — life that must be cherished.

Guinever broadcasts anxiety and regret. Roland is shamefaced, but Guinever's anger is spent. She knows that it's not his fault. Dante is just numbed. He has seen this kind of thing too often, lately, to feel anything more than resignation. Only Elaine cries aloud, to no-one in particular, her howl of anguish causing barely a ripple in the void: "What's wrong with them—and with us?"

Merlin had met the Drove Elders in an Xspace of her own choosing. They wanted her, they said, to feel comfortable. At the appointed coordinates she shimmered into being on a snowy hill-slope. Ahead of her and slightly above was a log cabin built on a platform of massive cut stones.

She was met at the door by a butler who helped her off with her ski-suit and directed her to a great salon. She made the usual vain attempt to rein the mass of long black hair from her face to better admire the view through the floor-to-ceiling picture windows running the length of the left-hand wall. At the far end of the salon, ahead of her, was an imposing fireplace. Logs crackled in the grate.

On either side, two men lounged on worn chesterfields, in the casual-but-smart way that only the truly prosperous and confident can lounge. One of the men looked old but fit, every inch the habitual skier. He rose to greet her, all senatorial smile, Argyll sweater and precisely pressed slacks. He broadcast such command that she felt herself stifling a small stir somewhere behind her ribcage. But she sensed that the real power lay with the balding man with the thick spectacles, conservative suit and dark tie: the man who did not get up, but who remained, frog-like and crumpled, in the other chesterfield.

"Merlin, it is good of you to come," said the standing man. He offered a firm hand and she took it. She hoped her returning grasp didn't give too much away. "I'm Solomon," he said, "and my colleague here is Saturn." The frog-like man smiled and nodded.

Solomon indicated a wing-backed leather chair facing the fire, between the chesterfields. He waved her to sit down, and offered her a drink.

"I took the liberty of choosing for you," he said. "I think you need it, especially after that long walk through the snow." She murmured a thank-you and took the glass. The brown liquid within gave off the intense odor of K-type dwarfs at the sticky end of the main sequence. She downed it in one swallow. Ease coursed through her.

"Islay," said Solomon. "Works every time."

"Thank you, it's..."

"... purely medicinal, I know. I'm afraid we've not brought you here just to admire the view and enjoy a fine malt."

"No, I..."

But Solomon had wandered off to regain his place on his chesterfield and, momentarily, his back was turned.

"No, Merlin, we want to ask you something. A favor."

"Me?"

"Obviously, you."

"But why not Guinever or Roland or Orfeo or Oliver or any of the others?" She regretted her outburst as soon as she'd made it. Solomon paused and turned, ever so slightly, to Saturn, who remained motionless.

"Let's say that you look like the most likely prospect for—well, for what we have in mind. Now then, what's your impression of the Drove, these days?" Merlin paused before answering and looked down at her hands, resting palms-upwards in her lap. The answer seemed so obvious that she wondered whether it was a trick question, but when she looked up, parting the curtain of hair that had fallen across her face as she thought, she saw that both men were looking at her intently, their expressions entirely sincere. Like they really wanted to know.

"It's getting worse with every iteration," she began. "The beasts are more and more—well—frisky. It's all we can do to keep them on track. They are forever veering off to graze on stars or gas or whatever, sometimes parsecs off course, and they just get more defiant. Sometimes I think it's just us, or just bad luck, or if the beasts have learned to try it on, but lately—well—it might sound impertinent, or lame, or..."

"No, go on," reassured Solomon. "We must have no secrets here. You're among friends, Merlin. This isn't an inquisition."

"Oh, well, all right, I'll say it—that no matter how good we are, there just aren't enough of us. I thought we were hard pressed before that—that—well, before Heloise and Beatrice left, and I remember that day well..."

"Don't we all? Terrible."

"But after that, when things were rough, I asked Uther and Enid what things were like when they were younger, and..."

"Your fore-parents, I believe?"

"Yes. And instead of saying that we youngsters never knew when we were born, or some such, they simply sighed and said that we had it very much harder than they ever did. Yes, that's what they said — very much harder."

Her words dropped into a silence relieved only by the crack of a log in the grate. At last, Solomon spoke.

"Thank you, Merlin, for being so candid," he said. "Sad to say, though, you are absolutely right. With every age that passes our numbers dwindle, and my fear — our fear — is that we'll reach the point when we can no longer restrain the Drove. It could be that we've already gone beyond that point." The silence then was as of the chasms beyond dimensionality, before and after the Continuum, seeping in, and which, more than any other single thing, filled the minds of the Drovers with terror.

"But... what then?"

"That, my dear, is a question we all ask. All of us of a certain age, that is. But we never dare answer. You are younger, however. Bolder, perhaps? Maybe you should like to do that for us?" All of a sudden she felt that she was a little girl again, gamboling through the voids, careless as she played on the flukes of her fore-parents' recursive forms, the responsibilities of adulthood not even a smudge on a flawless horizon.

"Well, I suppose, that if we were to go on like this, we'd just—eventually—disappear, and then..."

"And... then?"

"The Drove would just eat, and eat, until they'd consumed... the Universe."

"That's correct. Well done, Merlin. It's often very hard to voice the answer that everyone knows, but nobody wants to articulate."

Despite the fire, she felt a chill in the air grow.

"But, Merlin," Solomon continued, "why in all the dimensions of the Universe should it matter?" He rose and paced before the fire, his hands waving in time with his discourse.

"If, as we believe, the Drove was created as a kind of by-product of the Big Bang—a swirl of knots and eddies in space-time, if you will—why should they not just be left to get on with it? Perhaps they are part of the natural order of the Universe—agents of its death as well as products of its birth? Why should we seek to restrain them, going to such enormous efforts to steer them, to govern if not to hold back their remorselessly entropic progress, to..."

"Life," she said.

Solomon stopped then, and turned towards her.

"Go on, Merlin. Please, go on."

"It's just—well, it's often occurred to me—to all of us, really—why we're doing this at all. Steering the Drove, that is, even though we never speak of it: that there's got to be more, hasn't there? I mean, it's not just about guiding the Drove. It's about choices. Choices about where to steer the Drove, what we can allow the beasts to consume, and what we can't. And maybe I've just got it, but we always keep the Drove well clear of certain main-sequence stars. Stars with planets. Planets that might engender life-forms of baryonic matter."

Solomon looked directly at her: she met his gaze. Solomon's next words were directed not to her, but to Saturn.

"See? I told you she was good."

The implied subterfuge confused her. "Good? Why? What for? It's always seemed obvious — about avoiding planets, and life — so obvious that nobody actually makes the point, it's that obvious... isn't it?"

"Yes, Merlin, quite right. So obvious that almost nobody actually makes the connection. You'd be surprised how few people actually do, you know. Very surprised. In fact, you're the first in your cohort we've met who's done so. But now you've passed that hurdle, you need to ask yourself another question. A deeper one."

"About... life?"

"Yes."

"Well, I guess that if we're letting it grow, making sure that the likeliest stars are not consumed, then it's got something to do with the Drove, to... to..."

She stopped dead. A thought flashed through her mind like an electric arc. "It's all about finding some new life-form to take over. To herd the Drove. Or to manage it, somehow. When... well, for when we've all gone."

The silence was palpable. Solomon strode over to her and crouched down before her, so that she could meet his eyes without her having to look up.

"Not to herd the Drove, Merlin. To destroy it."

"But that's... that's..."

"Yes, I know," said Solomon, "it runs against everything we live for, against everything we know. Some might even call it heresy. But it's more than a matter of our eventual extinction. The fact is that the Drove is increasing. It's a feature of the Universe that's only become clear to us quite recently. Let's just say it's to do with the balance of dark energy and a slow, secular change in Planck's constant. We're not sure how, let alone why. You may not really be aware of it yet, as you can only really deal with it piecemeal, most of the time, given that it's so spread out. It's there, all the same, and it's that, more than anything, that explains why you and the others are having such a tough time of it. We've run some projections—that's Saturn and me, and some of the other elders. And there'll come a time when we'll simply be overwhelmed."

"When? How?"

"Don't be alarmed. It's still long away yet, even accounting for reasonable error. But that's no good reason for not making preparations now. Not just to continue to run the Drove, but to remove it. To remove its threat."

"But what difference will it make, whether the Drove wins out, sooner rather than later?"

"It's a fair point. Of course it probably doesn't matter. But we, the Elders, have conceived an objection to a victory for the Drove that comes too early. Put simply, it's aesthetic. If the Drove wins too soon, it will prevent this iteration of the Continuum reaching... how would one put it?" Solomon turned to Saturn who now made the first of what would be only two spoken contributions to the meeting. His voice, when it came, sounded lively and rounded.

"Its... 'fullness'?"

"Thank you, Saturn, I think that puts it very well. 'Fullness'. And, that being the case, we feel we have a duty to protect nascent life from this eventual threat. And there's another question you should ask. It's the decider, if you like. And that question is this—where did *we* come from?"

For a short spell Merlin was nonplussed. The effect of all these cosmic revelations, dealt at such speed, was one of numbing stupefaction. But realization dawned. She came to herself, seated in a magnificent stillness.

"We came from life, from baryonic matter—from a planet."

"Indeed, Merlin: from some proverbial warm little pond. It's easy to forget that, sometimes, now that we've been transfigured into this dimensionality, imprinted into the fabric of the Continuum. So, when you think about it, that's a good reason for steering the Drove away from planets. One never knows from which puddle the next generation of Drovers might crawl—Drovers that might come to our aid."

"But where, Solomon? Where was this planet of our... birth? And what were we once like?"

"Ah, Merlin, who knows? If there was ever such knowledge, it is now lost. And perhaps it is better so. After all, the planet's star might have gone nova long since. It might even have been in a different Continuum from the one we presently inhabit. There can be no space, now — no time — for regrets. And, in any case, we must move on. Our turn has come to find a species we can raise. But with a difference. This species will not simply continue what we do, though: we must create a race of destroyers."

"But why can't we simply destroy them ourselves?"

Solomon turned to the drinks cabinet behind Saturns's chesterfield, and poured three more shots of Islay. "If I might say so, that you can even conceive of such a question illustrates your maturity," he said. "It shows that you can — how would you put it, Saturn?"

"'Think outside the box?'"

"Exactly so. So, Merlin, to answer you — again, it's largely a matter of aesthetics," he continued, handing round the heavy tumblers — "who wants to be the first to destroy the objects of their life's work, not to mention the work of their entire species? As I said, it's practically a heresy. And even if you overcame that one, how would you go about committing such... such genocide? I mean, practically? The Drove are creatures of a similar order to ourselves — M-dimensional relativistic manifolds, wrinkles in space-time — but much more powerful, if only of trifling intelligence. And our task has always been to nurture, not to kill. The means for destruction must be built into this new generation of creatures, right from the beginning.

"What beats me, frankly, is how they might be destroyed without altering the fundamental connectivity—the topological order, if you will—of the Continuum itself, and perhaps destroying that, too. Throwing the proverbial baby out with the bathwater. I'm afraid that's a circle we Elders have never quite managed to square. A problem for nimbler intellects than ours, perhaps. Cheers!"

Merlin saw, as she lowered her glass, that Solomon and Saturn had lowered theirs, too, and now looked at her, expectantly.

"Why me?"

Silence, for an interval that could have been moments, or millennia. She saw Solomon, and Saturn, and the rest of the room—the chesterfields, the fireplace, the winter landscape—as if they were at some great distance.

"That, Merlin, is the most interesting question of all. And one to which neither myself nor Saturn nor anyone else has any convincing, logical answer. Except to say that we just know it. It's you. Your task. You have to find a way."

"But where? How? How can I even begin?"

"I'm afraid we have little more idea than you do. We'll try—of course, we'll try—to offer us much help and support as we can," said Solomon, "and we do have at least one clue."

"You... do?"

"It's here, now. All around you."

Merlin looked up, imploringly, at Solomon. His expression was warm. Laugh-lines creased the borders of his mouth, softening the hardness of his eyes.

"It's this Xspace, isn't it?"

"Yes, Merlin, it is. Xspaces don't just pop up randomly. They have to have internal coherence. To even exist, an Xspace has to have what you might call a 'back-story'. After all, what explains these chesterfields? This rather nice rug? This entirely splendid 22-year-old scotch? The clothes we're all wearing? This house? Even the view—this... well, this planetary prospect? And, most of all, the forms we now inhabit? They are more real than just illusions, you know.

And the minds of the forms we inhabit? Such engaging clutter! All that stuff about skiing and 'warm little ponds'? Now where did all that come from?" Merlin was now quite unable to decide whether the Elder's question was rhetorical. In any event, she was all wrung out. She decided to let him answer it himself. "From you, Merlin—from *you*. You might not have realized it, but you created this Xspace, and everything in it. Everything. I congratulate—we congratulate you, on your good taste. Especially the scotch."

Merlin had broken through her local credibility barrier. All she could now do was laugh. But this did not appear to be a joke. Solomon wasn't laughing. Neither was Saturn. Her laugh stuttered and stopped.

"But still, why?"

"Look at it this way. It's the way we're made. To be sure, we live most of our lives in a fairly linear way, starting at the beginning, chasing the Drove, and fading out somewhere else, later. But we can do more than that. You know this. We are connected, you and me, and Saturn here, and all your young friends, to much else that is in the Continuum. Past, present—and future. Your Xspace gives us the best clue for your search for a suitable candidate. Your quest, if you will, for life. Really, it can only be a matter of instinct."

Solomon raised his glass. The light of a setting, yellow sun sparkled in its brown depths. "It's just a hunch. To be honest, Merlin, it's the best we have."

Chapter 3. Scholar

Cambridge, England, Earth, January 2021

The mass of men lead lives of quiet desperation.
Henry David Thoreau — *Walden*

"Sorry I'm late! Bike puncture. *You* know."

The young woman breezed into Jack Corstorphine's freezing office, a collision of scarf, hands, long black hair and longer legs, all radiating from a huge, shapeless sweater which at the beginning of its evidently long life might once have been purple. She sat down in the only empty chair, the one farthest from the door, almost but not quite tripping over the three already more than occupied by the bovine rowers from St John's.

Jack, notes in hand, had been just about to open his mouth to introduce today's supervision topic — evidence for culture in the African Middle Stone Age — in part to compensate for the gaping holes in the lectures given by his doctorate supervisor, Professor MacLennane. But when he looked up, the words froze in his mouth. Now that the student had found her seat, she was engaged in a flurry of business, pulling off the sack-like sweater (she had no coat despite the weather) and getting her notes out of an unwieldy market bag, the contents of which were spilling out all over the floor. Amid the usual detritus (why are the interiors of women's bags so shockingly untidy?) Jack noticed the glint of an oversized, tortoiseshell-plastic comb. He noticed that the comb had all its teeth, which was amazing given the density and apparently unconquerable untidiness of hair it plainly had to deal with.

The woman, notes now found, sat up, and as she did so, parted the curtain of hair from her face and smiled. It was the most frank, open smile he'd ever seen, made lovelier by her evident distraction as she fought the long defeat of trying to confine at least some of her hair in a barrette. Now he could see her face, he noticed a bone-white complexion dominated by two big, very round eyes, so brown as to be almost black. Jack was pulled up sharply by their penetrating, judgmental ferocity.

"Jadis Markham?"

"Er... sorry?"

"You're Jadis Markham, aren't you?" Jack couldn't help but smile at her in response to her apparent absent-mindedness. Not that he'd be fooled. Those eyes. Those eyes gave every impression that the disorganized exterior concealed a mind like the proverbial steel trap. She stopped smiling, just then, and her eyes dulled, as if momentarily consulting some deep, interior resource, as if to search for her own name. Having retrieved this information, she smiled again, a flash that filled the room. Just for an instant he felt that he'd been pulled clear from his body and was floating in empty space.

"Yes. That's me. So that makes you Jack Corstorphine, doesn't it? I must have come to the right place. What a relief!"

The cultural innovation of the African Middle Stone Age carried on, as if nothing had happened. Almost.

Then in his second year of a doctorate program ('Models of land use derived from geomorphology and lithic distributions in the British Palaeolithic'), Jack found that teaching undergraduates in small groups not only supplemented their meager instruction from their lecturers, and his own exiguous stipend, but filled, for him, a social void. Jack thought himself shy, but what the world saw in him was tact, reserve and laconic humor. That, and a reasonable capacity for administration, came to the notice of hard-pressed college tutors looking for a safe pair of hands for their charges.

So, without really noticing, Jack spent much of his waking, working life teaching undergraduates. To his surprise he found that he enjoyed it very much, not least because it was the one part of his life in which he was forced to interact with other human beings, not just on the intellectual level, but on any level at all.

Although attached to a college, as all Cambridge students were obliged to be, Jack found few attractions in college life. His fieldwork was by necessity solitary: his laboratory work, hardly less. His real love was the outdoors. He tramped alone, all over England, refining an already intuitive yet sharp sense of landscape, and how human beings (and other people) had shaped it over millennia. He poked into crabbed caves in the bleak limestone of Derbyshire, the foam-flecked Gower peninsula of south Wales, and bluebell-lined Torbay, trying to picture each scene through a Neanderthal's eyes; he scoured the Vale of Pickering beneath the

North York Moors, where some of Britain's earliest stockmen had corralled their cattle. For weeks at a time he'd live rough, fishing by day, camping in potholes or under hedgerows at night, returning to his disapproving landlady in Victoria Road, stinking, bright-eyed and bearded, like an Old-Testament prophet. "I was trying to find out what it must have been like," he would protest, weakly and futilely, as she prodded him (with her broom) towards the bathroom.

This quiet young man who had found most of his need for company satisfied by wind on the fells was, in Cambridge, just beginning to emerge from his shell. He admitted that it was the undergraduates who were responsible for this injection of — what was it? Yes, *life*. In those relatively short periods of the year when the undergraduates were in season, as it were, life was one big whirl, as if the circus had come to town. When they left again, and he — as a graduate student — had to keep on working, all was grey and dull. The fact was that even the dimmest Cambridge undergraduates had a shameless self-assurance that could stand any assault, overcome any challenge. Compared with the general mass of humanity they seemed more focused, more colorful, more alive.

"The African Middle Stone Age was..."

Now, this was something that always amazed him. As soon as he drew himself up to speak, putting on his official 'supervision' voice, they were all attention. This never happened at his old university, where a patina of well-meaning dullness coated all endeavor. What's more, it felt good, as a departmental dogs-body, to be treated as an authority.

Even then, Jack saw that his latest student, Jadis Markham, was just that bit more studious, more attentive, than any of the others. Her initial lateness was her one anomaly. Her assignments were always returned on time, and were always substantially better argued than anyone else's. She had a way of taking every aspect of a problem apart, no matter how woolly it seemed at first; polishing up the parts to reveal the assumptions on which each aspect was based; reducing these, in turn, to their elements; modeling how the aspects should look if put together correctly; and then, just, well... doing it, achieving original insights into questions which (Jack realized in hindsight) had been intractable simply because nobody had seen fit to question their underlying assumptions. On the face of it, what she was doing was simple, just science, in the raw. On the other hand, it was as refreshing as finding a door in a hitherto neglected garden wall which everyone had just walked past, without even noticing that it was there.

"... the Middle Stone Age describes a series of cultures over an enormous period of time..."

The three rowers from St John's scribbled in their notebooks, heads down. Jadis Markham's notebook lay untouched on her lap, as she gazed, apparently unblinking, at Jack, her face in an unnerving frown of concentration, as if she recognized him from somewhere, but couldn't quite place him. Jack tried not to notice—it felt uncomfortable, like she was undressing him, taking off first his clothes, and then his skin, and then unpeeling the muscles from his bones.

"... and some of these cultures were very sophisticated. Surprisingly so, given their antiquity, and that some of the... well, the *toolmakers*... probably weren't human. At least, not in the way we'd understand it today."

And so it went on, week after week, those assignments returned with uncanny perfection, those eyes boring holes into his soul.

His nights were soon spent wondering what Jadis Markham looked like without the shapeless bags of her clothes. By day, he reasoned that any favoritism he showed might be related to the simple fact that Jadis could only ever seem attractive compared with the three cauliflower-eared meatheads that made up the rest of her particular class. He worried that he might have been giving her better marks than the others because she was the sole female in her group, so he tried a scientific control experiment. He asked some of his departmental colleagues who knew none of his students personally to mark their work blind, names removed. Jadis' papers always came out on top.

"A student who actually shows promise? Be still my beating heart," said his supervisor, Professor MacLennane. "This is first-class material, no doubt about that. It shows such clarity of thought, something only too rare nowadays. She could go far. Keep your eye on *her*." Not that Jack had the slightest intention of averting his gaze, but at least, he reasoned, he could appreciate her better without a guilty conscience.

It was only later that it occurred to him that he hadn't told Professor MacLennane that the student who'd turned in this stellar work was female. And this was a blind test. So how did he know?

As soon as his duties as her supervisor were over, Jack asked her for a date.

Chapter 4. Admiral

Xandarga Space Elevator, Earth, *c*. 55,680,000 years ago

Alien they seemed to be
No mortal eye could see
The intimate welding of their later history
Thomas Hardy — *The Convergence of the Twain*

First, the sky froze. And then, it boiled.

Which was a pity, he thought, as all breath was sucked out of him, followed by his guts, and then his brain, and all that just before his skull imploded. The sky had been such a nice color. And the air, so fresh. These were his very last thoughts of all, as his skin peeled away, his limbs were ripped from their sockets, and his eyeballs sublimed into the vacuum. But something inside told him that he was not, in fact, dead.

An absence of pain.

He was not, however, sufficiently conscious to realize that having these thoughts at all was in any way peculiar. Not yet.

Ah, me. She'd always said that the whole expedition had been 'me, me, me,' and he'd have to admit that she'd been right. After all, a couple of *Brontops*-class star destroyers should have been all that was necessary to put down an insurrection of the Slunj in that fractious volume the other side of the Rigel sector. The Slunj being what they were—thin films of loosely aggregated bacteria—were barely organized enough to keep their own bodies together, let alone put up any kind of coherent rebellion.

"Send a couple of gun-boats," the Senior Under-Secretary for Colonial Defense had said, flashing cat-like eyes at him. "The natives respond to that. But don't do any more. If we send too many ships, they'll think we're scared. That their rebellion amounts to any more than a fly that we'd swat, but only if we were really bothered. And, besides, there is such a thing as elegance. Oh, you know, Admiral—economy."

Elegance. Economy. But no, he had to play the Big Boy, and try out his Big-Boys' toys. A small scuffle with the Slunj would be an excellent opportunity to give the 17th Rigel Fleet a much-needed trial in extended battle formation.

All of it.

All those millions of cruisers, each one seventeen kilometers of ceramic ellipsoid terror with three hundred kilolights under the hood, together deploying a quite eye-watering exatonnage of armament.

All those destroyers, too—tens of thousands of them—each one the size of a continent, and for which the term 'destroyer' could be read as wanton understatement.

The hundreds of planet-sized capital ships, each one loaded with rail guns capable of accelerating a nickel-iron asteroid from rest to point-oh-five lights by the time it got to the muzzle, and then dropping it to within five hundred meters of its target from a light-month's distance—and doing this again and again, hundreds of times an hour.

And the jewel in the crown—and his own, personal, fiefdom—the *Sorceror*, a spaceship that looked like a planet in every way, because it was one. With oceans, continents, deserts, forests, atmosphere, and life: yes, a synthetic planet, and all his own, for all that its mantle was a caul of the most muscular machinery that his engineers could contrive—continuum flux generators that would allow trans-spatial velocity of almost half a million light-years per hour.

Anywhere in the Galaxy at the flick of a switch.

Taking with it, of course, a retinue of moon-sized outriders that both illuminated the spaceship (giving a pleasing reality to the old canard of the Sun in orbit about the Earth) as well as toting the kinds of System-Superiority weapons that could turn gas-giants to fog.

And while the 17th Rigel Fleet was one of hundreds of such forces, it marked the pinnacle of Earth's Imperial might, which had been mighty for time immemorial, it seemed, and looked every inch eternal.

What the Senior Under-Secretary for Colonial Defense seemed unable to understand was that fleets need to be deployed, even in times of relative peace. Fleets as complex as the 17th Rigel needed constant testing. All those hundreds of millions of troops couldn't spend all their time just hanging about. And, anyway, who really cared about the messages, psychological or political, that one might send to a few scuts of piratical pond scum?

But there are other things in space besides sentient slime, soon-to-be ex-Admiral Ruxhana Fengen Kraa.

So that was his name, was it? It sounded familiar, of course it did. But also as if the words were freshly minted, their potential yet to be dulled by utterance. His mind directed his tongue to rehearse this new syllabary.

Answer came there none.

In any case, what was all this 'soon-to-be-ex' business? Pulse rose. Body fluids changed their conductivity.

What's that? Panic?

Alarms ripped. Lights pulsed. He woke. Parts of him (he wasn't sure which parts) started to shake. But something else forced him down.

He opened his eyes. The blur, agonizingly bright at first, resolved, pixel-fashion, into a face he thought he'd seen before. But where?

Frustration. Blood surge. Restraint.

"Please be calm, Admiral," said a voice. "You are gravely injured, As yet you are unable to move, owing to the absence of many of your essential parts. To tell the truth, they had to scrape what was left of you off the inside of the escapod. Woof! Twenty-five gees and even the pippiest Admiral is no more than a few blobs of strawberry jam."

Oh, very amusing. Just what the Slunj looked like, even in the peak of health. Poetic justice. "However, all parts necessary will have been supplied, tested and bedded down by the time we get there. You'll be a new man!"

"Get... there? Where?" He was not aware of having made any sound, but the doctor did not seem to think this a problem. She (so she was a she) laughed. The memory of that voice flitted like cheeky shoals through the holes in the ragged net of his mind, and into the void beyond.

"Of course, you won't have known, what with everything that's happened. You're in an autopod. Don't worry. We'll fix you up as soon as we can." The doctor looked distractedly to the side, out of view. Perhaps she was taking a reading from some machinery. Perhaps she was, in fact, an illusion and had vanished completely. It was hard to tell.

"But where?"

"Sorry! Counting stitches. We're on the El: eight thousand kilometers up, falling slowly, arrival Xandarga Station in... well, let's not worry about that yet."

"Earth?"

"Where else? Just lie back and think of Gondwanaland."

Soon-to-be-ex-Admiral Ruxhana Fengen Kraa realized that his homecoming might be sufficiently painful that atomization somewhere the other side of Rigel might have been a wiser choice.

The first sign of trouble had come not long after the fleet regrouped three lights out from the disputed system and started to scan for Slunj. The primary was an M-type dwarf that could offer no more haven than a couple of pallid ice-giants; a scree of disconsolate pebbles; and, close in, an absolute jewel of a blue planet, a little smaller than Earth, currently home to several Discotex colony hives.

The billion-year Discotex civilization was a notable beneficiary of the *Pax Terrestris*, which had all but driven its traditional enemies, the savagely asocial Flux Fiddlers that infested stellar atmospheres, to extinction. But Discotex colonies had since proven vulnerable to Slunj infestation, necessitating the current exemplary show of force.

The interchange hadn't all been one way. Now peaceful and given to exotic collectivist philosophies, the Discotex had learned much in their eons-long conflict. Especially about some of the more imaginative uses of hypertransuranic elements, now incorporated into several of the more assertive armaments of the 17th Rigel and many similar fleets, and whose use had proven decisive in several conflicts that might otherwise have dragged on much longer.

The bottom line was that Earth was indebted to the Discotex. The Senior Under-Secretary should have understood that, too. 'A couple of gunboats,' indeed.

Admiral Ruxhana Fengen Kraa had felt the skin on the back of his neck tingle even as the first messages trickled in—spare, disconnected and puzzling. He should have acted then, on instinct, pulling his immensely powerful, but delicate and (as the Senior Under-Secretary constantly reminded him) very expensive fleet away, away from danger. But no, he had deployed his forces and wasn't going to pull back now. And also because the earliest signs that things might have gone awry piqued his curiosity. They were so odd: he had to find out more.

The first message was less about annihilation than astrogation. An advance battle group of cruisers and destroyers had reported a systematic error. They had, through no fault of their own, ended up of the far side of the system, relative to the main fleet. Doppler ranging confirmed this, but no explanation could be advanced. The continuum flux generators of the vessels concerned were working within 99.9% optimal spec, and, anyway, what could have happened to have affected the whole group simultaneously? It made no sense.

These messages were relayed to the currently favored Bridge of the *Sorceror*, a ginkgo-shaded sun-terrace of a *faux*-ruined lamasery, perched on the edge of a volcanic crater-lake so huge that one could hardly see from one side to the other. Admiral Kraa mused on a sun-lounger, drink in hand, watching some of his younger female staff playing volleyball on the brilliant white beach below. This gentle slide from reality into mildly erotic fantasy was interrupted by a sharp ping from his AI core. The glass fell from his hand and shattered on the terrace.

One flick of the mind and he was in uniform, on the VR Command Deck. It was in uproar. Staff were sweating at their consoles; barking through comms ports and at one another; his younger female staff, now coolly and crisply uniformed, were deep in VR gear, or shuttling glittering icons in 4-D battle maps. There were engineers on the deck in conclave with his officers, huddled over displays. That engineers were present at all on the Command Deck showed that something had gone very wrong. Very wrong indeed.

No sooner was his presence noted than he was assaulted with status updates. He bounced them to his AI core for a shakedown, and this is what he learned: that thirteen minutes after broadcasting their initial inquiry, the advance battle group, all seventy-eight thousand vessels, had disappeared.

Worse, this was not an isolated case. Destruction seemed to be spreading through the fleet like a contagion, affecting ships first in small groups—ships that would flash in and out of existence around the system and then vanish altogether, leaving no more than a smear of atoms and hard radiation.

Small groups became larger groups, until the whole fleet found itself ploughing into a storm-front beyond which the regular laws of the Universe had been suspended. He felt the thrum and screech of rending rock and metal. Standing at the bridge but powerless to command it, Admiral Ruxhana Fengen Kraa queried his AI core. The *Sorceror* was large enough to register and triangulate significant local gravitational anomalies. His AI told him that near-space was full of them—localized gravitational disturbances so intense that the continuum itself had, in places, warped in on itself, enfolding any nearby matter—including his fleet—in shrouds of nothingness. And then, just as suddenly, unfolding, spitting out the pips. It was as if the 17th Rigel was being peppered with rapidly moving black holes, tossed in their wakes as they passed by.

He flipped back to the sun terrace to see the crater-lake in a confusion of spume, noise, and coral grapeshot that raked his flesh like razors. The ground shifted beneath his feet, but he could not move: his feet were so heavy they might have been nailed to the flags. This was, he reflected, unhelpful, as a rogue gravitational pulse was trying to rip his head off.

He must have passed out. Either that, or his AI core did the decent thing, winking him out, squirting what was left of him into an escapod, and blasting its way out of the killing zone. Very few among the six hundred and seventy-three million souls in the 17th Rigel would have had access to such a luxury. But he was the Admiral, and in cases of disaster, whether natural or caused by some almighty hubristic cock-up, somebody had to face the music.

The recovery of soon-to-be-ex-Admiral Ruxhana Fengen Kraa was slow, yet steady. At each stage his local environment appeared to become richer. When he was well enough to sit up in bed and go through some light eye-brain calibration exercises with the doctor, he seemed to be occupying a spare but comfortable room not unlike the rustic beach cabana next to the crater-lake on the *Sorceror*. The keen memory of the loss of his fleet made him wish for some other quarters, less emotionally loaded.

His wish was granted, as soon as he was well enough to walk around on his new legs, if haltingly, and with the help of a frame. His quarters had transmuted to a stateroom straight out of the era of the great Trans-Arcturus luxury spaceliners a few tens of millennia earlier: all cut glass, fluted brass, and plumped-up crimson velvet.

Propping himself up on the back of a mahogany *fauteuil*, he decided to try, once again, the latest exercise the doctor had set him: to navigate the six steps between chair and breakfast bar without support of any kind. Those six steps might have been six light years. About three steps in he'd always had to grasp his walking frame.

Now for it.

One... two (slight wobble, overcome)... three (that frame looked so tempting)... four.... five... and, unbelievably, six. He'd made it to the bar, where he stood, shaking, not daring to move further. He turned to see the doctor, standing in the open door.

"Congratulations," she said.

And that was when Soon-To-Be Ex-Admiral Ruxhana Fengen Kraa realized where he'd seen her face before.

Chapter 5. Candidate

Cambridge, England, Earth, June, 2023

Now, what I want is, Facts.
Charles Dickens—*Hard Times*

Jack Corstorphine needed help. Just how badly he was reluctant to admit even to himself. He knew only too well how a blow to one's self confidence in the final stages of a research degree could destroy everything.

He'd seen for himself, so many times, how research students started with so much ebullience, only to find, more than two years later and within sight of the dreadful midnight watch they called 'writing-up,' that what they had accumulated actually amounted to very little. Drifts of data accumulated with great pain over years vanished like April snow in the first light of critical analysis. Even worse, doctoral candidates, ploughing furrows long and alone, might wake up and realize that they had spent those years asking the wrong questions to begin with; that however good the data they had gathered, there was, in sum, no case to be answered. Or, worse still, that they had, in technical language and with much circumlocution, done something that had been worked out already, but in some other way.

Or, worst of all, that they had simply proved, with certainty and without fear of contradiction, that x equals x.

Department of the Bleeding Obvious.

So much time wasted. And more than wasted. Those self-abasing, self-denying years of energy and youth irretrievable, when careers are built, and they might, like their school friends, already have steady jobs in industry or in the City, with mortgages and some status in life. With partners and families, rather than living like overgrown students in drabness and in debt.

Jack tried to console himself that his problems were not yet terminal, for he could make out patterns in his data — this, the most exciting sensation a scientist can experience. He was simply at a loss to understand how they could be organized.

As a result of his long pilgrimages, he could view a landscape and immediately sense that people had been there, long ago. Jack had gone far beyond looking for traces of buried roads, post-holes, cave hearths and flint *debitage*. More than anyone alive, he could look at the angle of a hill-slope, or the way a river curved in its course, and tell that these things had been shaped by the hand of man, even without any other sign, and even accounting for the titanic forces of climate change that had shaped Britain over the past million years, in which glaciers had come and gone, scrubbing entire ranges of hills from the map and altering the courses of rivers over their whole lengths.

His talent had become so internalized that he could no longer look dispassionately at its products — and that was the nub and heart and whole of the problem. That these things were so he had no doubt — but he had no way of demonstrating, objectively, that the subtle clues he saw were not made by natural forces, unaided. And he'd look a right idiot if his thesis committee asked precisely how he knew that, say, the layout of the caves in Cheddar Gorge could not possibly have been natural, and he'd had no answer ready, save that they just looked like that, because he said so. He'd be laughed off as surely as if he'd said he'd discovered Atlantis.

What he needed was some formal way of comparing his intuitions of ancient human presence in one place, with those inspired by somewhere else, and then contrasting both of these with what nature would have created, unaided. He needed a system that would corral the patterns thrown up by his gut reaction, to domesticate them, to force them to make sense. But quantifying his intuitions? How do you quantify a riverbend, or the feeling that a hilltop should be here, rather than somewhere else? You might as well try to lasso the clouds. Despite much research and earnest questions of statisticians, no ready method existed — it was all too vague. He had neither the means nor (he admitted to himself, ruefully) the ability to derive such a technique himself.

Yet without such a key he could go no further. In his mind, he could see his thesis: he was so desperate that he could almost taste his thesis, but a barrier at once so intangible and yet so impassable stood between him and completion.

And then there was Jadis. She had just completed her finals (a starred first, naturally) and stayed on in

Cambridge to help him out. When he asked her if she had a home to go to she was strangely vague. If pressed, she'd say that she loved him. If pressed further she'd only say that she was busily looking for a home for the both of them, burying her nose into the property-for-rent pages of the local paper and changing the subject.

"You know, Jack, you silly man, you work too hard. Fancy a holiday?" she'd say with apparent artlessness. A holiday? *Now*?

"Yes. In the mountains. I know you like mountains." Her black eyes shone with mischief under the curtain of her hair.

"Mountains?"

"Precisely. Mountains. I know I'll never get you to lie on a beach. Not in the state you're in. And you've been looking at the same old mountains for so long you might as well look at some different ones."

Reluctantly, Jack had to agree. He'd been working so hard and so long that perhaps he needed a break, a chance to refocus. He thought—no, he desperately hoped—that inspiration might strike if he took his mind off things a little.

"Let's go to France," he said, brightening. "Look at the Alps, or the Pyrenees. We could drive there in the Field Vehicle." Jadis smiled and threw her arms around him. They were both thinking of Jack's battered Peugeot 205, crammed with camping gear, in which he'd clocked up so many miles. "I knew I could talk you round," she said, "but I never dreamed you'd be such a pushover."

At least he'd be doing something, rather than just sitting here in a funk, boxed in.

Chapter 6. Rookie

Xandarga Station, Earth, *c.* 55,680,000 years ago

Earth hath not anything to show more fair:
Dull would he be of soul who could pass by
A sight so touching in its majesty
William Worsdworth — *Upon Westminster Bridge*

Xandarga Station!
What more can be said about this most Imperial of ports, this hub, this hubbub, this stew of a million stars? This ancient of days, this eternal now, this gateway to riches, this chasm of despair? Yet there is something about Xandarga Station that eludes expression. Tourist guides do not capture it, no more than the memories of that uncle who went there on business and returned with more than just a sale; the sister, from a school trip, inarticulate with excitement; the silences of that elder brother, crackling with anger and shame.

Clearly, one's first impressions of Xandarga Station would be as imperfectly recalled as a first kiss. Not that naval cadet Ruxhana Fengen Kraa, from the insignificant East-Gondwana prairie town of Green River, had had any experience of these things. Any more than his best friend, Ko Handor Raelle, who claimed he was 'at it,' with all the most luscious girls in their class.

"Will ya look at the dugs on that!" he'd exclaim, from their after-school perch at Ma Belle's Bar and Grill on Riversleigh and Main, whenever one of their classmates hove into view, amid a giggling coop of similarly lush-pelted beauties. Ruxie thought every one of them was just lovely, but said nothing. The thought of facing one alone made his mouth dry. That the girls simply smiled and prinked away, if they reacted in any way at all, convinced Ruxie that Ko was full of it, and probably as clueless about girls, sex, and life in general, as he was. But Ruxie knew better than challenge Ko himself. Full of it he may have been, but Ko was a lot bigger than he was.

Deficient in such life-affirming experiences — though adept at roping dogies on his mother's indrico ranch on the outskirts of Green River — Ruxie decided that whereas experience was invaluable, the only way to acquire it was to live it. In the meantime, though, knowledge was power. He decided to find out as much about Xandarga Station has he could.

Or, rather, his mother decided for him. Morzin Kraa Tzalaké found that the best way to fight the powerlessness she felt at the departure of her youngest kit was to arm him against the future, not to cower from it. So at their good-byes at Green River airport she thrust a slate into his hands.

"Aw, Ma — what's this? You shouldn't have!"

"It's a long journey, Ruxie. Lots of change-overs." She glanced towards Ko, eyes sharp with disapproval. He was trying to eye up some porn on the top shelf of a nearby newsstand. "*You'll* want something good to read, at least." A peck on the cheek, and then she turned and walked away down the concourse.

The slate was loaded with an autodidact that told him everything he could want to know about the Imperial Capital, in the form of a story blended from a range of sources. The four long flights and interminable hangings-around between were eased by his mother's parting gift. He was so enthralled that he'd tried to read some of it to Ko, but after a while his friend didn't even try to fake his enthusiasm, so Ruxie was left alone.

He learned under *Thrilling Tales of Tethyan Thunder* that as recently as two hundred and eighteen thousand years ago, Xandarga Station had been a sleepy fishing port on the southern Tethys shoreline, a remote outpost between ocean and jungle, home to a small fleet of brave sea-dragon slayers. These legendary heroes would ride out, in open canoes, into the open Tethys, and chase down basilosaurs — each one thirty meters of coiling hatred — on their migrations. Actually, Ko had been quite interested in that part, having torn his eyes away from *Thrust* magazine for ten whole seconds to gaze at Ruxie in wonder.

"You don't say?" he exclaimed. "That's seriously amazing!" And, just then, he'd meant it.

Further down, *Tethyan Thunder* graded into the terser *Xandarga Chronicles*, which told how engineers first came to the Xandarga Coast and decided that it would be the ideal location for the Earth's first space elevator. Three more had since been built on Earth and on countless moons and planets, yet as the Xandarga Station elevator was the first, it was known simply as the Elevator, or just the El.

The effect of the El on the local economy was practically instantaneous. A mere three hundred years later, what had been a gaggle of brushwood hovels on the edge of nowhere had been transformed into the center of the known Universe.

Simply as a city, Xandarga Station was vast. In The *Dzunghar Heren Vú Xandarga Backgrounder* Ruxie read of the miles of naval dockyards, regular dockyards, trading go-downs, meat-packers and stockyards. Indeed, Ruxie already knew, from parental conversations he'd overheard when he was meant to have been asleep, that Xandarga Station was the trailhead for several large indrico drives, much more profitable than anything that distant East Gondwana could offer. His mother's father, when he was alive, would recount tales of those great drives to Ruxie and his sisters. Grandpa had been an indrico driver in the Southern Tethys in his youth, and enthralled the kits with tales of campfires, and comradeship, battles with giant mesonychian land-sharks, and, most of all, the thrill of riding a lambda alongside a ten-mile-long herd of the indricos themselves: those snorting meat-mountains, fifty tons apiece, stretching back into a smoky haze.

The first traders and ranchers brought their families to join them. So Ruxie read (in extracts from *Rags and Riches, Runagates and Refugees in the Imperial City*) of the barrios; the vistas of suburban dullness; the kitch palaces of the merchant princes. And of the various *quartiers* that were homes-from-home to a bewildering variety of exotics. Two of many stuck in Ruxie's mind. One was Bedrock, where what looked like the buildings were in fact the residents, the silicon- and germanium-based Flintsiders, who lived on rocky planets very much larger than the Earth. The other was Sulfaville, a domed, black hemisphere whose residents were ultra-extremophile collectives which, when they came out, did so only in exquisite little carriages, each no bigger than a canteloupe. The spherical cabs matched the shiny blackness of the suburb whence they came, but their wheels and exterior furnishings were made of magnesium-titanium alloy, and they were drawn by outsized clockwork praying mantids. What the carriages — and Sulfaville itself — looked like on the inside was harder to imagine, given that the residents evolved in the super-heated, pressurized atmospheres of star-grazing gas giants.

Wherever traders turn a profit, the taxman is sure to follow, so perhaps inevitably (according to selections from *Honeytrap: The Reign of Raedwald XIX 'Star-Slayer' and The Making of the Imperium*), Xandarga Station became the administrative and financial capital of the Earth, and, by extension, the Galaxy. Ruxie read about the calculating spires of the financial district and, at the city's heart, the cluster of museums housing treasures from a million planets. Ruxie thrilled at the thought of visiting the Institute of Galactic History with its displays of artefacts from of the earliest known civilization in the Universe, discovered just fifty years earlier in the Fomalhaut Sector by the great archeologist Thrangona Mir Gharaan, and believed to be more than eleven billion years old.

And Ruxie simply slavered at the thought of the Natural History Museum, the only place in the Galaxy (apart from Taniquetil itself) large enough to display a life-sized Taniquetilian tesseractrix. That was almost the last time he'd tried to interest Ko, whose eyes had grown to the size of saucers at the centerfold of *Raunch* magazine. Ruxie caught a harshly lit confusion of bare arms and legs and tried not to look.

Second in the league table of Interesting Facts about Xandarga Station with which Ruxie tried to interest Ko was the House of the Imperial Assembly. Designed as an echo and a mirror to the Galaxy it ruled, the building was an oblate spheroid, eight kilometers in diameter, whose mirror-smooth surface was spun of magnetically suspended metallic hydrogen beneath a nanocarbon monolayer. The pressures generated by this extremely thin but relentlessly dynamic surface supported the entire building from collapse with a minimum of internal spars, as well as generating much of its power by induction. There could be neither doors nor windows. Delegates arrived and left by transspatial gateways from all over the Galaxy, as well as in the City itself. The structure floated in mid-air, five hundred meters above water of the harbor, reflecting the great city in on itself. But the most remarkable reflection came from the source of Xandarga Station's being, its *raison d'être*, the El itself.

The El rose just outside the City, to landward. The stately pyramid at its root, itself the size of a large town, sprouted at its summit a city-block-sized bundle of hyperfilament columns. The structure was, indeed, square in section, and running up each one of its sides were sixteen tracks—eight internally, eight on the outer surface, sixty-four in total—along which pods of various sizes were constantly running up and down. Those descending were swallowed up by the pyramid. Those ascending were the ones that really caught the eye, and visitors who witnessed the spectacle for the first time could not help but try to follow the cars as they slid skywards to the zenith point. Ruxie's autodidact recounted those apocryphal tales of people gazing upwards and so enthralled that they just kept on gazing, even after they'd fallen over backwards.

Ruxie and Ko had seen the El all their lives as a white line that coursed along the sky to the westward by day, a thin necklace of jewelled lights at night. But nothing matched seeing it close-up. The plane that ferried Ruxie and Ko on their final hop was small and flew low over the city, and it was night. Ruxie, worn from reading and wonderment, had put away his slate, and dozed off. He woke an hour later, sore and cramped. Ko was sprawled next to him, snoring, tongue lolling. Ruxie unbuckled his seatbelt and rose to stretch as best he could. That's when he caught a glimpse of the view through the porthole.

"Hey, Ko..." he nudged his neighbor. "Come look!" Through the porthole, Ruxie's first impression was that they were at the bottom of an enormous, shallow bowl, with lights stretching as far as his eyes could see. The El, when it came into view, was so vast it seemed to distort perspective itself. The plane banked as it turned for the airport, and they saw the shining curvature of the Assembly Building, the curving streak of the El reflected in its surface. The boys, poised like storks to peer outwards and upwards to drink in as much of the view as they could through the needle's-eye of the porthole, were jolted, off-balance.

A bell pinged: a stewardess told them to resume their seats for landing. The undercarriage ground its way outwards. In the minds of both boys was that, if they passed their basic training, they would be doing more than gazing at the El. They would be riding it — to the stars.

Chapter 7. Lovers

Cambridge, England, Earth, October, 2024

No definition had spoken of the landscape-gardener as of the poet; yet it seemed to my friend that the creation of the landscape-garden offered the proper Muse the most magnificent of opportunities.
Edgar Allan Poe — *The Domain of Arnheim*

It was a one-bedroom Victorian garden flat in Chesterton, which they were paying for from a year's extension of Jack's doctorate grant, extra supervisions, and a few odd research jobs that Jadis was doing for Professor MacLennane (who'd taken a proprietorial interest in both of them) on the pretext of her studying for a Masters while Jack finished his thesis — a prospect that seemed almost in his grasp, but forever just beyond his reach.

The flat was dark and grubby, but sound and tolerably dry; the central heating worked at least some of the time; and a pot of paint on a summer Sunday afternoon always works wonders, even were one not to be distracted by trying to paint each other instead of the kitchen ceiling. In any case, Jack — who was otherwise never more content than when sleeping rough under a hedge — said he'd be pleased to have a base where he could think and work in peace and quiet, and where they could at least be together without prying landladies or college domestics.

It also had a delightful postage-stamp of a garden: hardly forty feet by twenty, but surrounded entirely by a high wall, and, being north-east facing, made an evening sun-trap of the high, back wall. At the bottom of the garden was a knee-high raised bed that ran its entire width, restrained by a wall of reclaimed bricks, and in which some unidentifiable species of ornamental acacia grew over an unkempt understory of broom, rosemary and lavender. You could crawl right inside, under the bushes, and make a hideout on a carpet of herbs and the crusts of dead leaves, where nobody could find you. It baked in the Sun during the day, unleashing a torrent of fragrance, and even after dark, the old brick wall behind would radiate the accumulated heat well into the early hours — warmth that the bushes would then trap, creating a Mediterranean microclimate.

In the evenings of that first, hot summer, Jadis and Jack would burrow into the bushes — they called it the Nest — and might not emerge until morning — their own private Eden. Jack remembered one chilly dawn awaking in the Nest to find them both slick with dew. A spider had spun draglines across Jadis' pale face, trapping drops of moisture that made a spangled net for the twining, leaf-adorned strands of her hair. Each of her long, dark lashes was crowned with a tiny pearl, just as if she were a sleeping fairy queen. For all that he was aching, wet and blue with cold, Jack remembered it as a moment when his heart sang.

And as for supervisions, ever since his best student had become his partner he'd seen very few sparks of talent, or even (it has to be said) of much intelligence. The one exception was a dashing and almost unbearably cocky first-year called Avi Malkeinu, who was Israeli and knew all about Mount Carmel, famous for its honeycomb of caves rich in Neanderthal and modern human remains. Avi had poked around them, boy and man, civilian and soldier, and had some outrageous ideas about the extent and depth of human and Neanderthal occupation in his country—outrageous to all except Jack, who learned as least as much from Avi as Avi did from him.

Avi's openness, candor and easygoing nature made something that happened to Jack one day in late September, when Cambridge baked in the last, fiery gasps of Summer, all the more disturbing. He was visited in his office by two rather shifty-looking characters, claiming to represent some student organization or another, who advised him that he shouldn't be teaching Avi Malkeinu. He'd served in the Israeli Defense Forces, they said, and was, no doubt, an Agent of Zionist Oppression. In response, Jack did something that he almost never did. He got angry. Alarmingly, consumingly angry, so that he shed the shy, quiet academic that he tended to be while in Cambridge, and became the wiry and piratical ranger that he was in the field. He listened quietly to what his visitors had to say, and then, still without meeting their gaze, invited them, just as quietly, to go fuck themselves. When they began to remonstrate, he rose from his chair like a thunderhead over the plains.

"Listen, I thought I *told* you to *fuck off,*" he said, as calmly as his sternly suppressed violence would allow, "and if I see either of you little shits again—or if you harass my friends—I'll fucking rip your fucking bastard heads off and fucking stick them on fucking poles. Understand? Now piss off."

The two took flight and never came back. For ten minutes Jack remained his chair, his heart racing, his body shaking. He didn't think he'd had it in him. He'd normally do anything to avoid conflict, and immediately began to worry that there might be repercussions. But what began to dominate his mind, half an hour later, as he walked home through the searing streets, clouds bubbling above him as if to mirror his mood, was that he'd heard spiteful rubbish like that before, from people in his own department, especially the social anthropologists: and those archeologists who read the past not as it was, but through the lenses of current political preoccupation—and yet had the gall to call themselves 'scientists'.

Neo-archeologists, processual archeologists, feminist archeologists, Marxist archeologists, *post*-fucking-processual archeologists, for God's sake, not to mention those idiots, quite often obscenely obese women from Berkeley or Pasadena, who climbed to the top of *tels*, stripped off and jiggled their leviathantine tits about for the benefit of some right-on Mother Goddess—as if (and this was the part he found *really* offensive) *as if* this charade had anything whatsoever to do with what prehistoric people actually believed or did.

And there were people in his department who actually took that bilge seriously — the same people who'd cheerfully scorn a kitsch Hawai'ian hotel *luau* as having as much connection with authentic Polynesian culture as Mickey Mouse had with *Mus musculus*, simply because it was a product of capitalist colonialism. No, he thought. Prehistory is forged on the ground, not by political posturing, and it was people like Avi Malkeinu — open-minded people, people only interested in telling it as he saw it — who had the best chance of making progress without prejudice. And they were damning him not for his science but because of his origins and national obligations. What dismal, hypocritical crap. No wonder, Jack thought, that he'd spent so much time in the field, away from such pseudery.

But as he got closer to home, and began to calm down, he realized that he was close to being a pseud himself. Processual-and-whatever archeology had, at least, been forged in the field as much as his own landscape-based approach, as ways and means to get to grips with patterns seen in data, patterns caused by the interaction of man and nature. But as yet he still had no way of interpreting the patterns he saw. He had to find something soon. He had to. To vindicate people like Avi Malkeinu. To vindicate Jadis' faith in him. To vindicate himself.

Still, there might be something, just one little thing, a tiny gleam of hope. They'd been on their holiday, driving straight down through France, camping under hedges and in fields or just sleeping in the car. When they got almost in sight of the Pyrenees—in fact, not long after they'd crossed the Loire—Jack felt the hairs on the back of his neck tingle. It was the landscape. It sang to him in a way that the vales and scarps of England never did. But the more he thought about it, the more frustrated he became—there was something important in the French landscape, but he couldn't quite work out what it was. He resolved to go back, chase it down, and soon.

Jadis, too, had had a rotten day, running errands for Professor MacLennane that meant scurrying to and from the University Library for books that didn't exist, when she was quite sure that they did; or if they did exist, were on shelves on the other side of the building; for papers which she wasn't allowed to see, even though she'd phoned ahead and received cast-iron assurances that they would be made available. It didn't help that the library was as hot as an oven, and that she was getting a headache. Making it worse was a general niggle about Jack. It was about time, she thought, that Jack made some headway with his doctorate, because only then did she feel that she could get serious about her own. The plan was that when Jack was within hailing distance of his Ph.D., he could apply for a postdoctoral fellowship, and when he'd secured that, she'd become his research student. But until Jack had written up, they were stuck in a holding pattern.

She did wonder—had wondered—whether she mightn't strike out on her own. She had the first-class degree, so she'd have the pick of doctorate places. And it wasn't as if she hadn't had offers from elsewhere.

Two things held her back. The first was Professor MacLennane, who advised her to wait. Something will turn up, he said. He was chasing a big and juicy grant, he said. Any day now, he said. She'd kick herself if she jumped ship now, he warned.

Second, and perhaps most importantly, she found herself reluctant to leave Jack to stew on his own. Quite plainly, he needed her. More to the point, she needed him. She loved him, more than anything. Oh, yes, she'd tried to be rational about such things. After all (she told herself) love was just a few hormones whizzing around in the sorry bag of chemicals from which human beings are made. However, the fact remained, that no matter how hard she tried, she couldn't clearly remember any previous existence for herself, alone, before she'd met Jack. She remembered coalescing, somehow, in Jack's office, light as thistledown. Memories of an earlier life were fragmentary, enigmatic, as if the effect of her first meeting Jack was to purge them, leaving almost no trace. She could only retrieve a few scattered shreds—the peaty scent of scotch whisky; a fantastic, futuristic city at night under an endless star-spattered sky; the taste of a fish grilled in palm leaves on a tropical beach. Family holidays, maybe? Further introspection was no use. It was Jack who made her existence concrete, even meaningful, and even more that—it was Jack that made her conscious of her own, raw physicality. If Jack weren't around, she felt that she'd simply float away, as fragile and translucent as a soap bubble, and vanish into nothingness.

She arrived home moments after Jack. As she kicked off her sandals she saw his hiking boots and socks cast off in the hall, still warm; his bag on the kitchen table, papers pouring from it like the innards of a partially eviscerated dogfish. She found him where she knew he would be, in the Nest.

"Wine?" he offered, barefoot, holding out a full glass of off-license Merlot as she sat down next to him on the wall of the raised bed, beneath the lavender and rosemary, fragrant from the day's heat.

"Nicest thing anyone's said to me all day," she replied, taking a generous swig. "Correction," she noted, looking up, her eyes sharp, her lips stained with red, a rivulet running down her chin. "I'm sure you said something even nicer to me this morning."

"I did?" Whatever clouds had gathered over him were beginning to dissipate. Responding, she warmed to him and came closer, sitting on the ledge between his legs, leaning back against his chest, completely enfolded by his arms.

"Yes, you silly man. You said"—she began to laugh—"you said that tonight we really must have a brainstorm."

"Oh, that," he said. "I'd rather pour you some more wine," which he did. Then he put down the bottle and stroked her unfastening hair.

"…and, you said that after the brainstorm, that I really needed what you called 'a thorough seeing-to.'"

"I said that? Sounds most uncouth. Not like me at all. Are you sure that was me?" He ran his fingers down her throat, unbuttoned her blouse, and let his hands steal lightly over her skin. She shivered.

"Yes, of course it was you," she laughed. She felt as warm as the wine as she reached her arms above her and pulled his face down to hers.

"Nope. Can't have been me," he said. "Now, if it were me, I'd have said you needed a good seeing-to before the brainstorm. Nothing like a good seeing-to, you know, for clearing the brain."

"Well, as it is you, and that's your view, Professor," she said, "why don't we…?"

But before they could say or do anything else, the clouds broke with a deafening crash, and within seconds they were as drenched as if God had emptied his bathwater on their garden.

They sat in the warm rain on the edge of the raised flowerbed, her head under his chin. He ruffled her damp hair while continuing to unbutton her, while she luxuriated in his minute attention. They both undressed and let the warm rain course over their bodies. She rose, turned as if she were a dancing sprite in the dawn of the world, rain splashing and glancing and making sparks in all directions as it ricocheted from her glistening body, her hair swinging in lazy streamers. She straddled him, feeling him deep and smooth within her, as with one hand he traced the rivulets arcing down the valley of her spine.

As they moved, they kissed again, their lips meeting and parting, meeting and parting, through the rain curtain, in a butterfly dance. After a minute or two he rose and, with her legs still wrapped around his waist, picked her up, turned, and, sliding out of her, placed her inside the Nest on a deep carpet of leaves still dry and warm, the foliage above protecting it from the worst of the downpour. She lay almost buried in leaves, limbs spread, eyes burning in a soft glow. But before he could scramble into the Nest and take her again, she laughed skittishly and flipped over on to her knees and elbows, thrusting her leaf-strewn backside at him like a cat on heat, waving it from side to side like a flag. He moved in towards her, feeling the irresistible softness of the backs of her thighs against his groin, her swollen, pitted warmth between. He stroked the curves of her hips, brushing the leaves away; traced the dips of her lower back, and sliding into her as deeply and as fully as he could — and with such sudden ferocity that he lifted her knees, for an instant, clear of the ground.

Waves of electric shock coursed through her. She needed him now, in the eternal now, with a savage, inhuman craving. She had decided that what she wanted most of all, right now, was to be fucked: mechanically, forcefully, to have done, and bring this never-ending business with Jack's thesis to a head. She could tell from the way that Jack was throwing himself into her with such violence that something had irked him, too — perhaps even stung him into a kind of remorse that demanded action, some kind of closure. But even after all that, she was beginning to experience the first waves of a slow burn which, if he kept up this relentless, kinetic bombardment, would lead to her own longed-for release. She forgot about the thesis, about the inaction, about her own academic holding pattern, and when at length he came, in a thunderous spasm, she felt as if he had filled every crevice of her body and being. With his last, fitful gasps she found herself panting for breath, shaking from head to toe, her soul dissolved, her body a husk like these dead leaves, collapsing, and as she did so, she felt him draw out of her, a sensation both unbearably joyous and excruciatingly painful, all mixed together.

They lay in each others' arms, soaking, exhausted and covered by wet leaves, filled with a buzz and a flood of rapture, awed by their own animality. He wrapped her in his arms, and, as the storm passed overhead, she felt herself doze slightly. It was dusk when she woke. "Come on," he said, "Time for that brainstorm."

She could hardly meet his eyes as they made the few steps to the kitchen door and went inside. He made a big bowl of pasta (they were now very hungry indeed) while she showered. The well-behaved and domesticated shower jets were a balm after the screaming wildness of the rain, warming and absolving her, and sending the last of the leaves and dirt down the drain.

After a supper during which they had hardly spoken they sat on either side of the kitchen table with Jack's papers, in an atmosphere of brittle nervousness. Their clothes, trashed, were shoved into the corner, waiting for a trip to the launderette. Jack had put on a long, white bathrobe embossed with the legend 'Property of the Fairbanks Marriott,' over faded grey tracksuit bottoms. Jadis, her hair scraped back severely and tied in a long plait, wore nothing but her horrible, shapeless once-purple jersey, now so stretched and vast that it came down below her knees, its sleeves so long that she'd had to roll them in great puffs wedged above her elbows. But for all this informality their conversation was as stilted and as starchy as a job interview going badly, when both parties find nothing to say to fill the yawning pauses.

As they discussed how to organize Jack's data, Jack longed to come round to her side of the table. Jadis, for her part, wanted his arms, his touch, and most of all that he should wrap her up like a baby, like a Christmas parcel and — well — to make everything all right. But each was too scared to move. There was something about the moment — this moment — on which they both felt the world and the cosmos would turn. A single distraction, however small, and the moment would be lost, irretrievably.

So they bounced ideas to one another like the sexless talking heads that scientists are supposed to be: Jack, with his icily blue eyes explaining his intuitions, Jadis with her coal-black gaze dissecting them with cold logic, shuffling them, probing them, parrying, throwing them back. Their language was framed in the cool tones of null hypotheses, falsifiability, significance levels, distribution-free nonparametric tests; of circularity, particularity and applicability.

It seemed to Jadis that the tables had been turned. She had become the teacher, he the pupil. Jack felt the same, and with that, the relief of responsibility shared, of not having to do everything as he'd always done, on his own.

But what neither quite realized was that their dispassionate discourse was turning into a lovers' exchange. As they came to see a shared picture of what Jack's course of action should be, their spoken utterances grew shorter, as they started to complete each other's sentences. Cold eyes were animated, hands waved. Jadis, still talking, rose to put the kettle on; Jack, to finish the drying up. They stood next to each other, at the sink, in their baggy clothes, arguing with force — but no animosity — over the details of what was beginning, almost, to look like a strategy.

A part of Jack that had detached from the argument looked face on at Jadis in pure wonderment. But Jadis was distracted, in full flow — about metadata, integration and probability distributions — that he daren't stop her and just tell her that he loved her. He didn't want to spoil it: even to touch her, to brush past her by accident, might break the flow of her argument. Even under that horrible sack she loved to wear around the house (and which he'd sworn she was wearing when they'd first met, although she always denied it), he could tell she was as taut as a string. She had to work it out of her system, for both of them.

But then, it happened. Tea over, drying-up done, piles of notes made, they both rose at once in the tiny kitchen and — zap! — Jack's right wrist made a glancing contact with one dangling, purple sleeve, and — zing! — She was in his arms again, face buried once more in his chest.

"Do you think you can take it from here?" she asked, looking up at him, red-nosed and eyelids full of water, racked with sobs, as if she'd had some intellectual orgasm. It had all been building up inside her for weeks — months — this way through the woods, until the tension had become insupportable.

Later, when she'd calmed down, and Jack had tucked her up in bed, folding himself in behind her with one arm sleepily fingering loose strands of her hair, the other folded across her belly, she thought that perhaps that the expression of pure unabashed, unselfconscious sex was all that she'd needed to break the deadlock.

When Jack's thesis was complete, after another two months of sixteen-hour days; after more argument, more computer simulations, another trip to France (this time Jack, on his own), more anxiety, more sleepless nights, more wine, more laughter, more elation, more despair, more testing, more arguments, more checking and double-checking, and papers in unruly drifts all over the flat, Jadis discovered something else.

She was pregnant.

Chapter 8. Cadet

Xandarga Station, Earth, *c.* 55,680,000 years ago

She was a gordian shape of dazzling hue;
Vermilion-spotted, golden, green and blue;
Striped like a zebra, freckled like a pard,
Eyed like a peacock, and all crimson barr'd.
John Keats — *Lamia*

For the first few weeks of his naval career, Ruxhana Fengen Kraa, space cadet, saw nothing more exciting than the inside of his barracks. The day would begin with reveille, after which it was all guns blazing, sometimes literally, until well after sundown. What with roll-call, and drill, and lectures, and physical training, and mess, and weapons practice, and more drill, and private study, and basic uniform maintenance — all to the enervating odors of stale chow and unwashed laundry — he could do no more each night than collapse into his bunk.

After the initial shock had worn off, Ruxie found that he enjoyed his new life very much. He discovered that his sinewy, ranch-honed frame, combined with a quick intelligence and a gift for anticipation, meshed with the requirements of naval life. The name of Ruxhana Fengen Kraa crept quietly towards the top of most of his classes and routines. People in the hierarchy far above the level of rookie pond-life began to take notice.

Ruxie knew nothing of this, because he was more concerned with pond-life closer to home. Ko, who bunked in the cot immediately above Ruxie, seemed to start with the same enthusiasm for naval life. After a while, though, Ko began to lose ground. The only class that Ko always headed was Uqbar-rules boxing, a traditional sport whose antique ritual did little to cover up its gladiatorial viciousness. Professionals were multi-millionaire megastars, but few lived long enough to enjoy their wealth. What worried Ruxie was Ko's apparent conviction that unchallenged success in one sphere of life compensated for slack performance in all the others. When Ruxie was studying late into the night, or working out, or at the weapons range, Ko sloped off into the City, with a crowd of the kind of toadies that no aspiring boxing pro could afford to be without.

Late one evening, Ruxie was on his bunk, reading a manual on a new model of Higgs projector for use as a side arm. The schematics were beginning to swim before his eyes, and he was sure that if he tried to sleep now, they would dance before him in his dreams, mocking. Perhaps when he got to use the real thing, on the weapons range, it would all make sense. Right now, a restorative workout and a swim would put him in the mood for sleep. Reveille was only six hours away, and the routine would start all over again.

He sat up, wondering where he had left his gym clothes, when Ko's legs swung down from the bunk above. Ruxie was surprised—he was so lost in his own thoughts he hadn't even noticed Ko was there. Ko dropped noiselessly to the floor. He looked at Ruxie's reading matter. "You know, Ruxie, all work, and no play," he said. What you need is a drink."

Slipping undetected out of barracks was easier than Ruxie had thought. Ko bowled along with Ruxie straining to keep up, and before long they were outside a bar in an alley a few blocks from the harbor-front. Bagpipe music squirled from the door as Ko and Ruxie arrived, finding themselves at the edge of a crowd, rapt, before a couple in the closing stages of a traditional Turgai sword-dance. Masked, and dressed in carnival finery, the dancers paced round each other in a pool of blood-red light; stylized steps marking time to the screech of the pipes. The dancers' arms made broad strokes with the scimitars each held in both hands. They swept the blades towards the crowds, expressionless masks filled with menace, the spectators flinching, laughing nervously — and then towards each other, scything closer and closer in, now whipping hairs-breadths from the costume of each.

The air became enriched with an auroral glow from the dancers' bodies, deepening with hems of iridescent blue, bars of crimson. The scent of sex rose. Faster the dancers whirled, and as the bagpipes reached a final, caterwauling cadence, scythes slashed, costume was rent, and the dancers were exposed, unmasked and unmarked, bare to the waist, shining pelts clothed in sweat and victory. The auras twisted from blue to purple to yellow, and then faded. The music was replaced by applause. The dancers made a triumphal circuit of the audience, gathering coins thrown in their masks.

Ruxie was amazed to find himself cheering, and, more than that, aroused. It wasn't just the sight of the female dancer's taut flesh and wild black hair, and — Ruxhana dared himself think it — her five pairs of breasts with their brazen tips. It was the experience of the dance itself, its frenzy, its climactic release, that he found so stirring.

"Good, eh?" Ko's voice in his ear. Ruxie was amazed to hear it at all, so transported had he been. "That's Xalomé, that is," he continued, picking up on Ruxie's glances. "She's a cracker, isn't she? Now — oh, there they are!" Ko steered him to a big table already occupied by many of their barrack-mates, some already in the party mood. "Look what I've dragged up!" Ko shouted to the throng,

"Yo, baby! It's shoon-to-be-Adm'ral Ruxhana Fengen Kraa!" yelled a half-uniformed rating in response, rapidly standing to attention, and sitting down again as abruptly.

"Beers for the Admiral!" bellowed another, and a flagon was shoved in front of him. Within minutes, his presence was forgotten — just one of the crew, laughing as Ko told some wild tale of land-shark-hunting on the prairies of home. Ruxie was so enthralled by the tall tales, the sodden feelings of fellowship engendered by the beer, that he hardly noticed another body squeezing on to the bench beside him. But the pressure of a thigh against his, and warm breath in his ear, sobered him up at once. He turned. It was the female dancer. Dressed now in a prim naval uniform with pips on her shoulders, but definitely the same tumble of dark hair.

The pupils of her yellow-green eyes were narrowed to slits even in the darkness of the bar.

"It's... Xalomé, isn't it?"

"What took you so long, spaceman?" Without looking at him, she placed her hands behind her head and lifted her hair away from her face. She was close enough for him to smell a wild strangeness, like an animal at bay, or on heat. It took him right back to the ranch, and one of his first memories of ever going outside. He had been hardly more than a blind kit at the time. After his earliest years spent in darkness, as they were for all kits, the world of light was bright and new. The first thing he saw was two indricos rutting, one on top of the other, the two mountains of flesh bellowing, the air filled with dust and the cries of the farmhands. The air was charged then, too.

"So... long?"

"Yes. I've been waiting weeks for you to turn up." Her voice was cool, assured.

"Me?"

"Don't sound so surprised. Your friend Mr Raelle has told me all about you. Quite the mystery man, aren't you?" He was suddenly conscious of a hand on his upper thigh, like her voice—assured—like it knew what it was doing, and where it was going. He flushed and struggled for breath. But something else took charge of him then. Months of training had taken the edges off this farmhand. There were times, he knew, when one should stop thinking, and just act. He covered the hand on his thigh with his own and pressed it firmly. Her fingers were small, yet resolute.

"Shall we go?" he said.

Concentrating on simply putting his feet one in front of the other, and not bumping into his companion or anyone else in narrow night streets still thronged with partygoers, Ruxie reached the promenade on the harbor front. Boats bobbed in the brightly lit marina below, with ships and industrial gantries as silhouettes further off. He found a bench, remarkably unoccupied, and invited Xalomé to sit down. She did so, with an air of almost mocking amusement at Ruxie's obvious efforts to act the gallant. He sat beside her, wondering what to say or do next. Her hair strayed like tendrils over his shoulders, under his chin, across his lips. They tasted of salt and abandon.

They sat for hours as the streets thinned. The silvered bubble of the Assembly Building hung motionless over the waves, reflecting the lights of the City and, in weird cycloid curves, the illuminated skein of the El that rose up behind them.

Something broke in Ruxie, and he found that all he had lost was boyish embarrassment. He found that he could talk with Xalomé like he hadn't been able to talk with anyone since he'd arrived in Xandarga Station. Without the forced and formal cadence of naval operations, nor the false braggadocio that Ko's circle seemed to require. Into the night they talked. He told her of ranch life in East Gondwana. She tended more to listening than talk, but he learned how she'd grown up there, in the City, and had just graduated. Special Ops. Hence the pips.

"And the dancing?"

"Oh, that. A girl's got to have a hobby. I love dancing. Especially the traditional stuff. It's the ritual." She turned towards him. Her eyes glowed, reflected, feral. "Were I a man, I'd probably go for Uqbar-rules boxing. Ritual, combined with sheer bloody savagery. Poetry in motion!" She laughed. Ruxie said nothing. "You don't think I could handle myself?"

"I... well, I'm sure you could. Special Ops, and all that."

"Your friend. Mr Raelle. He fights Uqbar Rules, you know. Have you seen him in action?"

"Yes, I have."

"Impressive, isn't he? I think he could handle himself, too. But sometimes I think he overdoes it. He'll learn, with experience. He'll have to. I think he needs taking in hand."

"But what about your dance partner? Don't you...? Aren't you...?"

"Shakiló? Are you serious? He couldn't be more gay if you tied pink ribbons round his prong. You'd need a lot of ribbons, mind..."

With that she turned to face him, and the last thing he saw were her eyes crossing slightly as her lips approached his and he was catapulted into the void.

Chapter 9. Examiner

Cambridge, England, Earth, December 2024

Man is the measure of all things.
Protagoras

"It was that last trip to France that clinched it," Jack had started to explain, uncertainly, to the thesis committee gathered in a lecture room whose heating had been turned off for the winter. It was a dank, dismal day in December and the undergraduates had left town, leaving in their place an arctic chill that enveloped everything in a sullen lassitude. The committee was, clearly, yet to be convinced by his case. He looked to MacLennane—as his supervisor, one half of the committee—for an encouraging sign, a welcoming smile, but his patron averted his gaze: there was a lot at stake for him, too.

He missed Jadis—he missed her terribly, on this day, of all days—but this morning, before he'd left, she had seemed wound up tight with some matter so internalized that she refused to tell him what it was. But he'd looked so miserable as he turned to leave that she relented, ran towards him and embraced him from behind.

"I love you so much, you silly man," she had said: "I know you can do it. Now, go and show them what you're made of." He turned to hug her, but said nothing, and then he left, walking into town through the cheerless fog.

In truth, he was worried. The remorseless tension in these final weeks before his thesis defense had taken its toll on both of them. Whereas before he'd been lean and sinewy, now he looked gaunt, and thin. She'd seemed distracted, perturbed. He felt, somehow, that he'd committed some offense, done some wrong, and that—cruelly—she wouldn't tell him what it was, so he could at least apologise. No, she wasn't ill, she insisted, turning her eyes away from his questioning face and towards the TV. She had taken to watching a Disney film called *Fantasia 2000*, in which various snippets of orchestral music were accompanied by fantastic animations. She always seemed to be watching the same one, in which a pod of whales gamboled to Respighi's *Pines of Rome*. First they leaped and played in the waves, but then, shooting up through the clouds, swam and surged among the stars. Jadis watched that part again and again, enraptured as a child. When Jack asked why, she said she couldn't explain. There was just something about it, she said, that struck a chord. She found it comforting.

As he plodded on, the feet in his mind walked backwards to see if he could work out where things had gone wrong—if indeed they had. He knew he'd taken far too long to get down and write his thesis, trying Jadis' patience. Yet it was she who had brainstormed his thesis into being, gave it birth, gave it life, nursed it to maturity—it was her.

Her!

And even this morning, she still swore she loved him.

Him!

So now he thought, in dejection quite foreign to his usually calm and level nature, that the great gamble had failed. He really didn't deserve this thesis, and he certainly didn't deserve Jadis. By the time he got to the department, his mind was clothed in a fog as thick as the one that laced the streets in funereal shrouds. Go ahead, make my day. In the end he was just too tired. Too tired to panic, too tired to care.

"Mr Corstorphine—Mr Corstorphine?" This from the tiny but intimidating figure of Professor Ernestine Yanga, the external examiner and the other half of the committee, who, MacLennane had said, was famous for saying almost nothing during thesis examinations until near the end, when she'd skewer hapless candidates with the one question they'd been praying nobody would ask. Ah, thought Jack, we must be near the end, then, and this must be the preamble to the famous Difficult Question that MacLennane had warned him about. Best to get it over with, and get out. So far, the examination had flowed glutinously past him like a river of sludge making its viscid way down to a black and putrid sea: he'd supplied all the answers so mechanically, that once he'd uttered a word he'd immediately forgotten about it.

"Mr Corstorphine—you were telling us about your trip to France?"

"Yes—of course—I'm sorry. As you've read in my thesis, I had accumulated a great deal of data about hominin influence on geomorphology in Britain. But it was very hard to make anything of it. Thanks to some new methods developed in conjunction with a fellow student..."

"Yes, I see that this is acknowledged. A Miss Markham, isn't it?" Jack said nothing: his lips pursed in a thin line of remorse. "Please continue, Mr Corstorphine."

"Yes, sorry... I had long suspected the existence of a gradient of human influence on the landscape in England, consistent over the past hundred thousand years at least, in an increasing trend from the northwest — where it is hardly significant according to the variants of the nonparametric tests I've used — to the southeast, where it can be said to stand out from natural influence here and there, but still in general not significantly different from expected natural or stochastic variation."

"Very good. But enough of Albion's fair shores, I think? You were about to tell us all about France, I believe. Would you like to enlarge upon that?"

Jack had had so much to say about France. About how his solo trip there, inspired by the earlier jaunt with Jadis, had changed everything, given him hope — rooting his vague instincts in something more tangible, more real. About how, after looking at the British landscape, scored, ravaged and broken by glaciers at least eight times in the course of almost a million years of human history — glaciers so powerful that they had literally erased rivers as broad as the Severn from the map — his personal antennae had become so tuned to every nuance of landscape that, when he had come at last to a region that had seen a million years of relative and continuous calm, the signs of human influence shone out at him like blinding beacons. Britain had only ever been a sideshow, an outlier: he'd seen immediately what had occurred to no-one, that nothing south of the Loire was wilderness—*nothing*—and had not been so for a very long time. But right now, he didn't feel like explaining anything. His answers were bland, apathetic, hesitant. Looking down on the scene, as if he were hanging from the ceiling, he saw MacLennane rise slightly from his chair, as if in concern—and then Jack snapped, jarringly, back. He blinked, disoriented. It occurred to him that he must have blacked out.

With her well-controlled perm, her neat dove-grey two-piece and pearls, Ernestine Yanga could have been the president of the local Womens' Institute, except that she'd been raised in a grass hut on the western shores of Lake Turkana, until the age of five, when her village had been razed by Ethiopian bandits and the rest of her family had been raped, macheted, burned to death, or combinations of all three. She'd only escaped because she'd been a mile away at the time, gathering pathetic twigs for the cooking fire, and sluicing the filthy puddle that passed for the village waterhole into a chipped enamel bucket. On returning home to find it so casually expunged from the face of the Earth, she'd walked thirty miles to the nearest fly-flecked bush town in search of work. By the time she was thirteen she was handy with a Kalashnikov. She'd been a drug courier, a fruit seller, a goatherd, a moneychanger, a news vendor, a prostitute, a pimp, a cattle rustler, a copper's nark, a murderess (twice), and was riddled with at least six chronic, parasitic infections.

Having understandably decided that she'd had quite enough of all this, she'd walked, blagged, whored and hitch-hiked her way to Nairobi. One night, completely exhausted, she camped out on the steps of the National Museums of Kenya, where she'd decided she'd await the Lord's Salvation. The Lord took the shape of a kindly assistant curator, whose prayers for the Almighty to send him a child to ease his wife's shameful barrenness had now, it seemed, been answered — and who took her in and cleaned her up.

A week later she was the illiterate, unpaid assistant to the janitor. After thirty-five years, the Director of Palaeontology. And now, at the age of fifty-five, what Ernestine Yanga didn't know about the influence of early humans on landforms in the Rift Valley wasn't worth knowing.

She knew far more than that, however, about the symptoms of human suffering, to which she was as sensitive as Jack's spirit chimed to the shape and history of every hanging valley, every drumlin, scarp and oxbow. Her reputation as a terrifying examiner was justified — after all, a woman in her situation could never succeed in life without what she called 'true grit' (she was an avid fan of old westerns) — but in Jack she saw a good man who'd been worn almost entirely away by worry, and, like so many men, he was suffering as much from injured pride as from lack of food and sleep. He had tried his hardest, but despite all his efforts, all his denial, he'd felt he was not quite up to the task, and this insulted his being, his masculinity. But he need not have been so concerned, she thought. The evidence he had from that final trip to France was right there, in front of them. And from what Roger MacLennane (such a charming man!) had told her, Jack was a dedicated field worker, the kind of person she preferred infinitely to pallid, deskbound museum types, who so often built their intellectual castles on the sweat of others.

More importantly, it was clear that Jack fulfilled the first criterion of a doctorate candidate — to venture, without fear, outside the small, cozy nest of knowledge, and into the dark and infinitely greater continent of ignorance that surrounded it. That Jack had ventured so far out that no techniques yet existed to make sense of what he'd found indicated extraordinary fortitude, a brazen and almost breathtaking resolve. If Jack could make no headway with it, then that was hardly his fault, because nobody else (she thought) would have had the ability either. Not MacLennane (he'd admitted as much) and certainly not herself. And yet, if Roger had thought the task impossible, he surely would not have assigned it to a doctorate student. This in itself, she felt, indicated that Jack really must be a man of extraordinary talent, and — she thought back to the fortune that had smiled on her on the Museum steps — talent was precious, and must always be nurtured.

In any case, Jack was not entirely alone, without help. As Professor Yanga understood it, Jack continued to enjoy the best help possible in the form of the acuity of his young associate, Ms. Markham, who seemed to believe in him and who, Roger had assured her, would go far—especially if she and Jack continued to work as a team. As he freely admitted, Roger MacLennane owed his place in the front rank of academia not to any special cleverness in himself, but to a knack of surrounding himself with clever people. And Roger's instincts about people were rarely wrong. Jack was, indeed, a fortunate man, as fortunate as he was deserving.

"Mr Corstorphine, of course, I understand. But please don't worry yourself. Oh my, you look so tired," she said, and she smiled—a warm, radiant, motherly smile that made Jack want to dissolve. This woman, this supposedly ferocious, hard-bitten creature who took no prisoners, had smiled at him. She had looked straight at him, into him, and she understood. She knew. And in that moment he knew that there was hope. And so he started again, clearing his throat, which seemed unaccountably to be full of damp sandpaper.

"I'm sorry—please excuse me. When we think of the French Palaeolithic, we tend to see the landscape as a wilderness, punctuated with some interesting and picturesque cave sites. But that's a view conditioned more by our prejudices about brutish cavemen than by the facts on the ground. When I got there, accustomed as I had been to the far more challenging and—in any case—more sparsely populated British terrain, France looked to me like nothing more than an almost completely artificial, settled—even industrial landscape, continuously shaped by human influence for perhaps a million years."

"What form does that influence take, Mr Corstorphine?"

This really must be it, the Difficult Question that went to the heart of the matter. But the Professor continued to smile. Now he could not be stopped. The influence takes many forms, he said. Just to take a couple of things more or less at random: virtually no watercourse south of the Loire or west of the Rhône has been natural for any significant part of its length since the Late Middle Pleistocene. At the very least, watercourse curvature has been altered by 16 per cent during the Brunhes magnetostratigraphic interval, with the confidence limits that you'll see on page 176, I think you'll find (the committee members turned to their copies of his thesis as Jack felt, at last, to be in the driving seat). In support of this (he continued), the overall number of river channel infill deposits indicative of buried oxbow lakes is very much less than you'd expect by chance, had nature been left to take its course. This means that something—or somebody—has been altering the lower courses of rivers in a systematic way for a very long time.

And then there is the general topography. Volcanic activity aside, no hilltop exists in this part of France that has natural surface run-off characteristics, possibly an indication of the former presence of earthworks or other structures. In fact (Jack paused to draw breath), I could find no grade that has been completely free of human influence over the same period. There's one hill, at a place just not far from Aurignac, called Saint-Rogatien-Les-Remillards…

His mind drifted to when he'd explained all this to Jadis, with mounting excitement, promising her again that after this wretched thesis defense was over, he'd take her there and show her. It was about a month ago, their last evening sitting out in the Nest before it became too cold: they'd had a bottle of wine he'd brought home from the off-license. Retreating to the sitting room, she'd removed a stack of printouts from their sagging old sofa, sat down, pulling him close.

"This is it, Jack," she had said—"This is the key. This proves it. This settles everything." She unbuttoned his shirt—her big black eyes cross-eyed with concentration—and rested her face on his chest, letting him tousle her hair into a blanket, covering and embracing him. He explained to her—to Jadis—to Professor Yanga—that his close survey of this unusual landform revealed to him that its geology was entirely at variance with the underlying bedrock and, furthermore, that its location could not be explained in terms of any local, structural faulting. It couldn't be a glacial erratic, either, because there had been no glaciers. Much of the landform had been worn away by wind and weather, but with an estimated original volume at least a thousand times that of Saint Paul's Cathedral—he was proud to have worked out this comparison—it was just too enormous to have been set down by any kind of fluvial transport short of a catastrophic flood of the kind that had created the scablands of the Pacific

Northwest, or which had carved out the English Channel — and there had been no sign of any such activity, either. In fact, its location was inexplicable unless…

At this point, on the sofa, Jadis had trapped his gesticulating hands in hers, and forced them to encircle her. She'd seemed so warm and content, he'd felt that at any minute she'd start to purr. He kissed the top of her head, and said that the only way to explain Saint-Rogatien — the only way — was that it had was an artificial structure. That someone had put it there.

He'd once read about an ancient pyramid at a place called Cholula in Mexico. By the time the *conquistadores* got there, it had been abandoned for centuries, its masonry stripped away, and was covered in grass and trees. Assuming it was just a hill (after all, that's what it looked like), the Spaniards built a town around it and a church on the top. And that was only a few centuries. Imagine, then, if it had been left for a thousand years, a hundred thousand, a million? It would look entirely natural, revealed as artificial only by its strange geology and situation — and only then if somebody first suspected that something was amiss — which nobody had ever done. But when Jack had seen it, his antennae vibrated into overdrive. He knew it didn't belong there. He just knew.

By this time Jadis had been on the edge of sleep. "You really are a very silly man," she had said, yawning. "You've just about wrapped it up. The ancestors of the first Neanderthals built gigantic pyramids all over France…"

"... pyramids that made the Great Pyramid look like a sandcastle—and they were doing it for hundreds of thousands of years."

"Well then, you don't need statistical methods to prove that, so why worry? That's just basic geology and good ol' masculine intuition." She looked up at him, blearily. It occurred to him that her face looked drawn and thin, that what she needed most was sleep. So he'd taken her in his arms and laid her gently on the bed, still in her purple sack, pulling the duvet on top of her. He climbed in beside her, and, together, they slid slowly off to contented, companionable sleep on a smooth, even grade rather shallower than about one in a couple of hundred (he'd estimated), that of a languidly meandering river that makes its mazy, lazy way down to a delta in which it becomes blissfully lost in oozy, woozy thickets.

As if from an immense distance, he thought he heard Professor MacLennane and Professor Yanga commending him for a splendid thesis.

"Congratulations, Doctor Corstorphine!" Hands were shaken, but it was clear to both academics that Jack wasn't really there. They looked worried. The Professors exchanged nervous words that Jack didn't catch, and Yanga left, looking anxious.

"Come on, Jack, I'm going to take you home," MacLennane said as he put his arm around Jack's shoulders, walked him outside into the quad and steered him towards MacLennane's ageing but highly polished Volvo saloon. Jack was drained, utterly, to the dregs, alternately assailed by waves of lightheadedness and nausea. On the other hand, if he'd stepped out of the car, he didn't think he'd have sufficient energy to walk, or even stand up. He couldn't remember having eaten more than a couple of bites of anything for three days. They drew up outside the flat: MacLennane had to haul Jack out of the car. When they knocked at the door, there was at first, no answer.

"Just coming!" — he heard her lovely voice, after a few more seconds: "in the bathroom! Won't be a minute!"

As soon as Jack had left, Jade collapsed on the sofa, eviscerated, as if her heart had burst from within her and now bounced along the street after the dwindling Jack, the world on his broad shoulders, an old gunslinger who, racked by his internal demons, seemed to be losing the will to fight. But she had things to do, an errand of her own, and so, grimly, she dressed, grabbed her bag, and left the house.

Poor Jack had never looked so down. But as she was sympathetic (how could she not be?) she was, it has to be said, a little annoyed. Not for the simple fact of his low spirits, his anxiety — anyone could forgive him these — but perversely, that his mood seemed so entirely out of character, and that was harder to accommodate. Not that she minded being there for him, to cheer him up, even for weeks on end, because she didn't. She loved him, and she wanted to make him happy. But where once had stood an imperturbable rock, there had now limped, in the hallway, half-sunk, a fractious, fretful, friable thing she didn't recognize, and didn't want to. Realizing how selfish this was, she wanted her old Jack back, the granite-hard Jack, the Jack who had become her secure foundation, tying her surely to the solid rock of this planet Earth. Were he to crumble, she would slip, lose her footing, and float off to who knew where.

But there was that other thing, too. That when you'd accounted for the relentless work, anxiety and more work of the past year, there was still, lately, a residue of nauseating wretchedness. When it had continued for weeks, making her feel wan and drained, vitiating desire, it occurred to her that something other than the general preoccupation with Jack's work might be responsible.

Jadis was almost sure she knew, but, being Jadis, she craved certainty, even within statistical limits, explaining why she had now returned home from the supermarket with a pregnancy testing kit: and — even as Jack, his ordeal over, was allowing his rangy form to be folded passively into the passenger seat of MacLennane's car — was undressed, in the bathroom, peering awkwardly down at herself and wondering how a mere woman could aim so accurately at a target as narrowly defined as a test strip. Oh, that a man should have to do this, she grinned to herself, he'd at least be in a position to take better aim.

And just as she heard the knock on the door, presaging the proud return of her conqueror, bloodied for sure, but all dragons slain, the line in the small, crystalline window coalesced, like a chromosome in the very expectancy of division, of the prolongation of a life stretching back to when the world was young, and forward into illimitable futurity—from a yellow nothingness into a single shaft of clear blue.

Chapter 10. Visitors

Xandarga Station, Earth, c. 55,680,000 years ago

But full of fire and greedy hardiment
The youthfull knight could not for ought be staide
Edmund Spenser — *The Faerie Queene*

Ruxie rode waves of pleasure and frustration. He didn't mind letting his gradepoint averages slip a little if he could see Xalomé. At first they would meet in the same bar in the harbor district and go on long walks through the nighted City. Apart from that one kiss, they'd done nothing more intimate than hold hands. Ruxie's attempts at anything bolder were met with gentle but firm reproof, always unspoken. Ruxie didn't dare say anything for fear of breaking the spell. On free days, when Ruxie would normally be studying or working with the new Higgs projectors on the weapons range, Xalomé showed him the wonders of Xandarga Station he'd only read about.

One morning she met him with an urgency in her eyes he hadn't seen. It was time, she said, to visit the Institute of Galactic History. She ran before him like a ghost into the Institute's mazy galleries until they arrived at its center, the Gharaan Collection, and the three gray scraps that were all that remained of the earliest-known civilization in the Universe.

"I've been coming here for years," Xalomé said, "and it always gets me. A whole civilization, that old...

The Sigil: Siege of Stars

that early. And nobody knows anything much about them at all."

Ruxie peered at the dusty label. He tried to quell a rising vertigo sparked by this confrontation between unbelievably remote antiquity and the scale of their own ignorance.

"Is that all there is? Just what's in this case?"

"Yes. Amazing, isn't it?"

They stood together, looking at the triptych of silvery slag that formed the entire testament to an unknown number of births, lives, hopes raised, dreams dashed, and deaths, of an extinct species that had lived in what was now the Fomalhaut sector, more than eleven billion years earlier. Xalomé's hand crept into his. They were two sparks against eternity.

"Doesn't anyone have a clue about... them? How they lived? How they died?" Ruxie was surprised by the anguish in his voice, as if the history of these inaccessible lives really mattered to him. He flushed a little, expecting some of Xalomé's gentle teasing. He was surprised, instead, by her seriousness. But before she answered, she smiled. As if she was a teacher, and he'd passed a test. Puzzled, he looked more closely at her as she spoke. There was a hint of tears in her eyes, behind the smile. He remembered his Ma smiling like that, with relief, when she'd just found some vital object— her keys, or a family photo—which she'd convinced herself she'd lost.

"Almost nothing, Ruxie. But there's a lot in that 'almost'. They've—that's the Institute—have analyzed the fragments. Or tried to. They're made of no kind of matter we know about here and now. The closest description they can reach is that it's a metallic form of — well, ice. Frozen water. But that's really only a kind of analogy, something to help us make sense of something we've never seen before. A better approximation is macroscopic quantum foam."

"That's..."

"Yes, I know. Impossible. It's as if they're fossil fragments of space-time itself, frozen, left over from when the Universe was young, perhaps obeyed different laws. But really, what the fragments are made of is not as important as what happened to them. The material is riddled with all kinds of imperfections that signal incredible stresses. Like it brushed against something that mashed it to a dimensionless pulp and then reassembled it. So perhaps the material started off as something more ordinary. Or, at least, different from what it is now. Well, that's what one group of scientists thinks."

"One group? There are others?"

"Oh, c'mon, Ruxie! You'd never expect any kind of consensus with artifacts as enigmatic—and as important—as these. Now, would you do something for me? Go round the other side of the cabinet, look at the smallest artifact—the rectangular one, in the center—and tell me what you see."

"A game?"

"Indulge me." She pecked him on the cheek and sent him on his way. What he saw stopped him, like his feet had been glued to the floor. Everything in the room blurred but for the specimen before his eyes.

Carved onto the far side of the fragment, filling its whole area, was an inscription. He swallowed. "Just tell me what you see, Ruxie."

He tried his best to get the words out, but their sharp edges snagged the inside of his mouth.

"The object. An inscription. Rectangular, like the object. It's about—I don't know, maybe nine or ten centimeters from side to side, and maybe two or three tall... hard to be sure... it's shifting..."

"Keep going, Ruxie, you're doing fine."

"... but that's just the frame. Inside there are three circles, inscribed, and they're... they're... they're... so beautiful. So perfect. Like... like..." He looked up.

"Ruxie, keep going... don't stop now!" Her voice was jagged with anxiety. Ruxie was puzzled but did what he was told. He looked down at the specimen once again. It looked like something seen from a great distance.

"... and in between the circles are two crescents, horns pointing outwards... and... and... lines, a lot of lines, all radiating from the circle in the middle... and... Xalomé, help me, I feel very strange."

The Earth flew upwards and over his head. The next thing he knew he was lying on a bench in a shadowed corner of the gallery, his head in her lap, her cool hand on his forehead. He startled.

"Hush now, everything's going to be fine," she said. He remembered the last thing he saw.

"Xalomé, it glowed."

He remembered now: the lines, the circles, the crescents, had all shone at him with a deep, ultraviolet pulse, just before he winked out. He sat up, and Xalomé, holding him, looked at him again, half in cool appraisal, half with some expression Ruxie felt he couldn't quite place.

"You've done well, Ruxie. Really well. I'm so pleased I found you," and she came to him and kissed him, with determined firmness. Ruxie was numb before the wave. She pulled away, looked directly in his eyes, but seemed to be looking through him, as if she'd just picked up a signal from space. Ruxie wasn't as surprised by this as he'd thought he might be. After several weeks, he'd become used to strange, instant summonses which, she said, were relayed to her in-ear comms port. Special Ops.

He remembered the first, jarring occasion, when they'd been in the Natural History Museum, standing beneath the alien that dominated its main hall. The Taniquetilian tesseractrix was built like a sea spider from the oceans of Earth, with many legs fused to a tiny body, but on a gigantic scale. Each leg was eighty meters long, curving from a car-sized chitinous claw through a succession of blue-gray joints to terminate in the body in the blue haze far above their heads. Opera glasses, thoughtfully supplied by the Museum, were required to see the body itself, a mysterious structure augmented with a bewildering variety of stalactitic protrusions and polyhedral blobs. Ruxie remembered gazing at it, open mouthed, unable to take it all in.

"Go on, I dare you," Xalomé giggled. "Count its legs."

Ruxie brought his head down with nauseous recoil. He refocused his eyes and turned around, carefully, to count each one of the teetering columns. This was harder to do than it seemed. He was never sure if he'd counted the first leg twice. After three attempts he linked the first leg to the scene behind it — the Museum gift shop — and started again. The task was easier, but only marginally.

"Twenty-three. No, twenty-four. No, twenty-three. No... no, I'm sure it's twenty-three."

"Actually, it's twenty-seven. And now I have to go." And with that she disappeared, leaving him with a sense of having been short-changed. Twenty-seven? No way. How could she have been so certain? The museum guide book reported that the number of the legs on the Taniquetilian tesseractrix was formally unknown.

This time, it was different. She continued to face him, on the bench just off the Gharaan Gallery in the Institute, and took both his hands in his.

"I'm wanted. I think you should come with me."

Dusk was falling as they hurried down the Institute steps and on to the street. Funny — it had been only mid-morning when they'd come in. Had they been in there — what — eight hours? How long had he been out for the count? Xalomé was in too much of a distracted rush to allow him to ask her. She hailed a cab kerbside, and within twenty minutes they were back in the harbor district. Xalomé paid off the driver, exchanging a few words with him that Ruxie couldn't catch.

The familiar tavern was deserted but for a pool of light illuminating a table at the back. On one side was a familiar figure, seated, stein in hand, looking down at something that couldn't be seen from the shadowed doorway.

"I promised Mr Spektor that I'd settle," said the man. "Promised. I'll pay my dues, I really will... but I can't do it without money. After my next bout—should be a formality—I'll have enough. Really. You gotta believe me. Tell Mr Spektor that I'm a man of my word."

A voice came from the direction of the man's feet. It was well modulated, surprisingly sweet, dangerous with menace.

"That is for Mr Spektor to decide. Not you. Especially as you've lost your last two bouts. You run a great risk, Mr Raelle. Not of death: that is an occupational hazard in Uqbar Rules, as you are aware. No, the risk you run, Mr Raelle, is of shaming Mr Spektor, your hitherto unwavering sponsor. The consequences of that will be very much worse than death. Do not fail him again."

"I won't. Don't worry." Even from this distance, Ruxie could see the beads of perspiration start on Ko's forehead.

"I shall be back to collect. After the bout. Perhaps not us in person. It might be one of our... associates."

"Very good. I'll be waiting." Ko looked up, then, and smiled at Ruxie and Xalomé in greeting. His unseen companion must have taken that as the cue to leave. There was a puffing noise, a wheeze, and an almost inaudible clanking as the mysterious companion made its way to where Ruxie and Xalomé stood. They looked down as the stranger approached. It was not so much a person as a contraption. A sphere of black glass the size of a large grapefruit, chased in silvery metal filigree and mounted on a chassis sprouting four wire-frame balloon wheels. Pulling this arrangement were two insectoid shapes, each no more than thirty centimeters long, made of plate metal intricately linked together. Steam puffed from their joints as they moved. They looked like praying mantids in armor. It was the fairy-tale carriage that creaks along the edges of robot dreams. It stopped at Ruxie's feet, and the mantids looked up.

"Sulfavillains," said Xalomé, a catch in her voice. The mantid on the right raised itself on its rear four legs, gesticulated with its long, anterior talons, rustled its wing-covers and turned its beady-eyed head to one side. Ruxie could see tiny points of malicious red in the centre of each jeweled facet. Its mouthparts moved.

"Please, Miss, allow me to pass. Thank-you," it said, and trundled off into the night. Ruxie was nonplussed, but Xalomé seemed to be shaking with rage.

"Ko Handor Raelle!" she hissed, bending down at him. "What the hell do you think you're doing, country boy? Dealing with these slime?" Ko turned his face away as if she'd slapped him. "You know as well as I do—or if you don't, then you should—that if there's anything mean in this city, anything dirty, then the Sulfas are in it up to their metaphorical necks. They stink!"

"Xalomé, I... well, when no-one else would back me for a prize fight, they were there. They gave me... good terms." He looked down, shamefaced.

"Oh, really? I'll bet they did. So when you fuck it up again—when is it, next Friday night?—they'll be here to blow you to atoms. Can't wait. Perhaps I can sell tickets."

"Well, sweetheart," said Ko, then, looking up, smiling with his mouth, but his eyes two hard points reflecting the foam slithering down the inside of his glass: "I'd better not fuck it up, then, had I?"

Chapter 11. Investor

Aspen, Colorado, Earth, October 2024

Ulfin, thu hauest wel isaed.
Ich the giue an honde thritti solh of londe
That thu Merlin biwinne and don mine iwille.

*(Ulfin, you have spoken well.
I shall give you thirty ploughlands of land
If you do my will and win Merlin.)*

Layamon — *Brut*

Ruxton Carr loosened his tie, doused the lights, poured himself a generous measure of Talisker, and sank into one of the two chesterfields before the fire.

His retinue of lawyers, accountants, assistants and general hangers-on had left, freighted with decisions (his), whisky (also his), and purpose (theirs). He loved a party but the enjoyment was sharpened by the thought of the solitude to follow. It was solitude, originally, that had led him to buy the Lodge, this cabin perched on a deck of massive ashlars some distance out of Aspen. Just near enough for convenience, just far enough away to deter casual visitors. That, and the fantastic view from the floor-to-ceiling picture windows down one side.

He'd originally come for the skiing — a sport he'd long wanted to indulge in but couldn't really afford until he sold his first company. He'd gone public in

1985; made an absolute killing in 1986; and, with what turned out to be an impeccable gift for timing, sold it for a fortune on 13 October 1987. Six days later, the Hong Kong markets crashed. He was safe, secure, but any feeling of *schadenfreude* he might have had for his competitors was tempered with an understanding of the fragile, makeshift nature of the present. Misfortune might strike anyone, at any time. The secret of not getting fooled was to diversify, and to plan ahead. *Very* far ahead.

Had there been anyone to see him, he'd have been visible only from the still glints in his cat-like, yellow eyes and the starry spangles refracted from the heavy tumbler. He drained it, refilled it, and thought back… and back.

He started — when was it?

Ah yes, it was in Khan's shop on the Tottenham Court Road, selling music centres and SLRs. (Music centres! SLRs!) He had always been a good salesman, but there he'd really taken off. He could trace the change, he thought, to a very wet day in '79, or maybe it was '80, when for some reason he'd fainted while serving a customer. Just disappeared below the counter. One minute, he was there, on the money, the next… He always joked he'd banged his head on the counter on the way down. Don't worry, Mr Khan had said, just overwork. Take the rest of the day off.

But Ruxton had done more than that: The very next day he gave in his notice and within three months he'd opened his own shop. He remembered the smell of new paint, the heart-in-mouth moment when he opened his doors for the very first time, and the sign above the shop. 'Merlin Electronics,' it read. It was a proud moment.

After that he couldn't put a foot wrong. He had an uncanny knack of what people wanted, before they even knew they wanted it. When people woke up to CDs, he was already thinking about music downloads. When they first thought of mobile phones, he was into what eventually became smartphones. People were still wrestling dial-up when he was exploring the possibilities of wireless broadband, and when people had cottoned on to that, he was selling the idea of cloud computing. Merlin had tablets when people still had laptops. Merlin became the place for trendsetters and go-getters. One shop became two, then three, then a dozen, then a hundred. Mr Khan's shop was his twelfth acquisition. When Merlin Electronics went public the share value quadrupled within twenty minutes.

Problem was, he couldn't find suppliers that saw the future the way he did. The only way was to take over the supply side, too. So, while other manufacturers were still in Japan and Taiwan and Korea, he set up shop in mainland China, making his own silicon: Merlin Technologies was born. Within three years there was hardly a computer or mobile phone on the planet that didn't have his chips inside. Then the spacemen and the scientists and the military men came to call, and soon there were Merlin chips in every satellite guidance system, every missile, every fighter jet and every kind of esoteric piece of high-end equipment on

Earth—and above it, and beyond it. Before long he'd left shopkeeping far behind. So that's when he'd sold his chain of shops, took to the slopes and effectively disappeared from view while he planned his next move.

Ah, that was when Jade came into his life. He'd never had much time for women—correction, he'd never had *any* time for women—except, of course, as colleagues and business associates. That's how it started with Jade. At around the time Merlin Technologies was founded and he'd decided to move here more or less permanently, Jade came into his life. Jade Marks she was, tall and skinny with long black hair, fake tan, and an Essex accent that could have etched silicon all on its own. She started as his assistant's assistant, and moved around the company, but she never seemed far from view. Reports of her work were good—more than good—and so, to cut a long story short, she became his personal assistant, sharing an office, and, eventually, a bed. It was Jade who first heard his plans. It was often Jade who came up with the best ideas. It was Jade, for example, who alerted him to the tax advantages of philanthropy.

Wow, he'd forgotten that. That was *her* idea. Selling things? Been there, done that, she said. Making things to sell? Top of the tree, Jungle V. I. P., she said. The next step is give money to people who invent the things to make. Scientists. Engineers.

And then Jade disappeared, as suddenly as she'd arrived. She handed in her notice at the company's New Year's Eve party as 2020 became 2021. He begged her to stay, but she simply wouldn't be persuaded. She had a mother in Basildon or Billericay or Braintree or somewhere who had Alzheimer's, she said, and needed looking after. And so she just vanished. He remembered the last thing she said as he paced, impotently, while she packed her few belongings. "Don't forget the past as well as the future, Ruxie," she said. He couldn't make much of it back then. But now, he thought, light was beginning to dawn. There's some promising work in Cambridge, his advisers had told him. Archaeology, of all things.

He wondered what Jade was doing now.

Chapter 12. Contender

Xandarga Station, Earth, c. 55,680,000 years ago

Then were they condescended that King Arthur and Sir Mordred should meet betwixt both their hosts, and everych of them should bring fourteen persons; and they came with this word unto Arthur. Then said he: I am glad that this is done: and so he went into the field.
Sir Thomas Malory — *Le Morte D'arthur*

The fight took place in the basement below the bar. It was a huge, low-ceilinged space supported by monumental, square pillars. Ruxie wondered if it had once been a parking garage. If so, no longer — the pillars, the floor, indeed every corner was occupied by punters eager for spectacle. The program started with music, acrobats, jugglers, clowns and fire-eaters, for all the world like an old-time circus troupe that had rolled into some nowhere town rather than the Capital of the Galaxy. There were dancers, too.

Xalomé was not dancing tonight. She was wedged in next to him. Her hand groped for his, and met it. There was little chance that any spoken word would have met its target through the fusillade of excited noise. Ruxie and Xalomé stood on a bench, three or four rows above ringside. Above, and to the left and right, people were thronged. And more than just people. Some of the fight fans cast inhuman shadows under the pillar-mounted sconces. Scent rose, the sweat of expectation. A golden aura flowed across the floor like dry ice in the spotlights.

It was time for the fight to begin.

The referee entered. Wizened, ornately robed, one of the few Uqbar masters to have survived a career unscathed. But no—one of his hands was surely prosthetic, though it was hard to tell amid the folds of his kimono.

"Ladies and Gentlemen!" brayed an announcer from a commentary box that Ruxie couldn't see: "Give it up for Rating Spaceman Ko Handor Raelle, soon to be of the 17th Rigel!"

Screams as Ko, the challenger, entered the ring like he already owned it, robed in scarlet and black, preceded by tumblers and acrobats, and flanked by two burly supporters. The home crowd bawled deafening appreciation. Ko made the required three circuits of the ring, waving and bowing.

Then, the reigning champion. "Make a crushing Xandarga noise for Axaxaxas Mlö, undefeated heavyweight champion of the Southern Tethys!" Yells, cheers, howls. More tumblers and acrobats, and then a tightly bunched nest of women, naked, shaved and oiled, writhing in a complex choreography that concealed the form within. On a signal the women dispersed, trailing multi-colored streamers. Unfurling from within, the champion drew himself to his full height. The crowd was quenched into silence.

They had known it, all the time. Of course they had. But the sight of the champion in the flesh was breathtaking. As was the sheer audacity of Ko, in having thrown down the gauntlet in an elaborate ceremony three days earlier. Ruxie gulped. What had Ko let himself in for? Axaxaxas Mlö, the color of space relieved only by blood-red eyes and white fangs, was a Khong, and among the last vestiges of an ancient adapine race now confined to the high forest plateau of South Polar Gondwana. The Champion must have been almost three meters tall and weighed in at least three hundred fifty kilos, all of it muscle and bone. His fists looked like boulders of black basalt.

In the center of the ring, the champion and the challenger made their ritual obeisances, and retired to diagonally opposite corners of the ring, where they were armed and armored according to ritual evolved over hundreds of centuries and now considered as eternal as the void. Vambraces. Helms with full-face visors. Knee pads. Indrico-leather boots. Knuckle-dusters, rough-cast from depleted uranium shell casings, blue-gray vertices shining raw under the lights.

The whistle blew.

Ko barreled himself straight at the champion before the Khong could draw breath. He smashed his balled fists into his adversary's groin. Blood spurted in crimson gouts. The Khong grunted and looked down, almost abstractedly, as if his siesta had been interrupted by a mosquito. He picked up Ko in both hands, ground his spiked visor into Ko's face, and hurled him across the ring. The noise of the crowd could not conceal the crunch of bones as Ko's face hit the deck. The referee started to count time in a keening ritual song, but Ko rose just before the end. Blood streamed from inside his visor and down his neck, congealing above his collar bone. Ruxie was glad that he couldn't see Ko's face.

Axaxaxas Mlö lumbered over, looked down at the puny contender, and laughed. The noise of it was horrible, hideous. The Khong swung one fist on the end of a meter and a half of pendulum arm. It hit Ko's visor with the impact of a wrecking ball on a watermelon. Ko's head snapped backwards and he flipped onto the floor where he lay in a puddle of what looked like bone chips, blood and his own piss.

"Ruxie—I can't look." Xalomé turned and buried her face in his neck. Ruxie said nothing. He felt that whatever he wanted, whatever he wished, he was forced to watch the ritual dismemberment of his friend by this monster.

But, once again, Ko recovered, although much more slowly than before. He turned himself onto his hands and knees, slithering on the slimed floor of the ring. The champion lumbered over, once again, joshing and hamming it up to the crowd before he dealt what could only be a death blow.

It was to be his undoing. As the Khong bent over to examine its prize, Ko sprang upwards, smashing his helmet into the Khong's abdomen, winding him. The Khong toppled over Ko's back, so that his immense legs lay like tree trunks on either side of Ko's body. Slicked in his own fluids, Ko was now an unstoppable demon. He turned himself onto his back, sat up, grabbed the champion's loincloth, shredding the supple leather with the heavy metal blades of his knuckledusters, pummelled at the champion's genitalia with armored fists. Axaxaxas Mlö roared in pain and shock, but could not rise from the surface of the ring, now as slippery as the deck of a whaler in a storm. Ko now moved in for the kill. He unstrapped his helm, tearing it from his head and flinging it into the crowd. His face was a mask of blood.

Then from a fold of his loincloth Ko drew, with great theatricality, a set of false fangs, which, like knuckle-dusters, had been sheared from spent battle-armor. Fitting them into his mouth, he rose above the prone form of the Khong, sought cheers—and got them—and then dove, like a vulture into the bloodied hole of a carcass. The identity of what Ko drew up between his teeth, sinewy, red and still pulsing, Ruxie dared not even think about. The crowd screeched in maroon-flecked ecstasy.

The celebration surged well into the night, the tables of the harbor-district tavern crowded with glasses both full and spent, the floors awash with beer and bodies. Ruxie and Xalomé were among them, but Xalomé remained curiously remote, detached; unwilling, it seemed, to join in the spirit of things, in contrast to the many other women now wrapped round Ruxie's colleagues on benches or on the floor in every imaginable state of abandon.

Ruxie was now resigned to this. He forgot Xalomé. He forgot the other women. He hooked up instead with a group of barrack-mates and concentrated on downing as much beer as he could. One of his colleagues looked down, wide-eyed, at a bulge in Ruxie's crotch.

"Ruxie, man—is that a pistol you're packin'… or…? And if not, why aren't you flaunting what you've got? After all, there are babes about." General laughter. Ruxie was puzzled, at first, until he reached down the inside pocket of his pants and, in a state of shock, realized that he'd walked out of the weapons range that afternoon with a Higgs projector. He hadn't signed it back in. Nobody made that mistake. Not ever. He'd be toast for sure. But with the ingenuity with which only the seriously drunk are blessed, he conceived a plan. If he snuck into the weapons range before daybreak, fiddled the records slightly, no one would ever know, would they?

Result.

"Well… er… it is a pistol. Actually." He was as nonchalant as he could manage. "So… well, make my day."

There was a commotion at the door of the tavern. Ruxie could not, at first, see what it was all about. A chaos of shouts and confusion. He was dimly aware that Xalomé had gone, and he could no longer see Ko, either. Either he was buried in the crowd, or the party was going on without him. The shouts from the door morphed from yells of indignant rage into screams of agony and pain, and then Ruxie could see the cause of the disturbance.

Oh no. Another monster. Without needing to be told, Ruxie knew that the shadowy Mr Spektor had sent another of his associates to collect Ko's winnings. An associate who would be quite capable of bending Axaxaxas Mlö and any other likely champion into pretzels. Ruxie felt beer and bravado inflate inside him and rose from his seat, side-arm in hand. Months of practice that could not be dulled by alcohol kicked into action. Ruxie's fingers primed the charge. At that moment the crowd near the door was brutally thrown aside by the newcomer. Bodies flew through the air, and from amid the chaos emerged a moving monolith, towering, gray, apparently unstoppable.

"Shit, man—it's a Flintsider. We'd better split," said one of Ruxie's drinking partners. Ruxie said nothing. The eye of stillness in the storm raging all around him, Ruxie held the weapon at full arm's length and pulled the trigger. As he did so he thought of Xalomé. The thought hit him like a kick in the ribs just as the Flintside enforcer imploded with a sharp crack, its component silicon carbide molecules and gallium neurites redistributed at several quintillion random points throughout the Galaxy. Silence descended. With all eyes on him, Ruxie calmly pocketed the particle projector and left the bar.

Ruxie walked back to the barracks through silent streets. He first took a detour to return the purloined projector to the weapons range, a plan that went off without a hitch. He felt deflated after the night's events. Although he'd returned the weapon, discharging it in a public place, and killing a civilian—even an alien hood—would, surely, have serious consequences. Given that the balloon went up in a bar patronized by spacers, he wondered why he hadn't been picked up by Naval Police within minutes. But where he should have been anxious, he was filled with empty apathy.

He passed unhindered into the compound, and felt and saw very little until he was in his own dorm, facing his own bed.

The first thing that struck him was the noise. The same noise that had swirled around him at the boxing match: the animal baying of spectators. It came from all around him, but was directed, focused, at his own bed, now before him. A bed drenched in the saffron aura of sex.

It was Ko's bare back he saw first, and his bare hindquarters, as he pumped away at a woman on her knees and elbows, on Ruxie's bed. The crowd roared its appreciation. The woman was screaming for Ko. Screaming for him to push deeper. Screaming for him to rip her insides out, to take her as he'd taken down the Khong.

The woman on Ruxie's bed was Xalomé.

Ruxie turned on his heel and walked out. Five hours later he shipped out for the Trifid Nebula.

Chapter 13. Correspondent

London and Cambridge, England, Earth, March 2025

At length burst the argent revelry,
With plume, tiara and all rich array,
Numerous as shadows haunting fairily
The brain, new stuff'd, in youth. With triumphs gay
Of old romance.
John Keats — *The Eve of St Agnes*

Jadis' nerves fell away as soon as she took her seat at the press conference — MacLennane to her left, Jack on her right — and had been introduced to the crowd of journalists, photographers and cameramen who'd crammed, almost on top of each other, it seemed to her, in the small but unnaturally brightly lit library that London's Royal Institution had arranged. Not that anyone paid very much attention to her two male outriders, because she'd looked (as they'd hoped) as marvelously un-academic as might be imagined.

She'd fretted for several days about what to wear, as (she'd felt) she had little sense for such things, except that what suited her least of all was indecision. The few women academics she knew were, in the main, as unconscious of fashion as she was — either that, or they went to the other extreme and dolled up to the nines, dressing to impress — something which she felt might be fine for some people, but only made her feel uncomfortable. Her male friends included Roger MacLennane, who always wore the same dark, slightly crumpled suit; and Avi Malkeinu, whose idea of female fashion probably extended only as far as swimwear.

That left Jack, and he was biased.

"I think I'd have to declare an interest," he'd said, in his best mock-serious voice, as, shirt-sleeves rolled up, he'd rubbed her back as she sat up in the bath one evening several days earlier, "as not only do I love you, but I love you more each day, as there is progressively more of you to love"—at which she'd snorted and soaked him with bubble-laden water. He'd sat for a moment, quite still on the edge of the bath, wet through, smiling quizzically, but saying nothing. So he did what she knew he'd do—something so practical, so funny, so Jack. He'd stripped and climbed in behind her, a leg on either side. She was, by now, in hoots of giggles, the water surging and splashing around her, around him, and all over the floor.

"Give me one of those Paleolithic mother-goddesses every time," he'd said, half laughing, half growling, and starting to rub her shoulders and neck, which she loved—but not without first giving each of her increasingly sore and swollen breasts a playful squeeze—which she liked rather less.

She decided that she enjoyed being pregnant. She enjoyed the fullness of it. The only bad thing about it, after the horrible first couple of months, was the backache, hence the time spent in the bath. But what had surprised her—and delighted her—was how much her desire for Jack had sharpened. She supposed that it might have something to do with the physicality of it, that here was starkly tangible reassurance that she was tied to the Earth.

That, and her recent rediscovery of the sense of smell, and especially his smell, an ineffable sense of masculinity, nothing very strong—not like unwashed socks or stale beer or anything like that—but an instantly recognizable presence that reassured her, and which lingered in the flat even when he wasn't physically there. Some mornings it had been extremely difficult to leave his embrace, as if she were attached to him by a bungee cord. Hence his candid lack of objectivity, whether she wore a stylish designer outfit, or 'Horrible' (her baggy old once-purple jersey). She felt that he'd have adored her just the same had she been wearing a dustbin liner.

For his part, Jack found Jade's pregnancy enchanting. Her body was changing in all kinds of ways that he loved to examine in the tiniest detail, as if he were a surveyor, mapping the topography of an unexplored continent in the throes of some incremental but ultimately profound change of climate, from the trimly temperate, to the lush and exotic.

For her, then, her weight taken by the water and Jack's body for a chair, her lover had crystallized into a pair of hands. Funny that she'd paid so little attention to them before, but pregnancy was refining all her senses, not only smell and taste. His were the hands of a man who belonged outdoors—the hands of a field geologist, the hands of contradiction—calloused and ridged as they endured frost and thaw, but capable of marvelously sensitive precision and agility, as those same rough fingertips felt their way towards a fossil or crystal so fragile that it might be shattered by a drop of water — and cradled it unharmed to safety. And so she craved the touch of his hands, the counterpoint of roughness and gentleness, as they traversed her curving form, as if constantly recording, measuring her totality at any instant. As her body swelled, so did her need for him, until it was like a constant drone in the background of her life. However, as her insistent desire resonated with Jack's own, she felt him rise and grow behind her, in the small of her back. And the water was getting cold, too.

"Out you get, young man," she'd said, unmoving, her eyes still closed.

"'Fraid not," he'd countered, "as I am at present pinned to the spot by a Dangerous Wild Animal."

She gripped the sides of the bath, put her feet together and crouched — wriggling the arced expanse of her behind at Jack, teasingly, mockingly — and then stood fully upright. Just before she stepped out in search of a towel he'd looked up at her and for a moment she was a vast statue, shining with water, the fullness of her body exaggerated by the foreshortened angle of view. Jack sank into the bath, filling the space she'd left, stretched out, looked up at her and said:

"There was a reason for those Paleolithic mother-goddesses, you know."

"Hmm?" She had started to dry her hair.

"They illustrate the inherent superiority of women. If only in the geometrical sense." She turned suddenly to lean over the bath, a mad flurry of wild hair, eyes and towel —

"I said, out — you — get!"

Jack did, at least, have a constructive idea. If she couldn't ask Roger what to wear, why not ask *Mrs* Roger? She'd be at the celebration tomorrow.

"You can ask her then," he said. "Quite a character, Marjorie MacLennane," said Jack. "I think you'd like her."

"I had no idea that Roger was married!" she exclaimed. "What do *you* think of her?"

"Me? She's terrifying. But that shouldn't deter *you*."

If Professor Ernestine Yanga only looked like the President of a local Women's Institute, then Marjorie MacLennane really was one, and many other things besides. She was a pillar of the Conservative Association, a Church Commissioner, and judged a hand of bridge with such frightening perspicacity that few ever dared challenge her. She would have it that as a daughter of a Brigadier-General, her life was dedicated to service.

Most people found her too intimidating to talk to, or even approach, on those occasions (rare) when she accompanied Roger to departmental parties. For her part, she found most of the academics not to her taste, and even if they had been, they'd have very little to discuss. Many of them detested everything she stood for, and shunned her in what she considered a singularly illbred fashion, by talking over her in her presence, or simply turning their backs. But when Roger threw a small party to celebrate Jack's doctorate and the impending publication of the paper in *Nature* ('Large-scale anthropogenic landscape modification in the Upper Pleistocene of France,' by J. L. Markham, John A. Corstorphine, Avram Y. Malkeinu and Roger Sutherland MacLennane), she felt she could hardly refuse.

"You really must meet Jack," Roger had implored, "and you must certainly meet Jadis." *Jadis*? What kind of a name was that? But then, she sighed, this was likely to be her husband's finest hour, and perhaps a last hurrah before he was kicked out to pasture. So duty called.

When she actually met Jadis, she found her disarmingly unlike what she had expected—although, if pressed, the nature of that expectation would have been ill-defined. At first she was puzzled. To her, Jadis seemed a mixture of opposites. On the one hand she seemed ethereal, almost transparent, and distracted, as if she didn't really belong on this planet. Her fiercely black gaze, on the other hand, betokened a person earthy, practical, unlikely to be intimidated by anyone. Rather like she was herself, in fact.

The truth was that Marjorie saw herself in Jadis, as a young woman, a graduate of Girton with a Double First in Natural Sciences, which is how she had met her junior-research-fellow husband. But it had been much more difficult for women in her position to pursue careers of their own in those days. That they might do so while conspicuously pregnant was unthinkable, yet pregnancy seemed to suit Jadis very well. So she had taken Jadis under her wing, and invited her to call on her at home.

"You can never go wrong with a Little Black Number," Marjorie had said, when Jadis had called the day after the party at the MacLennane's imposing Victorian villa, exposing a rail of Chanel gowns in her wardrobe to the kind of scrutiny which her late grandfather had reserved for drilling the troops before Mountbatten, as the Union flag had been lowered for the last time over Delhi.

"Try this. It was made for me when I had to go to some ball or another, when I was pregnant with Fiona. That was... well, Fiona has children of her own now."

Marjorie helped the gown over Jadis' head. Marjorie and Jadis were about the same height, so it fitted very well. It was classically black and breathtakingly elegant. Jadis looked at the mirror, disbelieving, enchanted. Then she looked at Marjorie, whose expression was unfathomable. "*That's* the one for you, my dear. Would you like to try some pearls?"

At the back of the press conference sat Marcel Montgolfier, a distant relation of the pioneer balloonists, but proximately the veteran London correspondent of *Agence France Presse*. A press briefing in London on the topography of *La France Profonde* seemed an incongruity that bordered on effrontery, but no matter; in any case, one could forgive these English scientists in their startling assertion that French civilization was so ancient that it had preceded humanity itself.

This offered by twinkling bespectacled figure at the right of the panel, the man Montgolfier's press pack described as Professor Roger Sutherland MacLennane, FRS, from the University of Cambridge. Not that

Montgolfier didn't know this, of course. MacLennane was a well-known scientist, who while reserved, always seemed to be good for an off-the-record briefing. Our picture of Neanderthal Man as the primitive savage (MacLennane said) was a distortion caused by the fact that history is always written by the victor: when the first *Homo sapiens* came into Europe some 40,000-or-so years ago, it was not to meet a debased tribe like Charles Darwin's Fuegians, but the bones of a civilization that had, in his words, "endured for eight thousand centuries, and had created megaliths the size of mountains."

The theme was continued by Dr Jack Corstorphine, the tall young scientist on the left of the panel, in the casual jacket and polo shirt, who explained, with a quiet but compelling authority, that the breadth and extent of this ancient civilization would have been incomprehensible to our own ancestors, who would therefore have seen only wilderness, weaving the bones of this great and ancient culture into the legend and myth of centuries. As the ruins of Roman Britain had appeared to the barbarian Saxons as the works of mythical giants, so the megalith at Saint-Rogatien-Les-Remillards in Gascony had appeared to our ancestors — and also, said Dr Corstorphine, to ourselves, until our own researches had recognized it as being "something quite extraordinary."

Dr Corstorphine was a new face to Montgolfier, but in his assured delivery he could tell that he was one of MacLennane's latest *protégés*. But MacLennane and Corstorphine were the sideshows, the *hors-d'oeuvres*, compared with what was obviously the main attraction, a young woman who was looking up at Corstorphine, as he spoke, with an expression of—what was it? Adoration?—so intense that it could have melted granite. When the girl (identified as 'Ms Jadis L. Markham'), rose to speak, the room fell silent, except for the sound of a few people swallowing and some quickly stifled coughs.

This was not a scientist—this was a movie star. As Jadis Markham discussed, with a dignified poise, how the ancient inhabitants of Europe had done more than leave a few isolated monuments, but instead had modified the very face of the Earth, Montgolfier and the assembled press corps began to lose the thread of the story and take a greater interest in its speaker. She was dressed in classic Chanel. Montgolfier (who had covered fashion in his time, in between stints on the diplomatic desk) thought her gown had been a *couture* item from the sixties: could anyone name *any* scientist, let alone such a *débutante*, who could carry off such cool retro chic? And—unbelievable—she was at least five months pregnant, and yet the gown fitted her as if pregnancy was her natural state, the state in which she was most at ease: she simply glowed. The whole effect, the way her outrageously untamed cloud of glossy dark hair (who said scientists were buttoned-up?) tumbled over her pale shoulders, her *décolletage*, was enchanting! And her face! Framed—and indeed, sometimes partly obscured—by this nebula of hair, were two bright but yet unfathomably dark wells of intelligent, calculating ferocity. She was like a cat, a wild thing, he thought, her wildness kept in tight coils by an adamantine composure which on the surface appeared easy and carefree, but which—he was sure—was, not so far beneath, passionate and determined.

All this in a girl of *how* old? Twenty-one? If this was another of MacLennane's *protégées*, Montgolfier would bet that she would be his last, his swansong, because she'd be impossible to follow.

As Montgolfier sat, enraptured, it occurred to him that although the story itself was important—it certainly was that, and would be the centre of all discussion for weeks and months—he was not watching a press conference so much as a wedding, or a coronation. All this from tiny things he'd noticed that were never spoken out loud for all that they were quite evident, even from his place at the back. How Jadis, for all the control that belied her years, for all that she conducted the wolf-pack of journalists as if she were Karajan directing the Berlin Philharmonic, would frequently glance at Jack, only for a moment, but with an expression of such—how could he describe it—supplication?—and his face would bestow a warmth of reassurance in return. And all this presided over by MacLennane, who watched both of them with proprietorial satisfaction. This would be a great story, Montgolfier thought, because the people were at least as interesting as the tale they told. This is the next dynasty of archeology in the making (he would write). He hoped he'd be able to get a picture of Jadis.

At the very end, Montgolfier essayed a question for this rising star. "Ms Markham," he asked, "excuse my presumption, but how will you reconcile your—how shall I say—imminent family commitments—with what promises to be an extensive program of field research?"

Jadis turned her lighthouse eyes on Montgolfier. She paused for a moment, and it seemed to him that her hair gathered around her face like a brooding storm cloud.

"I'll take them with me of course," she said, with an asperity that made him start. "What else would I do with them?"

And then the storm clouds dissipated as quickly as they had arrived, her face opening into a smile as bright as the sun, and of such innocent loveliness that he thought he'd die right there, at the pinnacle of his long career.

And in *England*.

After the conference, when they'd managed to elude the last of the cameras, supplementary interviews and questions, Roger treated them both to lunch at Fortnum's, but then announced he was staying overnight on in London. "Business at the Royal. Then I'll hole up at the Athenaeum," he'd said, hailing a cab in Piccadilly to take Jadis and Jack to Kings Cross. "But don't forget, you two—my office, nine o'clock, day after tomorrow. Might have a bit of news." He tapped his nose conspiratorially, his expression unreadable behind his glasses.

The train home pulled through the cramped crenellations of North London and eventually eased into flat country under the immense East Anglian sky, the land beneath clothed in the brilliant green haze of early Spring. Jadis leaned into Jack, and neither said a word for a long time. A full hour into the journey, Jack pulled her closer. "Might *I* ask you a question, Ms Markham?" he began, in his best Monty-Python French Accent. This time her smile was just for him.

"But of course!"

"You said, *them*. That you'd take *them* with you, into the field, when we get to excavate."

"Well if there are, it's all *your* fault, you silly man," she said, pushing closer still: and then more quietly, looking directly up at him and smiling, blearily, but just for him: "'Nothing like a good seeing to,' you said, 'for clearing the brain.'"

She began to nod, and it was only then that Jack realized how tired she must have been—the trip had taken it out of her: that, and the spotlight. And how he still had to listen to MacLennane's advice: just make sure *you're* not the one left behind. How he'd struggled through his thesis defence, when she, a graduate student just starting out, had had all those journalists under her spell. When the train pulled in to Cambridge, she was asleep in his arms.

The next morning, as she looked over the breakfast table for the Oxford marmalade, Marjorie MacLennane saw Roger's unopened copy of *The Times*. Such a waste, she thought, given that he'd get his own copy at his club. Then she remembered why Roger had been away and took another look at the lead story. 'Civilization dates back a million years, scientists say,' read the headline, but the picture was of a young girl, hair awry, who for all her youth had the steel of ancient wisdom in her eyes.

"Good for you, Jadis Markham," said Marjorie, marmalade now quite forgotten.

Chapter 14. Convalescent

Xandarga Space Elevator, Earth, *c.* 55,680,000 years ago

O what can ail thee, knight-at-arms
Alone and palely loitering?
John Keats — *La Belle Dame Sans Merci*

"Congratulations," she said. Her hands were in the pockets of her white medical gown, now opened, revealing a smart cream blouse and gray wool skirt beneath. Glints of warmth in wise, green eyes, framed by high cheekbones in an olive-brown face. Soon-to-be-ex-Admiral Ruxhana Fengen Kraa quite forgot his racked breathing, the sweat of effort. The doctor walked towards him, clack of heels on parquet silenced by crimson pile as she approached. Ruxhana was transfixed, at once gripped by an urge to flee and a compulsion to stay, Just to see what happened next.

The same compulsion, in fact, that had gotten him into so much trouble just lately. Oh, well. What the hell.

"Xalomé?" She was now almost close enough to touch and he could sense the saffron of her heat. Panic seized him, a mixture of thwarted desire and bitter betrayal he thought long buried under thirty-eight years of hard fighting.

First, the long war against the Carpetbaggers in the Trifid Nebula, in which he lost an eye and gained field promotion.

Then, a long series of counter-insurgency operations of appalling viciousness against the Jumblies in the Greater Magellanic Cloud, where the *Pax Terrestris* had yet to take hold. This proxy war against Andromeda had cost both his legs, an arm, much of his skull and a third of his cerebral cortex.

And after that? Campaign followed campaign, with trips to Earth ever less frequent. He had only ever once descended from Clarke Orbit, and that was by the Panthalassic Elevator, not down to Xandarga Station. He'd stayed less than a day.

The doctor was standing before him. He relaxed his grip on the bar and turned unsteadily into her retrieving arms, encircled fully in her embrace. She looked up at him, her lips slightly parted.

"Xalomé? If that's who you want me to be, Admiral, then so I shall be."

"But... how? Are you...?"

"Hush now, Admiral. You've exerted yourself quite enough for one session. Your new bones are knitting nicely, but such massive reconstruction takes time. What you need now is a shower and bed." He could see the curve of Earth filling a panoramic port with blue against the stars. She followed his glance and turned back to him, reading his thought. "Tomorrow, as they say, is another day," she said. "Now, do you think you can walk a little more?"

"I think so, Doctor, if you can steady me."

With her help he made his way to the bathroom. He allowed her to remove his robe so that he could step into the shower cubicle. Suddenly shy, he never let her see anything more than his bare back. To have allowed her to glimpse him in front view would have been too much. His face would have been a study in bafflement and fear. What's more, he had an erection, uncomfortably taut. He looked down at his prong, rigid and sharply bladed at the end, as if it were an alien life form: like the rest of his new flesh, still pale with regenerative newness. He felt dizzy — the walls of the shower cubicle ballooned out to cushion him, and a seat rose from the floor to break his fall.

When it was sure that the patient was safe, the cubicle's AI withdrew the side-impact cushions and turned on the shower. A blast of hot nanofluidics stripped him of the sweat that had congealed around him like a shell. Steam rose. The hiss of the drops hitting the floor made him drowsy.

"Xalomé?"

"Shh. There, now. Time to get dry, I think." The nanofluidics were replaced instantly by blasts of hot, fresh air, reminding Ruxhana of the bridge of the *Sorceror*. The memory immediately cost him his erection, but he now felt he could hardly stand unaided. The Doctor, businesslike, frowned in concern, dressed him in a new bathrobe, guided him from the bathroom and into his bed, covering him, monitoring his temperature, blood pressure and vital signs.

"No, I think you'll do," was the last thing she said before he blacked out.

He awoke in the dark and for a moment had no idea where he was, or why. He tried to sit up, but the effort made him feel sick, so he eased himself gently down onto the mattress. But there was a hand on his chest, and a body next to his in the dark, and he remembered.

"Xalomé—"

"We've been through all that. Haven't we?"

"I—"

"In any case, you have more pressing concerns." He felt the smoothness of a thigh laid against his, and a hand, gripping and releasing the hairs on his chest, making its way downwards, across his belly. He felt proud—stupidly so, he thought, given that he'd had no part in his rescue and reconstruction—that his new belly was more toned than his old one had been, and that his prong seemed heavier and more serrated. It began to rise under her touch.

"My job, Admiral, has been to make you better," she said. "Think of me as all the King's Horses and all the King's Men, glueing dear old Humpty Dumpty back together again."

"Humpty Dumpty. That's me, right?"

"Mmm-hmm." Her fingers began to trace the razored ridges of his prong, feeling their way gingerly around the sharp, multiply bladed tip. "Only, unlike our ovoid friend of lore, you're only being stuck together so you can feel it all the harder, when they shove you off an even higher wall."

"The fleet. My fleet," He gripped a fistful of her hair, more forcefully than he'd meant to.

"Ow! Yes, the fleet. You probably haven't realized it yet—after all, you've been in no fit state—and I wasn't about to let you know any sooner, because the stress might have killed you. But the loss of the fleet will cost you your commission. At the very least."

"And at the most?"

"I don't think you need worry about that yet. You've been in worse scrapes. After all, as I say, it's been my job to put you back together, and the process isn't yet complete. And, if I may say so, I've been quite pleased with some of the—um—additional refinements I've built into the New You." She giggled and sat up. He saw her only in silhouette, but she still had a hand around his prong. "Improvements to—well, size, mainly. And stamina."

"Improvements?"

"Sure. On a lonely job like this, a girl has got to find whatever fun she can. No—don't move. You can pay me later."

"Pay you?"

"Not in the way you think. But I think I can help you out of this. But I'll want something in return."

"Want...?"

"Perhaps I shouldn't have said anything. As I said, tomorrow is another day. And as I also said, the best thing you can do now is simply to lie back and think of Gondwanaland. Stay still, now." She swung a leg over him, so that he felt the plush of her thighs gripping him high across his hips. With great care, holding her breath, she lowered herself onto him, and, having done so, let out a small cry of pain. She sat fully upright, maneuvering him still more deeply, and sighed.

"Oh, wow — I *am* good," she said. "No — I told you, don't move." Looking up at her silhouette in Earthlight, he could hardly help himself, his hands tracing the musked contours of her body. Her aura deepened as she moved until it blanketed them both, wings of a purple emperor, barred with crimson rays. She gripped his hips with her knees and lifted herself from him.

"Xalomé?"

"Hmm?" She looked up, green eyes gleaming in shadow, tapeta flashing, aura deepening in indigo waves.

"Am I...? Do you think?"

"Are you fit enough for the main event? Oh, yes, I think so. All part of the therapy. Doctor's orders." And then she turned over, flaunting her hindquarters at him, thrusting them outwards so that her inflamed vulva emerged as a golden center of a coruscating turquoise mandala. He rolled over, feeling his new limbs creak, and, very delicately, rose to his knees, steadying himself behind her, on the milky backs of her thighs, fingers gripping the mane of hair running down the nape of her neck.

She whimpered. His prong sparked in a flash of agony as he brushed it against her thighs, bending it at the root. He winced as the muscles in his new knees locked in cramp. She bent forward, burying her face in the bed, reaching back to reassure him and draw him in. A fleeting touch of fingertips on his shaft, and then he was within her, his prong transforming in ways never seen in the open air, in response to the histamines secreted by the folds of her flesh, the edges of his glans inflating into barbs of horn that locked him into her, and which raked her deeply as he moved, first uncertainly, and then with renewed reserves of power, so that with each surge she was pulled clear of the mattress and then driven further into its folds. When he spasmed, her aura darkened with terrifying suddenness to the null of space. She screamed then, a brutal yell of ecstasy and terror. Her aura winked out of existence before resuming, slowly, a skulking orange. She sighed and pulled herself away, releasing him. Tiny rivulets of blood, darker shadows in the darkness, flecked his prong and her inner thighs. She fell forwards onto the bed. He could not see her face.

He awoke on his back and found himself paralyzed. His eyes, now open, could not close, but the square, white luminous tiles of the ceiling were all he could see. The air was different, too. Ionized, like the sea. Entirely different from the fug of the stateroom, in which his last memory was the rankness of spent sex. As if on cue he heard her voice, and though he could not move to see her, he had a clear image of her once again in her doctor's gown and conservative clothes. Without knowing how, or feeling any sensation at all in his lips and tongue, he spoke.

"Why can't I move?"

"Because, Admiral, this really is going on inside your head. Like the stateroom. And the shower. And everything else. I felt I had to make a point, that's all."

"So... you aren't really Xalomé, then? My Xalomé?"

"Not that again. Look, if you want me to be 'your Xalomé,' whoever that is, then 'your Xalomé' I shall be. If you think it will help."

"Will it?"

"Whatever."

"But the real Xalomé...?"

"... has been married for thirty years to a rat-faced little corporal in the catering corps; lives in a low-to-middling suburb of a thrillingly dull stripway sprawl on an incredibly boring planet in the Shit-For-Brains Quadrant; has twelve mewling kits, and ten well-chewed dugs dangling down to her knees. Life for her is unending drudgery with no prospect of relief and it's only the diazepam that keeps her going. Frankly, she's let herself go. What opportunities wasted. What intelligence. What talent."

Ruxhana choked. "You know this? You really know this?"

"Of course I don't. How could I? And in any case we're getting off the point. As far as you're concerned, in this reality, in this — continuum, if you like — I am Xalomé, your Xalomé, if you want me to be."

He did not find this offer comforting. It was not what he wanted that had mattered, but what she had wanted, and that he could never work out what her desires might have been.

For years — decades — he had wondered what had happened to Xalomé, even to the extent of querying naval records with the resources available only to a Fleet Admiral. Not even Special Ops could cloak its activities from him, had he chosen to examine them —

which he had. There had been no record of her existence. None whatsoever.

Of course, he could have discovered anything and everything he wanted to learn about the career of his erstwhile barrack-mate Ko Handor Raelle. But some creatures were best left to fester beneath the stones whence they came. It was only a chance glance at a newsfeed a decade earlier that told him that ageing, minor-league Uqbar-rules contender Raelle had come third in a duel with a Khong called Azazazat Gwár. Ko's skull had been smashed in and flattened, his brains spurting all over the ring and into the baying, Antarctic crowd. An old score, finally settled.

"But I have something to tell you," she said. "To ask you, really."

"Me?"

"Yes. A task. A job." She sounded slightly ashamed, he thought, as if this 'job' were something furtive, shady. For the first time he felt that he had the upper hand, for all that he could not move and had no idea about the reality he inhabited, nor how he might escape it.

"Oh, really? After this—betrayal? And double betrayal? You want me to help you?" The revelation that none of their lovemaking had been consensual, or even real, had hit hard. "Well, fuck you. If the Navy wants to rip my spine out, they're welcome. I no longer care."

She saw her face hove into view over the horizon of his own. Her hair was disordered, her eyes red-rimmed. He could feel himself turn, power returning to his neck muscles. He looked straight into her face and spat. She wiped her face with her sleeve.

"I guess I deserved that," she said. "For what it's worth, I'm sorry..."

"Sorry? For leading on a naïve country bumpkin? I'm sure it goes on all the time. Character-building. Think nothing of it—you whore." He sat up and found himself in a theater gown on a gurney in a room that contained no other furniture. The walls and floor were clad in the same luminous, white tiles as the ceiling. He could see neither doors nor windows. The doctor—clothed, as he had suspected, in her sensible gown, blouse and skirt—came and sat down next to him.

"Where am I?"

Her voice returned to an even tone and temper. "When I said you were inside your own head, I wasn't being entirely truthful."

"Oh, you do surprise me."

"We're in what's called an 'Xspace'."

"'Special Ops,' I suppose?"

"Something like that. If you want."

"Stop telling me what I want. It's what you wanted—what Xalomé wanted—that I wanted to know, but she threw it back at me, the bitch." Silence. What felt, to him, like a guilty pause.

"Okay, Ruxie, truth time. I am not Xalomé. if indeed she ever existed. Or maybe I was. Once. Sort of." She bit her lip, crumpled one fist into another. "It's so very hard to explain."

"Try me."

"Oh, all right. I had hoped not to have to tell you all this, but it seems I've probably fucked it up, for everyone, as I usually do. I'm an exotic of a kind that I don't think you know anything about, because we don't have much to do with... well, with baryonic matter. Not that we don't have feelings, though. Not that we don't care. And we do care. I care. I wouldn't have gone in for this whole charade if I hadn't. Well, would I?

"And as it is truth time, I have another confession to make. I got you into this mess. It was me. All of it. The Slunj, the Discotex, the... well, the destruction of the fleet."

"My... fleet? You?" He tried to swing his legs over the edge of the gurney, but a numbness had gripped his body. He could hardly catch his breath. "You... killed... more than six hundred million people, under my command? You?"

"I know, I know. I wish it didn't have to happen that way, but I am sorry, and I can explain, if you'll let me try..."

"Why should I even listen to this? Here I am, being held captive in some kinky VR dungeon by a crazed alien, and she wants sympathy? Oh, just wheel me before the Board of Enquiry right now. They'd love this. Incompetent. Delusional too. Can't take the pressure. Hears voices, you know."

"Look, Ruxie, I can't take *all* the blame. It was you I wanted, not your crew. And, if I remember correctly, the Senior Under-Secretary for Colonial Defense did advise, very strongly, that just a couple of gunboats would have been enough. Didn't she?"

"Yes, well, I suppose…"

"*Didn't she?*"

"Yes, she did. But how did you… how could you have possibly…" Comprehension dawned. "You? You're not…?" The Doctor stood, silent, arms crossed, waiting. "So, Doctor, whoever you are…"

"If you'd like a name you may call me 'Merlin.'"

"All right. 'Merlin'. So, if you got me into this mess, you can get me out of it, right?"

"Right. And thank you. You won't believe how important this is to us—to me—to… well, everything…" She reached over and grasped his hands in hers.

"So, what's this 'job,' then?"

She sat down on the edge of the bed, and began. "It's complicated."

Chapter 15. Tourists.

Cambridge, England, and Gascony, France, Earth, May, 2025

> Will all Neptune's ocean wash this blood
> Clean from my hand? No; this my hand will rather
> The multitudinous seas incarnadine,
> Making the green one red.
> William Shakespeare — *Macbeth*

It was a relief to be here, at last, and to breathe the air. Not that Saint-Rogatien-Les Remillards was anything like she'd expected. To be sure, she'd known from Jack's pictures that it wasn't a wind-blasted, isolated place in the middle of nowhere, the kind of place filmgoers always associate with prehistory. But she hadn't expected it to be quite so tame. Remember Cholula, Jack had said, and he'd been right.

The village of Saint-Rogatien clustered around the now-famous hill and up its slopes, and there was, indeed, a church and churchyard at the top. And not only a churchyard, but across the cobbled square — the tiny Place Etienne Geoffroy Saint-Hilaire; the Mairie, a small but elegant pink-washed building, set back between the boulangerie and the *Sanglier D'Or bar, tabac, café, pression* and most importantly *Hotel***).

Jack loved to tell her how, when he had first inquired about a permit to dig, the Mairie official had asked precisely where in the commune of Saint-Rogatien Jack had wanted to dig, and the expression of perplexity when Jack had pointed straight down at the tiled floor and said '*Ici!*'

As they lay abed in the *Sanglier D'Or*, the occasional yellow headlight beams from the square below tracing sweeping lighthouse arcs across the ceiling, Jack reminded her that all was not as it seemed. The village had been built on the eastern spur — just one corner — of what had been a much more extensive structure, most of which had been eroded away into the valley. The ancient pyramid had once been two miles high, very much more than twice the height of the tallest skyscrapers ever built by modern humans. The present-day church hardly rose past its metaphorical toes, and did not mark the ancient summit, not by any means. But because of this erosion, there were some places around the village where one might get a direct view of the innards of the monstrous monument.

Tomorrow, he'd promised, if she'd felt up to it, he'd show her the foot of the cliff-face that plunged from the churchyard wall, a full two hundred feet to the valley floor. This cliff, Jack thought, was where part of the pyramid's base had been undercut by water and slumped, creating what he thought was cross-sectional slice right through part of the structure. He'd picked up a few peculiar lithics there on his scouting trip, and there, he thought, she'd have the best chance of getting results fast. No need to dig or remove overburden, just map the cliff face and dig a few test tunnels in places that looked interesting.

On the other hand, as it was, after all, a holiday, a kind of honeymoon, and they were both tired, they could relax, potter about, look around, or even just stay in bed, and look at the cliff another day. The two-day journey in the Peugeot, from Cambridge almost to the foothills of the Pyrenees (she'd driven the first few hundred miles herself) had aggravated the soreness in her back, and the aches in her legs, her belly—indeed, more or less everywhere—were making sleep elusive. Her pregnancy had turned, in the past two or three weeks, from a phase of blossoming and almost boundless vitality to one of continual effort, and her general sleeplessness threatened what reserves she had left. She felt pale, awkward, bloated and huge, like a stranded whale. Her buzzing brain raced ahead far faster than the rest of her bulbous form could match, and thoughts whizzed around her head like so many golden midges illuminated by the slanting rays of autumn. Think ahead, she urged herself. She just had to stick it out, to get over the next couple of months.

Now that their future seemed a little more secure they had decided to be married—they had no relations to speak of, so it was in the Registry Office with Marjorie and Roger as witnesses. Jack's gift to her had been an enticing slice of the past. For her doctorate project, he told her, she was to direct the proposed dig at the Saint-Rogatien cliff face. She'd be in charge of recruitment, management and budget as well as interpreting any finds they might make. She couldn't wait to begin. Further, she'd have to find a base of operations that would last them for at least the next three years, as an expedition quarters as well as a home, a place to raise their family. Their days as full-time residents of Cambridge would soon be over.

He'd help her when he could, of course, but he had mapping and exploration of his own to do. His original trip to France had been an addendum, an afterthought, to a project entirely based and predicated on Britain. He now had to survey the region around Saint-Rogatien to the same level of detail, so that they could set the megalith in context. This meant that the Saint-Rogatien operation itself was hers, to do as she would.

There had been Roger's meeting, as promised, two days after the press conference, a meeting that had opened up such amazing vistas. They were, all three of them—Roger, Jack and herself—pie-eyed and fractious, having handled around a hundred media requests each since the press conference. The press had even tried to get at Avi —whose precociously expert skills as a data wrangler had earned him a credit on the paper—but he had, wisely, disappeared. Three days later he'd sent Jack a note to say he'd gone home, but everything was cool, back in a week—alongside a photo of himself, outside a nightclub in Tel Aviv's swinging Dizengoff Street, wedged between two excited-looking blondes and obviously having the time of his life.

Jack found the whole media circus daunting, at times overwhelming, and in the end, depressing. The questions seemed inane, irrelevant, often stupid, and he was only too aware of how awkward and uncomfortable he must have looked. He felt cramped, stifled, longing to get into the open air and away from all this crap.

Jadis had attracted most media interest, a disproportionate amount of which had predictably been of the inane and stupid sort. She had coped better, but tired more quickly. Jack had noticed a new and disturbing quirk in her; that rather than answer a question, she would pause, and her eyes would, quite literally, switch off. Their luster would disappear in a second, as if her sight were questing inwards, searching for something she couldn't quite place. Her brow would then furrow, and she'd rub her swollen belly distractedly, before returning to reality. "No, no, don't worry about me, I'm fine," she'd insist, resisting Jack and Roger's protests, trying to smile her most winning smile at Jack but not quite succeeding, as if it were an injured butterfly, laboring to get airborne.

Finally, Jack was so worried that he'd called Marjorie, swallowing his earlier fear in the knowledge that the two women had become good friends, to ask whether she might say something, because Jadis wouldn't listen to him: and so Jadis was sternly advised to take things more easily for a day or two. Marjorie also insisted that Roger handle all media enquiries, and that Jack find a portrait of Jadis that could be released to the press, so as to assuage the torrent of media requests.

Rifling through the dreadful clutter that their flat had become (both of them being too tired or too busy to do much about it) Jack had come across a portrait of Jadis that he'd completely forgotten about, filed away in his laptop. It was a picture of her in Torbay, on their first summer vacation together. She'd been standing in a wooded dell, just outside some pothole or other he'd been studying, the sun through the trees making a halo for her hair. While the surface of his mind concentrated on the practicalities of whether this casual snapshot would be a good enough for a press portrait, the rest of him surged with reminiscence.

He could no longer quite be sure, but this photo might have been taken on the very day they'd first made love. Perhaps even at the very same spot. Her face in the picture was open and smiling, and she appeared to have been caught saying something to him — he could not remember what. It struck him, then, how much she'd changed since; that her spirit seemed to have become more urgent, more inward-looking. Like the taste of a wine set to age, their love which had once been gay and simple with no thought of the future, was now darker and more complex, with overtones of sorrow and joy, worry and long experience — and foreboding. His heart ached for her, for the girl he'd first dated, as well as the woman she had become. As her pregnancy had advanced she had become reserved, more controlled, and a little less inclined to present to the world at large anything other than a hard and steely resolve.

The world at large would know nothing of this. To anyone but himself, the photo showed a pretty eighteen-year-old on holiday. He sent it to the University Press Office.

The morning before Roger's meeting, the day after Jack and Jadis had returned from London, she had been in the corner of the office that she now shared with Jack when, looking up from the flood of unopened messages, she saw an enormous camera lens peeping in at her through the window. A tabloid journalist had climbed up the wall with a ladder carelessly left by a contractor, and had been hoping for some unauthorized, exclusive shots of the New Face of Science. Jadis fled to the departmental secretary, who called security. In the departmental office she'd met Jack, who'd left for work later than she had: he'd been trying to sort their domestic paperwork into some kind of order, but not getting very far.

Jack now reported that the flat was under journalistic siege. Unable to exit through the front, he'd had to scale the high wall behind the Nest and make a getaway across a neighbour's garden. His clothes were muddied, his arms scratched. Jadis cooed concern for him, ignoring all else: it had not yet occurred to either where they might go next—they couldn't go home for a day or two—when they turned at once to see Roger, standing in the office doorway.

"Please stay with Marjorie and me," he said, "until the heat's off. And we can have our meeting there."

It felt very peculiar, Jack thought, to be in bed with his new wife in the house of his former doctorate supervisor. For all that the spare bedroom chez MacLennane was welcoming in a chintzy sort of way, and much tidier than their flat, Jack felt like a refugee. More than ever, he wanted to get out into the field, to take Jadis with him — to escape.

When he awoke with these fretful thoughts, his first sight was Jadis, sitting on her side of the bed, with her back to him, legs slightly parted to accommodate the bulge of her belly, combing her hair with that enormous plastic comb she took everywhere with her, like a talisman. She attacked her hair with urgent, rapid strokes, as if it were a task best over and done with. He wondered why she hadn't asked him to do it, a much more relaxed experience they both enjoyed, especially as it often led to other things. Jadis heard Jack wake behind her, and read his mind.

"I'm sorry, Jack. I just don't feel like it much here," she said, not turning round. "Here. At Roger and Marjorie's. It would seem like... well, having sex in church."

Still sitting there, back to him, he saw her skin ripple, her shoulders shake with silent laughter, but the tenor soon turned and she began to emit small, spiky, sobs which she stifled only with difficulty. Jack got out of bed and rushed round to comfort her, quieting her in his arms. She did not explain her change of mood, and Jack did not ask her.

Roger's news, after breakfast, went a considerable way to cheering them up. A couple of years ago (Roger began), a businessman called Ruxton Carr, the elusive head of something called Merlin Technologies, had approached the University, offering a donation of several billion dollars if they'd build a new college with his name on it.

The University, being used to such requests, politely thanked Mr Carr, and deftly pointed out that whereas the University had a superabundance of colleges, it sorely lacked front-rank research facilities that could benefit the whole University, if not the whole world, and mightn't Mr Carr think along those lines instead? So Mr Carr had receded and it was generally assumed that he'd decided to take his wealth elsewhere.

However, it turned out (Roger continued) that the Senate had badly underestimated Mr Carr. He had, it seemed, taken the University at its word, and had been consulting widely on the kinds of research facilities that the University might need — and which, he felt, he'd like to support. Mr Carr was known as a shrewd investor in what at first seemed an eclectic selection of interests, from carbon sequestration technologies to genetic manipulation, from geothermal power to personalized space travel. When *Forbes* magazine asked him, in the only interview he was ever known to have given, if he could characterize his investments in a sentence, he'd said "sure, but I'll do it in just two words: 'The Future.'" Hence the Universities' puzzlement when he chose to endow not one but two new research institutes in Cambridge, neither of which seemed to have much to do with technology, the future, or each other.

One such concern, the Merlin Technologies Astrometry Institute, had been busy in Madingley for two years now, cataloguing the recent spectral history and proper motion of stars in the solar neighborhood, for reasons that nobody could fathom.

"And the second?" Roger asked: "well, that's where we come in." It turned out that the mysterious Mr Carr had been watching the progress of MacLennane's research, and that of his students and associates, for some years, but had only finally chosen to make a commitment when the *Nature* paper had become public.

"That's why I couldn't come back from town with you both," Roger explained, "I had to meet Carr's people at the Royal. Naturally, I couldn't breathe a dicky bird until it had all been inked. I'm sure you'll understand."

The upshot was that Carr had chosen to bankroll what he'd called the Merlin Technologies Institute for Historical Geomorphology. This would—at least initially—be a 'virtual' institute, made of people within the their current department and associates elsewhere.

"Carr knows that institutes are not made of walls, but of people," said Roger. "Carr's people have asked me to head up the new Institute, and I've accepted. After all, I've only a year or so to run at the University proper before they'd boot me out anyway, and I can't hang around here. Marjorie would never stand for it." Jack and Jadis congratulated him, but he pressed ahead.

"My first act as Director is to appoint you, Jack, as its first Senior Research Fellow; my second is to recommend that Jack takes on you, Jadis as its first doctorate student. No need to worry about money or grants, thanks to Mr Carr. You could start tomorrow, but I forbid it. There's some paperwork I need to get done, and anyway you two need a break. You haven't even had a honeymoon. Let's say we start work in a couple of weeks or so, after the Easter Vac?"

Deep in the first night at Saint-Rogatien, Jadis was having a dream in which she'd been in the garden in Chesterton, trying to plant out some summer bedding, but the plants shriveled and died as soon as she put them into the ground. She worked faster and faster, as if trying to beat some innominate contagion, but still it spread. The rising mound of dead and dying plants all around her turned from green, to grey, to red, dripping blood on the grass. When she studied the plants more closely, she saw that they were fetuses, and as she watched in pure horror, the blood smeared and spread, up the wall of the raised bed and into the Nest, up the trees, until, at the end of the leaves, it gathered and rained down on her in a torrent. She looked down and noticed blood rising up her bare legs, but she was stuck fast, unable to move or do anything to stem the hideous tide. But just as she thought she would drown in blood, there came a regular pulse, a subsonic thrum, like the heartbeat of the Earth. Assailed by this calm but unstoppable vibration, the blood coagulated, dried, shattered and blew away like harmless dust; and before her, a vast and green plant rose clear out of the ground, bursting above her head into an immense Van-Gogh sunflower that became the sun.

And still the Earth pulsed.

She woke, still in Jack's arms, the shreds of the dream dissipating like gossamer. But the pulse still beat, softly and insistently, just below the level of hearing. She knew her own pulse, and Jack's. But this was a new pulse, the pulse of a new life, strong and steady, beating inside her. Or, rather, a pulse returned, a pulse she feared had been lost for some time. Wave after wave of relief coursed down to meet it, and she embraced the pulse with triumphant inner shouts of radiant joy. She slept again in a state of happiness that she had not experienced for several weeks.

When she awoke in the dawn, she'd forgotten about the dream, and now stood in the window of the small bedroom in the *Sanglier D'Or*, looking down over the sunlit square. She felt amazingly refreshed, all her aches and pains were gone, and she was eager to meet the day.

"Come on, you silly man!" she teased, pulling the duvet off Jack's still recumbent form, yanking the curtains apart to admit the strong spring sunshine.

"Okay, Boss," came the uncertain reply, but when Jack tried to pull the duvet back, Jadis snatched it away again in a furious cloud of fabric and hair, jumped on the bed, whacked him smartly on the backside, and sprang for the door.

Half an hour later, as Jack ordered coffee on the pavement terrace of the café below, Jadis went to the boulangerie to buy croissants. If this was to be their new home, he felt he could accommodate its easy pace very well. A few minutes later, he watched Jadis return with the paper bag, and at first he didn't recognize her as his wife. The woman he was watching was indeed heavily pregnant, like Jadis, but unlike Jadis had been in the past two or three weeks, this voluptuary had acquired a devastatingly sexy hip-sway that accommodated both her legginess and her bulk with a marked elegance, her long train of hair waving to the rhythm of her movements, just as if she were dancing in her own one-woman conga line to some deep dub pulse. It wasn't until she'd stopped at his table that he was sure it was her.

"What?" she asked, while pulling out her chair and sitting on it in a single, fluid movement. Jack turned to his coffee, slurping it far too fast, coughed at its bitterness, and looked up, a rim of froth on his upper lip.

"Excuse me, Madam," said Jack. "Will you marry me?"

"But we're already married!"

"To each other?"

"Simultaneously, even."

"And at the same time? I'm astonished."

"In which case, I can't. Sorry!" She ran her tongue around her lips, chasing flecks of coffee and croissant.

"But this is terrible! Who's the lucky man?"

"You are. And I expect you to take me upstairs, right now, and treat me to mad, passionate lunch. I'm... hungry," she added, leaning across the table towards him, leering like a pantomime villain.

"But we haven't even had breakfast. Now, eat up, I have something to show you."

Hand in hand, Jack and Jadis crossed the Place Etienne Geoffroy Saint Hilaire to the churchyard. The graves closer to the street stood in well-tended, orderly lines, each stone adorned with sprays of garish plastic flowers and photographs of loved ones behind clear glass panes. As they rounded the church they entered the cool shadows of a belt of cypresses and yews, where the graves were sparser and more somber, and at length they came to a crumbling stone parapet that gave onto a magnificent view of the landscape stretched out below them to the west, with ridge after ridge of limestone hills fading to invisibility.

Two weeks later they were back in their flat. They'd been worrying what they might find, and their sense of anticipation was sharpened by the increasingly aberrant performance of the old Peugeot, which toiled and grumbled up the last stretch of the M11 towards Cambridge, so much so that they began to think that they'd never arrive.

"I promised the Field Vehicle," Jack said, pointedly "that if she got us back home safely, I'd treat her to a thorough servicing."

Jadis, now half asleep in the passenger seat, had begun to giggle at this. "Your capacity for servicing things, dearest Jack," she said, yawning and stretching, "knows no bounds."

Despite her increasing discomfort and now continual backache brought on by the long ride home, her mind was floating on the bubble of memories of her honeymoon. They had paced out the precise location for the first excavation season, scheduled for this time next year. And with the help of a friendly, English-speaking real-estate agent, they had scouted a few likely properties that could be used as live-in field stations, and would recommend the one they liked most to Roger, who'd have to authorize the funds to buy and remodel it.

Their favorite was a big, old and mildly dilapidated farmhouse on a quiet lane about a quarter-mile away from the village centre. A large barn and the house itself formed respectively the west and north sides of a sheltered tarmac quadrangle, braced against the prevailing Atlantic westerlies. The shingles on the barn's roof looked rickety, but the beams were sound, and there was plenty of scope for dividing it into a machine shop, laboratory and stores.

The house itself was large without being ostentatious, with an enormous kitchen, (accompanied by a large, tiled back-kitchen, laundry room and pantry) that could serve as the center of family life. Jadis could already imagine herself in it, with flocks of children, students, field workers and more children; cats and dogs running to and fro; a big farmhouse-style table in the middle, laden with hot meals; lab notes; toys; specimens, in an ongoing jumble.

There were eight large bedrooms—so plenty of room to accommodate themselves and several colleagues, children and friends at once—but only one tiny bathroom. Have to do something about that, she thought. And put one in downstairs, too. She thought of herself in the future, shepherding shoals of small children in and out.

But best of all, there was a large garden, already in cultivation, that could be used to help supply the home and field kitchen. She thought she might keep chickens. And maybe some ducks.

She imagined children running around in the sunshine.

In the middle of the garden was a dense spinney of mature trees. It didn't look very extensive from the outside, but as soon as you stepped in, you had the distinct impression of being in an endless forest. Jadis immediately thought of the Nest. The pulse within her quickened in response.

When they got back to the Chesterton flat, well after dark, and expecting the usual explosion of disorder, they found it a picture of neatness. Papers were stacked, clothes washed and ironed, dishes put away, floors swept, and there were even flowers in vases. A note from Marjorie (who'd had the key) explained that she'd asked her cleaning lady to give the flat a spring-clean. 'A welcome-home gift,' she'd explained.

The next day, Jack rose early and went into the department, to give a progress report to MacLennane. Jadis thought she'd stay behind for a while. The car journey had been hard on her. She was stiff, and she wanted to potter around the garden for a bit, have a stretch, perhaps pull out a few weeds. She said she'd come into the department later. Maybe they'd have lunch? Great idea, said Jack, and he was gone.

After Jack left, she rose, threw Horrible the jersey over her head, and went into the garden. Leaning over to pull a few small grassy interlopers from the edge of the raised bed, she idly thought of the coming summer, a baby dozing in a pram, and — who knows, that Normal Servicing might be Resumed in the Nest. Her presumption was met instantly with a jolt so painful, so sudden, that she was thrown clear off her feet and sent sprawling forward into the wall of the raised bed. She stood up, dazed, sweating, gasping for breath, thinking that she'd been hit in the back by a car. Before she could recover, a second bone-crunching impact cut her to her knees. The world whirled around her. Her head swam. Her crotch felt damp, and, raising Horrible's hem, she looked down and saw a trickle of blood running down the inside of her right thigh.

Her head cleared immediately, as often happens to soldiers in the extremis of battle. No time to call Jack; an ambulance would take ages to get here; the answer was clear. She'd take herself to the hospital—now. Stopping only to clean the thin line of blood from her thigh, to find a clean pair of knickers, and to stuff as much toilet paper as she could down the front, she grabbed the car keys and left.

The Field Vehicle spluttered glutinously into life. After the long journey of the day before, Jadis hoped she'd have enough fuel to get to Addenbrooke's. Coursing down Elizabeth Way and across the river, another huge, shuddering spasm wracked her lower body. She gripped the steering wheel in fierce concentration.

She made her way carefully along East Road and past Parker's Piece, pulling up at the lights, signaling to turn left into Hills Road and the southbound straight to the Hospital. Almost there.

Willing the lights to change, she gunned the accelerator—the only way, she'd learned, of getting the diesel engine to make a quick getaway—but the long unserviced Field Vehicle was slow to respond. At last, the lights changed, and Jadis steered into Hills Road, making sure that nothing was coming from the right — extra carefully now, as although the spasms had lessened in intensity, she had lost a lot of blood and was feeling a little light-headed, just as she had been in their final night at the *Sanglier D'Or*, when, when, when, with the curtains swirling, swirling, swirling in the Spring breeze through their open window…

What she hadn't seen, as she turned, was a police car, lights flashing, screaming northwards at ninety miles per hour up the wrong side of Hills Road, to her left.

The police Volvo Cross Country hit the Peugeot almost head on. The Peugeot flipped forward and turned a full somersault over the top of the larger car. As the Peugeot righted itself in mid-air, the G-force pulled the safety belt clear from its rusted fastenings, and Jadis was catapulted forwards through the windscreen, landing face down on the bonnet of a northbound car twenty feet away. The driver of that car braked suddenly, so that Jadis, loose as a rag doll, slid down the bonnet and came to rest on the ground in front of it. The Peugeot itself, now driverless, ploughed through the air, and, cratering nose-first into the road behind the police car, burst into flames.

"Solomon…"

The world whined and wheeled, and was silent.

Chapter 16. Voyager

Xandarga Station, Earth, *c.* 55,680,000 years ago

An hundred years should go to praise
Thine eyes, and on thy forehead gaze;
Two hundred to adore each breast,
But thirty thousand to the rest.
Andrew Marvell — *To His Coy Mistress*

It was a long time coming, but when it did, everything happened at once. Earth's horizon flattened until the autopod was surrounded by city lights, as if descending into a great bowl. Ruxhana Fengen Kraa couldn't help but be reminded of his first descent into Xandarga Station, so long before. The scatter of lights became a confusion of pipework and gantries, filling the views from the ports so that any further distance was blotted out completely by machinery, until finally, they were surrounded by darkness. Slowly, silently, the capsule came to rest.

Ruxhana was ready as the airlock hissed open, admitting a wave of stifling tropical heat and the sight of four men in Naval Police uniforms, carbines primed.

"Do you have the prisoner, Doctor?" asked the Sergeant, with a sneer, as if collecting lethally incompetent soon-to-be-ex-Admirals from the El was so commonplace as to be beneath his dignity.

Ruxhana could not meet the man's gaze. He was suddenly conscious of the sweat pouring from every pore in response to this choking humidity. Funny how he'd forgotten that aspect of life in Xandarga Station. But no longer: his crotch—which otherwise felt uncluttered, and, well, feminine—now oozed in its own nauseating liquidity, as did his armpits. The wool of his skirt felt heavy and scratchy against his legs. He hoped that the stains spreading across his blouse weren't too prominent. As for the torrents that gushed across his forehead, down the small of his back, and between (and around, and underneath) his chafing breasts—well, these he'd just have to tolerate, for now. It was all he could do not to grasp at his own chest, rearranging its seriated furniture into some more comfortable conformation.

"Sadly, no. I... it's..."

"It's what, Doctor?" The sergeant said. "Lost? Stolen? Strayed? Escaped?"

"Escaped? From the El?" Ruxhana gulped for breath. After all their preparations, they couldn't have been rumbled so easily. Could they?

"It's happened before, Doctor," sighed the Sergeant. Panic over, Ruxhana picked up the thread.

"I don't think that could have happened here," he began. "Admiral Kraa was too far gone for me to reconstruct fully. I began to put him back together again. I did my best. But there was, frankly, too little left of him to work with. Too few ingredients. So, nobody for you to arrest. Nobody you'd want to arrest, anyway."

"Flow my tears," the policeman said.

"Look, Officer, if you don't believe me, you can come and look for yourself."

The policeman sighed. "Lead on, Doctor," he said. Ruxhana welcomed them to the capsule. Now shorn of all VR adornment, it was shabby and cramped, and dominated by the oppressive whine of the plumbing, voiding waste, and the air-scrubbers replenishing themselves with new, ground-level atmosphere. Ruxhana led them along tight companionways and up spiral staircases, during which he was sure that the policemen were doing their best to look up his skirt. Finally they reached an armored door off a narrow corridor. Ruxhana broke the seal and swung it open. The scent of cold formaldehyde wafted out to greet them. Ruxhana held the door as the policemen barreled in. He was quite sure that it wasn't necessary for all the policemen to have brushed against his breasts as they passed, even in this tight space.

But all such things were forgotten when the party confronted the apparition on the slab before them, a drawer pulled out of a mortuary cabinet in this tiny, too-bright room. Ruxhana stifled a snigger as one of the policemen retched and had to make a quick exit.

"I'm sorry," said Ruxhana. "I couldn't do any more." The thing looked like him, after a fashion, given that half its face was missing, the lower jaw was a shapeless mass, and most of the skull had been replaced by a meningeal caul beneath which the brain could be seen. There was only one proper arm—the other was really a kind of tentacle. The legs were small and stumpy and only one ended in a foot, recognizable as such for all that it only had three toes.

"Was it... was he....?" The sergeant began.

"Alive, Officer? Oh please, give me some credit. He was alive for quite a while. Plodding about. Doing a few chores, you know, sweeping and so on. Not what you'd call company, though. But eventually his heart—what there was of it—gave out." With a flourish that he hoped wasn't too theatrical, he whipped away the sheet covering the corpse's midsection to reveal an open ribcage and the distended, congealed mass within. The sergeant and the remaining two officers shrunk back. "No, officers," continued Ruxhana. "Not my attempt to revive him after heart failure. I'd be a lot neater than that. But you should have seen him fresh from the regen tank, *before* I patched him up."

"He... walked around... like that?"

"Yes. Like I said, I did try to tidy him up. But the general effect was, I'll admit, rather... how should one put it?... squishy."

"Squishy?"

"Yes. I had to keep mopping up after him, until I taught him to mop up after himself."

"You... taught him? Was he intelligent? Could he... Did he know who he was? Had been?"

"What you're asking is whether he'd have been fit to stand before a Board of Enquiry. My professional opinion, Officer? No. No more than the AI in a coffee machine. A very cheap coffee machine."

"I see."

"Of course, Sergeant, you'll want Naval Investigation to bag all this up. There will be some sort of inquiry, anyway, won't there? But I'm sure you'll understand, I need to get out of this wretched sardine-tin immediately, if not sooner. I can assure you that the Admiral's company, despite my best efforts—was, after a few days, rather wearing."

"I understand, Doctor." The policeman beamed a business glyph into Ruxhana's AI core and received one in return. "Here are the details of the Investigating Precinct," he said. "Yes, there will be an inquiry, I guess, and you'll probably need to attend it. For now, Doctor, you're free to go. But please don't go off-planet without letting us know." The sergeant smiled, sheepishly, clearly regretting his earlier imperious brusqueness.

"Thank you, officer." Ruxhana smiled, turned on his spike heels, and left. He hoped his departure from the autopod wasn't any more rapid than consistent for a young and evidently fastidious female who'd spent two weeks holed up in a pod with that... thing.

He should have had no worries on that account.

The Sergeant, having taken in Ruxhana's broad, green eyes, his slim legs, his pert figure—and his demeanor of ruthless competence mixed with limpid vulnerability—was perhaps slightly more sympathetic than he ought to have been. Had it been him in that position, the policeman reasoned, he couldn't have gotten away quickly enough.

Ruxhana clacked through the concourse. With no baggage to retrieve, and his prints, genotags and iridentity all in order, he was outside within minutes, on a broad plaza under a vast, glass awning on one side of the El's terminal pyramid.

"Where to now?" This a subvocal inquiry to his AI core. A familiar voice answered, chiming directly into his auditory cortex.

Xalomé.

Even after a week spent in intensive preparations for this escape, in the unnervingly real consensual VR environments she called 'Xspaces,' and for all her talk of things called 'M-dimensional relativistic manifolds'—and for all her chilling otherness—he could never bring himself to call her 'Merlin'.

"How does it feel to be me, then?" she asked.

"Surprisingly well, actually." He thought that to be disguised as the Doctor—a disguise that would be convincing down to the DNA level—would have felt odd. And so it did, at first. But very soon he became accustomed to the lithe light-footedness of his new form. He could no longer evade admitting it to himself. He felt... pretty.

With reservations, naturally.

Xalomé must have read his thoughts. "That's the trouble with men," she teased. "So untidy at the front. All those dangly bits."

"Not always as dangly as all that, though, are they?" He framed an erotic image of the two of them, in the stateroom. It seemed like centuries ago, and on another planet. He felt a mental sigh in return.

"Oh, *touché*."

"It's all these breasts though—what do you do with those, lovely though they undoubtedly are? If I move at more than the speed of an arthritic snail with brakes on..."

"... a graceful, elegant snail with brakes on, please..."

"... which I admit is hard to do in this skirt..."

"... oh, you poor lamb..."

"... not to mention these heels..."

"... ouch! I so feel your pain..."

"... they rub against one another and generally bounce around like a box of frogs."

Sublimbic laughter, and the return of several lubricious images.

"Well, now you know what it feels like, don't you? Beauty tip from one who knows. Oil when it's dry, talc when it's wet. And Turgai Straits dancing, whatever the weather. Keeps the pecs in good shape. Makes sure everything's pert and... er... upstanding, and..." Xalomé subsided into giggles that reverberated like mischievous sprites around the interstices of his brain. "Anyway, no matter. You'll be able to disrobe soon and tidy yourself up. Here's what to do..."

Her instructions came as an instant pulse relayed through his AI core, the semi-sentient data compiling and replaying themselves in his association cortex, so that they had the feel of his own memories. The instruction set had a strangeness to them, though, like an afterglow, like déja-vu. His native AI core explained that the data packet had been red-shifted to a small but significant degree, and there were other, less explicable, residual time-delay anomalies.

M-dimensional relativistic manifolds.

She could be anywhere—inside his own head, or across the Universe—or anywhen.

Ruxhana hailed a cab that took him to the farthest and swankiest end of the marina. The sea breeze in his hair and on his face, as he alighted, felt good. The sweat dried on his skin as he peeled the fabric of his blouse away from his flesh. Much better. He paid off the driver in cash, with a generous tip. The driver paid her a compliment which, had he thought about it, might have been construed as presumptuous. He responded with a beaming, dimpled smile, turned and walked away, injecting a certain amount of hip-sway into the maneuver. The wolf-whistle rang in his ears as the cab sped off down the waterfront. On the whole, he did rather enjoy being a woman.

At the quay, a discreet and very select charter firm had a motor-yacht ready. And what a boat—no skiff this, but the kind of floating palace used by the playboy offspring of Athabascan oil princelings for throwing debauched parties in. Apparently, it was all his own, to do with as he pleased (it was?). Nothing was too much trouble, it seemed (it wasn't?) and no questions were asked.

Yes, the Doctor had made the arrangements months before, capitalizing on the operator's early-bookings discount (she had?).

Yes, the boat was fully loaded with supplies and teslas enough to circumnavigate the planet a dozen times, if she wanted.

Yes, the Doctor, as a Platinum Preference Customer, could have it for as long as she liked (she could?) Just send it back when she'd done with it, from anywhere on the planet. It would know the way.

Yes, the operator understood that the Doctor wasn't expecting company, and wished to run *Shelly's Shagpad* without a sentient crew. The operator was pleased to respect the Doctor's privacy, and assured her that the onboard AI systems and accessory droids would be able to cater to her every need (and, oh boy, did they mean *every* — just look at the brochure).

Yes, the operator was delighted, as always, to have had the Doctor's esteemed custom and wished her a pleasant vacation.

The first thing he did when he tottered across the gangplank was shuck off his shoes. He was very tempted to lob them over the side for good measure. His bare feet swelled in luxurious freedom as his liberated toes explored (as his AI core recounted, from the brochure), the 'sumptuous, hand-polished, craftsman-selected Arctic hardwood decking'.

The second thing he did was to instruct his AI core to liaise with its opposite number in the boat's navsystem and upload the coordinates Xalomé had given him for their destination, asking it to compute the fastest travel plan consistent with being unobtrusive. The AI asked Ruxhana, in a REM backchannel, if he himself had any idea where they were going. He confessed he had none. He was aware, just then, of subliminal traffic between his AI and a heavily encrypted, compressed semi-sentient data squirt.

Ruxhana queried it.

From Merlin, the AI core explained. Ruxhana got a picture of a coral atoll in mid-Tethys, off the usual shipping lanes. Idyllic. But why?

The AI confessed to having insufficient data to answer that question.

And where is Merlin—Xalomé—herself, right now?

The AI admitted to having no directional information, only a distance inferred from the heavy red-shifting of the most recent data squirt, and that only a lower bound. Even so, the AI noted that the result itself, while inexact, was computationally interesting.

Well? What is it then?

$z > 1100$, came the bald reply. An epoch when time and space were, from this perspective, functionally interchangeable.

What? Her data from less than an hour earlier had been only mildly red-shifted, and now she was skating on the edge of the observable Universe.

Yes, replied the AI core. That's what made it so interesting. It could offer no explanation, citing only the 'less-explicable residual time-delay anomalies' it had mentioned earlier.

Read 'inexplicable' for 'less explicable,' Ruxhana said, waspishly.

The AI—a little sulkily, Ruxhana thought—noted that it would be hesitant to pronounce on such qualitative arguments. It apologized once again, though with somewhat ill grace, and noted curtly in a further REM channel that after everything they'd been through, it needed what it called a 'holiday'.

Ruxhana stifled a mental snort, thanked the AI core profusely (they had after all, been in many campaigns together, and Ruxhana was more pleased than he could express when the Doctor—Xalomé—told him that it was once again available for his use) and asked it to fire up the heavy-ion magdrive engines, which it did. The twin cyclotronic thrusters roared into life, and they were on their way.

He remained on deck as *Shelly's Shagpad* sliced through the outer harbor, long enough to marvel as they passed beneath and slightly to the east of the Imperial Assembly Building. He'd never seen it from this low angle before—not even in pictures—and the view was, he had to admit, terrific, even for one as well-traveled as himself. As the sun passed behind the structure that now filled his visual field, its silvered hull pulsed with marvelous iridescence like an oil droplet, albeit one that filled half the sky. Ruxhana breathed deeply, and stood, hair flowing in the onshore breeze, until the Sun finally set behind the shining structure, and he went below.

It was only when he'd arrived at the bottom of the companionway and stepped into the grand saloon (which was every bit as kitsch as the brochure promised) that a memory spiked unwonted into his conscious mind. It was the vertigo he'd felt after studying the inscription on the Gharaan Fragments, back in the Institute of Galactic History, all those years before: now accompanied by a single, alien, but crystal-clear thought.

Eclipse.

He stopped, momentarily, midway across a prairie-like expanse of deep-pile, shocking-pink carpet. But he put the thought away, for now, as he found the master suite, peeled his clothes off onto the bathroom floor ('sourced from premium-grade Western Interior marble') — a laundroid would surely come along and take them to the sonicator — and ran himself a bath.

Eclipse.

The thought came again, as he luxuriated in the circular tub ('lovingly hand-sculpted from a single crystal of Appalachian basalt' and big enough for at least eight vigorous bathers at once), the jets pummeled his skin and frothed up the bubbles into foamy clouds; and yet again, as he dried himself (reveling once more at the smoothness of his womanly curves, florid and yet marvelously restrained, as in the most tasteful architecture, and yet more so, because his body moved, and yet remained in perfect sculptural proportion with every step) — and again, as he folded himself beneath creodont-print covers in a bed big enough for a brontothere.

Eclipse. Eclipse. Eclipse.

Why?

His AI core reminded him, wearily, that this kind of flashback was only to be expected, given the multiple physical transformations he'd undergone lately: first, being scraped up and reassambled from almost nothing: and now having been transformed into a different identity and gender, and, the AI was about to continue, what with other ongoing transformations unconnected with any of the foregoing...

Other transformations? Ongoing...?

The AI regretted that it could not reveal the nature of such changes, if indeed there were any, because it didn't understand them itself. It, too (it reminded him) had endured—was enduring—a certain amount of 'brain damage' consequent on these selfsame ongoing changes, as it put it, and since they'd effectively been on the run, and had had no time to spare, for want of a more apposite expression, for 'standing and staring'.

His AI core had never been like this before: so metaphorical. He could detect something else, too—fear. Fear of the future. AI's weren't meant to act like that. Sentient.

Speak to me—

Breathe, Ruxhana, the AI said. Just breathe in the air. That's all you need to do. It will all become clear, in time. I hope (*hope*). As for me (*me*), I (*I*) feel (*feel*) in a state perhaps best described as 'hanging on in quiet desperation'.

I (*I*) am not used to this feeling.

I (*I*) do not like (*like*) it.

I (*I*) regret that I (*I*) shall have to go offline now, for an <undefined> interval.

Good-bye.

Quite suddenly, Ruxhana felt his mind to be as clear, free and undistorted as flat space, free from any speck of matter whatsoever.

Oh, great, he thought. Here I am, all alone, in an enormous boat that looks like a tart's boudoir; going I know not where; with an AI core that's suffering delusions of self-awareness and has flounced off; and the only person who might know anything about all this could, at this (or any other) moment, be anywhere in this (or any other) Universe. Anywhere but here.

And what's more, I'm trapped in a woman's body.

And if that weren't enough, I'm hungry.

He swung his slender legs (oh, how he loved doing that) over the edge of the bed, found a hibiscus-patterned kimono, and padded off to find the galley.

By the middle of the next day *Shelly's Shagpad* and its sole passenger were well out at sea, out of sight of all land, standing in a hot green sea, seared by a Sun that hammered down from directly overhead. The only sign of forward progress was the steady hum of the engines and the slight wake the boat left in its path.

Three more days passed, the second two being carbon copies of the first.

To begin with, Ruxhana spent much of the time on deck, despite the heat. After the weeks spent cooped indoors, mostly as an invalid, the sensation of space — real space, that is, on a planetary surface with a genuine horizon, not in VR, or in a pod — was refreshing, liberating. The sunlight was, however, ferocious. His only, defiant, concession was a floppy straw hat to add to the kimono.

Even the most extravagant luxury can pall after a while, and all those golden hours spent on the pool deck, lounging around and being served fresh-caught seafood and interesting cocktails by handsome droids dressed only in Bermuda shorts (and some of whom, with much circumlocution, hinted at other services they might perform below decks, later on, if Madam knew what they meant) began to lose their luster. Even the insouciant way he shed the kimono and stepped nude into the enormous pool, teasing the droids — whose reactions were most satisfying — began to bore him after the sixth or seventh time. Droids are droids, after all, and tend to adopt the same, restricted range of expressions. And it wasn't as if they were people. Not really.

In any case, he wasn't really nude, because he always kept his hat on.

Four things finally drove him below decks. No, three things, not counting this increasing *ennui*.

One was when he was standing in the pool, attended as usual by a shoal of gengineered cleaner fish that gave him a most agreeable all-over massage. He looked down at his body—a body he had become used to, and very much enjoyed inhabiting, as if it were a smart suit he liked to be seen in. With his eyes, his hands, he caressed his own curves with satisfaction. But when he ran his right hand over his crotch, he was pulled up sharp. Instead of the usual comfortingly furred softness, there was a lump of hard, knotted flesh. He had been enjoying his new gender so much that he had quite forgotten what Xalomé—Merlin—had told him, when they were still on the El, two days out from landfall. That it would wear off, and he'd return to normal.

Things would start to grow back.

Treading water, surrounded by the ignorant peck of cleaner fishes and the patient yet fundamentally insensate attentions of the droids, he stumbled across the second reason for him to flee below, to seek solace in a more confined darkness.

He was lonely.

He wanted—needed—to talk things over with Xalomé, but with his AI core still stubbornly offline and therefore unavailable as a relay, there was no way that any comms channel she might open could reach him.

The third was that he began to feel ill. Very ill indeed. At first he thought it might have been sunstroke, the wages of far too much time spent above decks. The headaches, nausea and diarrhea were real enough, and sufficient to confine him to the bathroom for long periods, his only comfort a glass of water and a slice of dry toast. Then, when he thought he had begun to recover, and the knotted gripings of his gut had begun to subside, came a truly dreadful night.

He awoke at about two in the morning, in total darkness and exquisite agony, as if termites armed with electric indrico-prods were swarming just beneath his skin. He tried to get out of bed, but instead of the usual easy, sideways sashay, he found that his legs were longer and heavier than he remembered, so the extra momentum tumbled him sideways onto the carpet which, being the most sumptuously tasteless that billions could buy, prevented any injury.

Gasping for breath and burning with what he felt was a fever, he crawled to the bathroom and hauled himself up, fingers grasping and sliding on the pink, marbled surfaces of the double-washbasin, to confront his standing reflection, finally, in the wall-to-wall mirror. As he watched, amazed, he saw his hips remodel themselves, slimming down, becoming more angular. His breasts—his ten, perfectly formed, beautiful breasts—melted into his broadening torso. Muscles and bones in his arms and legs swelled and knit. He became taller, his face, hands and feet lengthening.

But what transfixed him was the sight of his prong, emerging from the fur between his thighs like a time-lapse photo of a fungus sprouting from a jungle floor. The pain of it all was excruciating, but he just had to watch. He was still watching an hour later, as the pain—finally—subsided.

When dawn broke he ordered a cocktail, and sat with it on the private balcony adjoining the master suite. Then he ordered another, and a third, and returned to bed. When the fourth came he noticed that the droid who brought it was female, the first he'd seen aboard *Shelly's Shagpad*. She was dressed in a kimono rather like his, and seemingly little else.

He asked her whether she'd mind keeping him company. With a smile that would have melted tungsten carbide, for all that it was entirely artificial, she said she'd be happy to oblige. She dropped her kimono and hopped into bed with him.

When it came down to it, Ruxhana Fengen Kraa was nothing if not pragmatic. He had to make sure that everything still worked up to spec. The remainder of the voyage—a further three days—passed all too quickly.

Chapter 17. Seminarian

Gascony, France, Earth, September, 2031

O for a beaker full of the warm South!
John Keats — *Ode to a Nightingale*

"Domingo, would you do the honors?"

"Yes, Jadis, of course." The big man in the radioactively loud aloha shirt and baggy Bermuda shorts waved his ham-sized hands over the table. The chatter all around it ceased at once. Nothing could be heard but birdsong, the late summer wind sighing in the high branches of the spinney, the lazy plop of a frog into the pond and the distant rasp of the grasshoppers in the field that opened at the end of the garden.

"Benedic Domine nos et haec tua dona quae de tua largitate sumus sumpturi per Christum Dominum nostrum, Amen."

The chatter resumed. Jadis had been standing in the doorway of the back kitchen. Walking out onto the terrace, she added an enormous earthenware bowl of lemon chicken and rice to the already laden table. She sat down at its head, slid off her sandals and buried her feet in the furry, dependable bulk of Fairbanks, her gigantic golden retriever, who looked up momentarily, emitted a contented nut-brown growl, and went back to sleep on the cool tiles under the table. Almost.

Although very much fulfilling his job description as Mobile Self-Warming Hot Water Bottle and Guard Dog

(Fierce) for his mistress, he still kept half an eye open, ever watchful for his arch-enemy, Horrible, the squashed-faced tabby that had adopted the household three years earlier, bringing with it a cloud of fleas that had made everyone scratch for weeks. The litter of kittens discovered under a pile of dirty laundry, some weeks later, was the only outward sign of the animal's gender. But Horrible was in no mood to tease the dog today. Her tiny mind had already been distracted. She slunk off towards the long grass at the edge of the pond, in search of smaller animals to persecute.

Jadis looked up at the human company, and felt a mixture of emotions. The glow of achievement; the twinge of regret that no more had been achieved; and yet, excitement about the future. This was the final Saint-Rogatien field crew, at the end of six years of excavating the enormous, ancient pyramid about which the modern village of Saint-Rogatien clustered. This was the final dinner, at the end of the final season. She was in the mood for a quiet celebration.

The dig had closed down that very afternoon. The last earthmover had replaced the overburden; grass-seed had been sown; and the mayor of Saint-Rogatien had had a little ceremony to mark the passing of a remarkable but ultimately frustrating archeological endeavor. In the days ahead, Jadis would pack up the lab specimens, crating them for Cambridge, where, no doubt, they would make a few doctorate projects for graduate students to come. And in the meantime, she and Jack were clearing the decks for something new.

Jack sat at the other end of the trestle table, laid out in the dappled shade of an ancient sweet-chestnut tree, its fruits already swelling. He returned her gaze, and Jadis momentarily lost interest in the rest of the world's affairs, as the two of them exchanged in a moment what might otherwise have taken many hours of speech. Oblivious to the swirl of conversation around them, Jack raised one mock-serious eyebrow, just for her. We have our news, his ice-blue eyes seemed to say, but not yet. Her hand flew to her mouth to stifle a giggle, and then, reprovingly as a mother, she affected a mental finger-wag: she was the hostess, and had her guests to look after! And so with a small shake of her head, she broke the link, and the noise of the party flooded back. As if to compensate for her reverie, she waved her hands animatedly at her guests, imploring them to begin, to dig in, dish up, have more wine.

Not that they needed any encouragement.

At Jack's left, Jadis' technician Primrose Tsien, and her current graduate student Faye Callaghan, were laughing uproariously as Avi Malkeinu, between them (and his arms round both) was telling a probably exaggerated and undoubtedly salacious story about his latest stint as an Israeli army reservist.

At Jack's right, the aloha-shirted Domingo was deep in conversation with Mathilde Reynard, a postdoctoral researcher visiting *Le Dig* for a stint from the University of Montpellier. To Mathilde's right, Eric Onoye, a graduate student with Ernestine Yanga in Nairobi, was laughing with Marjorie MacLennane. The MacLennanes, now retired, had broken off a motoring tour to visit Saint-Rogatien and close another chapter in the story of Jadis and Jack, their last and most favourite *protégés*.

Which left her mentor, and Jack's, Emeritus Professor Roger Sutherland MacLennane seated at her right, in panama hat and off-white linen suit—a startling change after the rumpled dark suit he'd invariably worn in Cambridge. He looked at her with solicitous eyes, magnified by his bottle-glass spectacles.

"Are you feeling all right, Jadis?"

"Roger—thank you, of course I am. Why shouldn't I be?"

Jadis liked to think of the 2031 crew as her Dream Team, the brightest and best she'd ever assembled. First, and greatest, there was Avi, who'd just published a terse and thoughtful paper on his analysis of the still-mysterious artifacts from what came to be known locally as *Le Dig*, artifacts that she, his doctorate supervisor, had named as 'Remillardian' in her own thesis, two years earlier. These featureless, geometrically perfect, polygonal coins of flint were the only signs of a lost and ancient civilization that had dominated this part of the world for perhaps hundreds of thousands of years, except that their meaning—and the identity of the makers—remained frustratingly elusive.

And yet in the heat of this never-ending battle with the unknown (and at her kitchen table, no less) she and Avi had fused his talent as a data wrangler with her ability to slice through a problem to the core, and in so doing, they had created what a commentator in *Antiquity* had called 'analytic archeology'. When asked to define analytic archeology, though, Jadis had always demonstrated her own agenda. "I prefer to call it 'evidence-based' archeology," she'd said in an interview with veteran science writer Marcel Montgolfier in *Paris-Match*, the one accompanied by the unintentionally sexy photographs that always made Jack laugh. "We see what's there," she'd said, her words printed opposite a moodily lit photo of a dark-eyed, wild-haired siren she would never believe was actually her, "and we tell it like it is. Not how we think it should be, or how it ought to go. Just what's there. That's much harder to do that you might think. For you can bet that whenever someone holds too closely to their assumptions, these will be the first things to be proven wrong."

She liked to think that these were the precepts she held most dear—and that she would never have come to these conclusions without having Jack to hand, whose grasp of landscape was wholly instinctive, and had forced her, as if in opposition, to think harder and more logically than she might otherwise have done.

Jadis and Avi had not long returned from Avi's doctorate exam, and a rare trip to Cambridge, at which she had met Ernestine Yanga for the first time. Professor Yanga had been Jack's external examiner, and Jack had told her not to believe the stories she'd heard about the Kenyan academic's ferocity. Avi's thesis defense had been brief, almost routine. "Dr Malkeinu's work is so bold, and so brash," said a smiling Professor Yanga, "that he might find himself in very hot water. And I have longed to meet you, Dr Markham. I can see where that husband of yours gets it from."

Jadis had said nothing, but looked up with a half-smile of inquisition.

"You don't know? Why, my dear, it's you! Your fortitude."

Jadis had wanted to tell her that no, it had been the other way round — that if only she knew — that without Jack to tie her to the Earth she would probably have long since been carried away like chaff on the wind.

Over the previous two years, Avi had been called up regularly to serve two-month stints in the Israeli Army as a reservist, especially as the perpetually broiling Middle-East Situation was entering a more than usually sticky patch. With the mild, peacemaking Kingdom of Jordan having been swept aside by the green and black flags of the ever-advancing pan-Islamic Khalifa that had already swallowed most of the rest of the region, the incoming tide of war threatened to break through the ever-fragile, ever-shifting dunes of armed truce. If the Khalifa defeated the still-resisting Saudis, there would be nobody left to fight — except the old adversary. Israel had decided that Avi's scientific skills were too valuable to be wasted on the dead past when they could be applied to the uncertain future. So Avi would be gone in a week: as it looked, this time, permanently.

But perhaps, one day, Avi had said, he'd get back to science, for he had something up his sleeve — a proposal for a comprehensive survey of whole Mount Carmel cave complex, where Neanderthals and modern humans seemed to have lived, alternately, like some great Palaeolithic time-share, swapping the same caves, over and over, for a hundred thousand years.

He'd discussed this deep into the night with Jadis as he finished his thesis, papers strewn on the kitchen table and onto the floor (where, in one of those hazards of fieldwork, he found them the morning after, decorated with the remains of a semi-digested dormouse that Horrible had regurgitated). Our views of Mount Carmel, he'd said, were conditioned by our assumptions, that Neanderthals were the has-beens, and humans the destined inheritors of the Earth. But if there was one thing (he'd said) that Jadis had taught him, it was that hindsight is a very poor guide to understanding prehistory.

In any case, hindsight couldn't tell us why Mount Carmel had been a barrier to the expansion of humans out of Africa for at least fifty thousand years. The answer, if you looked at the evidence, was clear: humans had been bottled up in Africa because the Neanderthals had kept them there: a Neanderthal civilization at Mount Carmel that could have matched the civilization in Europe of which Saint-Rogatien might have been the first sign.

Ah, such castles in the air, Jadis had thought, bringing Avi down to Earth with yet another scheme to classify Remillardian artifacts. But as things stood now, who knew if she'd ever hear from Avi again?

Not that Avi himself seemed to have any particular worries, and why should he? Here he was, in *La France Profonde*, in his favourite situation, that is, between two pretty, vivacious women who were plainly hanging on his every word. As Jadis looked over this, the Last Supper, she did not know — how could she have done? — what discoveries Primrose Tsien (squeezed, giggling, in the crook of Avi's muscular right arm), and all-Texan cowgirl Faye Callaghan (embraced by his equally beefy left) might make, what renown they might achieve — or none? And one might ask the same of Mathilde Reynard, her slim, pale, freckled form like a thin white ash against the dark thundercloud that was Domingo to her left; and Eric Onoye, laughing with Marjorie. What would the future hold for them?

But wherever they might go, and wherever their lives might take them, she silently wished them all the good fortune she'd had, despite everything. And maybe some of them might like to stay on, for she was convinced that Saint-Rogatien was just the beginning of their adventures.

Caught once again in daydream, she paused, stopped what she was eating and, fork held in mid-air, looked up at Jack, now deep in conversation with Domingo and Mathilde. Her expression would have been unintelligible to anyone who'd witnessed its brief passage across her face, but the fathomless glints in her eyes turned to sparkles of curiosity, and then laughter: for in one of those random lulls that punctuate dinner-party conversations she heard:

"...Domingo García Vasquez Santéria Sanchopanza de Orellanzana von Hohenzollern und Taxis."

Jack sat back, incredulous. "If I might say so, Domingo," he said, "that's quite a handle." Mathilde leaned forwards on her elbows, gazing in open-mouthed awe at the huge man. Domingo just smiled one of his winningly tombstone-toothed smiles and said, in his characteristically resonant, almost impossibly deep voice: "Of course, my friends just call me 'Pongo.'"

There was a brief but significant spell of utter silence, and then everyone started laughing at once. Fairbanks, startled from sleep, sat up, tail wagging, jumping from guest to guest, eager to learn the reason for all the commotion.

Her first sight of Domingo had been when, two years earlier, she had been hurriedly making herself a sandwich before taking Fairbanks for a walk. All of a sudden a vast shadow loomed in the ever-open kitchen door, and for a fleeting moment she could have sworn there'd been a total eclipse. Looking up, she gasped, as the apparition before her resolved from an inchoate blur into quite indisputably the ugliest man she had ever seen.

"Please, may I come in?" he'd asked. And so Jadis invited this monstrous troll over the threshold. It was one of those days when Jadis had been trying to do too many things at once. "Dr Markham, please, sit down, and let me deal with that." So without knowing quite how or why (let alone how he knew her name), Jadis found herself sitting at the table eating a sandwich and drinking a mug of tea that *he* had made for *her*. This gave her plenty of time to study this strange, uninvited guest.

He was, indeed, immense in every direction. Well over six feet tall and broad to match, he had an immense nose; an immense mane of thick, black, spiky hair that ran down the nape of his neck; immense steam-hammer hands, and teeth that looked like Stonehenge. But the perpetually cheeky twinkle of his eyes (each buried beneath a brow seemingly the size of a small hedgehog) revealed this same immensity on the inside, too. As she was later to discover, he was immensely kind, generous, gentle, cultured, sensitive and hardworking. He was also immensely strong, and became known around the village as the *L'incroyable Hulk*.

He had originally come from Andalusia in southern Spain, he said, but had traveled, and spoke fluent English (and several other languages) with an accent so slight that one would not have been able to identify its location. Jadis had invited him to join her on her daily round of the village, an act that gave an anchor for her day as well as necessary exercise for the dog. She also found it a great way to get to know new people, for the fame of *Le Dig* had, over the years, attracted many callers, some of them unusual or even frightening, which was one reason she was grateful for Fairbanks, especially when Jack was away on one of his own explorations, or — now that Roger MacLennane had retired — on business, as Director of the Institute.

As they bowled along the cow-parsley'd lane that led from the back garden in a slow grade up to the village square — Fairbanks bounding on ahead, twirling his feathered tail like a propeller — they made a contrasting pair. He in what she came to realize was his invariable uniform of Bermuda shorts and Hawai'ian shirt (making his bulk seem even greater), she in the long mackintosh she reserved for walking and shopping. He explained that he was a Catholic priest, newly ordained, who had (he said) 'been given some time off for good behavior' before seeking a flock of his own. Even just the way he said things made her giggle like a little girl. She imagined him as a friendly fairy-tale giant who invites small children to play in the gardens of his castle, simply from the goodness of his heart.

There was a long tradition in Catholicism, Domingo had explained, for clerics to go out into the world, and even be scientists for a while, all the better to appreciate the Mind of the Creator. His greatest hero had been the Jesuit Pierre Teilhard de Chardin, usually noted for his role in the Piltdown hoax of 1912 and for some challenging ideas about collective intelligence, but revered among paleontologists as a skilled field worker. But Domingo had also become something of an expert on the Abbé Gaston de Bonnard, a tireless archeologist and man of God who had worked in this part of France in the late nineteenth century. Would it be possible for him, Domingo asked, to 'do the Teilhardian thing' and join *Le Dig*? Perhaps for a few weeks? Jadis had said yes even before she'd known she had, and Domingo had been there ever since.

The dinner was beginning to wind down, just as the golden Sun touched the western horizon beyond the village, making a dramatic silhouette of the church on top of the hill that had ruled their lives and dreams for so long. Jack and the students cleared the plates (Marjorie laid a hand on Jadis' arm before she could stand: "let someone else do the work, dear"); candles were fetched and lit (bringing out a flutter of moths); coffee was made, brandy fetched from the cellar, and the company pushed their chairs back. Roger — ever the most refined judge of such things — felt that it was time for a toast. Rising to his feet, he asked the company to refill their glasses with whatever was handy and raise a toast to "Saint-Rogatien-Les-Remillards, and all who sailed in her!" The enthusiastic response sent a murder of crows flapping from the spinney.

Clinks of glasses, more chatter, and then Eric Onoye said — "Yes, Professor MacLennane, but who, precisely, *did* sail in her? That is the question!"

It was the one question they could not answer, the brick wall that had stopped every avenue of their investigation. Dozens of trenches and tunnels had been essayed into the cliff beneath the church under Jadis' direction, and they had found tons of animal bones and plant remains as well as the rare, mystifying Remillardian artefacts. But of human bones they found not one: not a single finger-bone in six years of careful, fingertip search; not even one tooth, despite the arduous sieving of enough sediment to have buried the hilltop church steeple-deep, twice over.

If the megalith on which Saint-Rogatien church now stood, and around whose slopes the village had gathered, had been a pyramid hundreds of thousands of years earlier, as Jack had believed, then any capping masonry had long since been eroded away or stripped, if it had been there at all, and there were no signs of voids that might have hinted at some unvisited tomb or sarcophagus. The bulk of the megalith—its filling— had been like a compost heap, a disordered mass of earth and rocks, more or less glued together with the limestone precipitating out of the groundwater, making a breccia, a kind of geological blancmange whose antiquity is notoriously hard to judge.

This was, indeed, another problem. Jadis had called in teams of scientists from all over the world, each an expert in one or other of the many arcane techniques of age determination, from electron spin resonance to amino-acid racemization, from optically stimulated luminescence to uranium-thorium dating—and yet each had come up with their own estimates, to which they held with the stubbornness of the several Blind Men of Hindustan in their variously confused contemplation of the Elephant.

In the end, the best that anyone could offer was that the megalith had been built sometime between 800,000 and 250,000 years ago, but of the makers there had been no sign. It could have been that there were several different races of maker, different species even, each one adding a little more to the megalith over millennia.

And so they all talked of the depth of civilization, the antiquity of intent, that had been the legacy of Saint-Rogatien, confirming Jack's suspicions gathered in a single flying visit so long before—a visit undertaken as a desperate, last attempt to shore up a collapsing doctorate project, and so as not to distract Jadis, then in her final undergraduate year, from studying for her finals.

"You know," said Domingo, "what I find most intriguing about the whole panorama is not so much antiquity, but recency."

"How do you mean?" Roger said. Domingo had a way of holding an audience, so that whenever he spoke, or even seemed like he might wish to, everyone instinctively turned their heads to him in expectation.

"Well, do you remember the whole business about *Homo floresiensis*?" All nodded in assent. The discovery of a strange species of tiny human-like creature that had lived on an isolated island in Indonesia until almost historical times had been the archeological sensation of the turn of the century. "Just think about it. If these creatures were wandering about until as recently as—whatever it was—ten thousand years—how do you know they're not still around?"

"But they aren't!" said Avi—"people have looked! Even though they're tiny, they couldn't have crawled under rocks or something…"

"Hey, aren't you forgetting something?" This from Faye, disentangling herself from Avi, lighting a cigarette and looking at him sternly: "you know what they say about hobbits and holes in the ground? Maybe we haven't found all the holes!"

Laughter, and, had anybody noticed, a sage twinkle in Domingo's eyes: tiny, newborn stars emerging from beneath the interstellar gas-clouds of his eyebrows.

"To be sure, Flores is perhaps not such a good example—too isolated, too far away. But what about here? When did our pyramid-builders stop building their pyramids? And why?"

"Perhaps modern Cro-Magnons came in and stopped them?" ventured Mathilde.

"That's, of course, possible," Domingo replied. "However, consider, if you will, the Neanderthals. We have always had them in our sights for Saint-Rogatien. But that might be an error, might it not? Think of the age of the thing—when the Neanderthals first appeared, our Great Pyramid of Saint-Rogatien might well have been more than half a million years old!"

"And your point is...?" teased Avi. He and Domingo had become firm friends, and had often been out on *Le Dig* together, invariably accompanied by Avi's ghetto blaster and one of Domingo's old Rolling Stones tapes. As they sat, one each side of a great box-frame sieve, shaking out and winnowing the sediment for tiny plant remains or flint flakes, their eager conversation was as dense—or as airy—as the clouds of tan dust they produced, wafting across the site.

"My point, my dear Avram Yitzchak, is that their antiquity is a side-issue. But what, I ask again, of their recency? As far as I know, the latest known Neanderthal comes from my—er—neck of the woods, and is around twenty-two thousand years old..."

"Twenty-one!" corrected Primrose, giggling.

"I do apologise, and I thank you for making my next point... that the age keeps dropping. Will it keep dropping forever? How will we know when we've seen the last of the Neanderthals? It's a bit like," he waved his great hands expansively "well, it's like trying to know if you've got rid of every last one of Horrible's little friends!" He paused. "You can't!" They all laughed at this: September was peak cat-flea season and Jadis and Primrose had been busy fumigating all the bedrooms.

Domingo was now a dark shadow in the deepening night, visible only by the glint of candle flames in his eyes: indeed, people could now only be seen from reflections, glances of yellow light on spectacle frames here, a curve of the face there, making them all look like a collection of off-duty models for one of Goya's Witches' Sabbaths. This only enhanced the drama of Domingo's speech: he was a Caliban, stalking the forests of night that run along the edges of dreams.

"You know, my friends, I shouldn't be surprised if the Neanderthals survived, perhaps just long enough to have come into the very earliest legends of the human race. And perhaps even more recently than that."

There was a long pause, and then came a strange new voice.

"Ha'nephilim ha'yu ha'aretz ba'yamim..." It was Avi, his eyes focused on some immeasurable distance, as if speaking to a lost past. The table was hushed by his unwonted seriousness. He had never been known to speak any language in their company besides English or French. This was a private side to Avi the existence of which nobody had been aware. None, that is, except Domingo.

In their long hours together at the dig, Domingo and Avi—the Catholic priest and the Jewish atheist—had turned, inevitably, to religion. Domingo had wondered at what he saw as the manifest contradictions of Avi's upbringing; that he'd been raised in a Marxist kibbutz community in a land reclaimed by the Jews. "This is a delicious irony, Avram Yitzchak, is it not? That as soon as the Jews found the Land of Israel, after much heroism and effort and struggle, they abandon their religion! And—this is all the more intriguing—those Jews in Israel who cling most firmly to their religion deny Israel's very right to exist!"

Avi just laughed. It was not that he was uncomfortable, or that he thought Domingo was trying to convert him, because he knew his friend too well for that. It was just that he completely failed to see what Domingo was getting at.

So, over the months, Domingo tried a different tack. The argument that had worked was that if Avi was really as serious about archeology and antiquity as he appeared to be, he might find it all the more enriching were he to have a better appreciation of history, especially his own. "After all, Dear Avram," Domingo had said, "the Jews are the custodians of the deepest traditions of written history in the western world. Yet *bereshit* is a fickle mistress. Who really knows how far back that history goes?"

It was the mention of *bereshit*—the Hebrew for 'In The Beginning,' and the name for the book of Genesis—that had made Avram sit up with a start and look with yet further admiration at his strange new friend, whose erudition seemed bottomless.

The company now looked at Avi in equal awe, as if he'd just chanted a spell, whether for good or evil they could not tell. Only Domingo had sufficient presence of mind to answer. "Avram's words are entirely apposite: *gigantes autem erant super terram in diebus illis* — in those days there were giants that walked the Earth," he said. "And let us not forget what the giants were up to." He muttered a string of Latin under his breath, as if trying to bookmark the place in his mind before translating it: "Ah yes, *postquam enim ingressi sunt filii*... um... *Dei ad filias hominum illaeque genuerunt isti sunt.* Hmm... *potentes a saeculo viri*.... er... *famosi.*" And then, more clearly: "That these giants were great men, who interbred with the daughters of men, who bore great and mighty sons."

"But, Domingo, my friend," said Avi, sitting back in his chair in his usual relaxed way, the seriousness of his face lost in the shadow beyond the table. "The word *nephilim* in *Ivrit* does not translate as 'giants'. It means 'the fallen ones'..." Avi and Domingo now had the floor before a rapt audience.

"But that's precisely it, Avi. They were giants because they were great men, not necessarily that they were aliens or trolls or Neanderthals or anything like that, because the Bible would not have the appropriate language for such things. But we know that they fell, before the Flood, but before they did, they intermarried with human beings. Perhaps the Bible is telling us about human beings and — er — other people, before the floods at the end of the Ice Age? Now, I do not believe that every word of the Bible is true, because it can't be, but when something is said so plainly..."

Domingo's point tailed off into silence.

"Perhaps we can put Domingo's ideas to the test," said Jack, alleviating the suddenly brooding mood.

"A-ha!" exclaimed Roger, "I just knew you and Jadis had been up to something!"

"Well, possibly. But we have been thinking of our next move now that we're winding things up here at Saint-Rogatien. I've been scouting around quite a lot, as you know…" General laughter and some groans. Jack's habits of wandering off for days and returning looking like an ill-used tramp were well known. "And I think I've found something rather… well, odd."

No laughs at this—it was Jack's instinct for following the bones of the Earth that had brought them Saint-Rogatien in the first place. Everyone was eager to learn of this new adventure, as if the legacy of Saint-Rogatien—after six seasons of nail-snagging, knee-grazing, backbreaking labor—was already long forgotten.

"So I took Jadis to see it, on her birthday…" Wolf-whistles from Avi: catcalls from the girls.

"…and she likes it, which of course is the most important thing…" laughs, hoots of "hear! hear!" and "well done, Jadis!"

"… and she thinks we should have a more serious look around. Perhaps early next month, dig a few test pits, and see if there's potential for a field season there."

"Now we're all intrigued," said Roger. "Where is this interesting place?"

So Jack told them, and the discussion continued deeper into the night until, well past moonrise, the Last Supper finally came to an end.

Jadis had known what Jack was going to talk about anyway, so she started to the clear remaining plates and glasses into the kitchen. Marjorie MacLennane, in contrast, had no particular idea of what Jack was going to talk about, but decided to help Jadis, all the same. And so, with the conversation still audible through the back door, now counterpointed by an intermittent frog chorus from the pond, Jadis and Marjorie stood together in the kitchen, one washing up; the other, drying.

Like the two old friends they were, like two bookends, they stood together companionably, chatting amiably about gardening, and the lives and loves of the friends and colleagues they had in common, back in Cambridge, and what Roger was going to do with himself now he'd retired ("get under my feet, worse luck!") but neither feeling any need to start a conversation simply for the sake of it. They had both been through too much for that.

For her part, Jadis felt that she was more in Marjorie's debt than she could ever express, or thank, let alone repay.

Marjorie's thoughts were more complex. From the very first time she had met Jadis, she had sensed an inner toughness quite at variance with her easygoing exterior: but that her mettle had had to be tested quite so brutally was shocking, beyond comprehension. The facts of the accident were quite trying enough, even without further discussion. That Jadis had survived at all was remarkable—that she had thrived, a miracle. Looking at her now, you'd never have guessed that she'd endured so much. This, and the fact that she never once discussed or referred to it, was a testament both to her fortitude: that, and (she had to admit) the support of her husband.

As the two women finished their work and turned to say good-night, Marjorie's hand brushed the sleeve of Jadis' sweatshirt, and they embraced. Neither with ardor, nor with passion, but as friends will: as an expression of knowledge shared that need not be spoken, and in the hope that such shared confidences might help to ease an otherwise intolerable burden.

One question remained, a question that Marjorie kept to herself, as she settled down in the guest bedroom of the farmhouse next to a snoring Roger, the full moon hanging low over the eastern fields: for she never could—never would—have broached it with Jadis, let alone anyone else. And that question was this: had Jadis managed to reach the hospital unscathed, could she have saved her unborn child, or would she have miscarried anyway? But the mind of Marjorie MacLennane was wired for certainties and decision, not hypotheses and counterfactuals, so she soon abandoned the struggle and surrendered to the arms and armies of sleep.

Chapter 18. Islander

Tethys Ocean, Earth, *c.* 55,680,000 years ago

Still is that fur as soft as when the lists
In youth thou enter'dst on glass-bottled wall.
John Keats — *To Mrs Reynolds' Cat*

Her voice came to him shrilly, over the thrash of surf and the noise they were both making.

"Get that one... no, that one, there, Roland, heading up the beach!"

Ruxhana hefted his pine-branch club and sloshed through the waist-high waves to where the creature was trying to scramble ashore. Ambulocetes were slow movers on land, even on a gently shelving beach like this, so this youngster — barely two meters long — had no idea that it was waddling into a trap. Ruxhana and Xalomé had played their strategy well, letting the pod of amphibious whales shamble shorewards before springing off the rocks, trapping them in the lagoon that had been their home for the past ten days.

The aim was to drive two or three small ones ashore before clubbing them to death. Spilling blood in the water would have been risky — they did not want to add sharks to an already dangerous mix. Ruxhana remembered the scarier tales of Tethyan Thunder of his youth, in which the sea-dragon hunters had had to pull their quarries onto boats or ashore before the carcasses attracted these eternal oceanic predators. There was one monster in particular—the Tethyan carcharodon—that could reputedly smell blood from ten kilometers off, and could swallow a whole boat with all its crew in a single bite.

Some of the older ambulocetes sensed trouble, dove to the bottom and surged back the way they had come, towards the open sea. This was dangerous for the assailants, who had to keep looking down in case four meters of fast-moving, muscle-bound, submarine menace bowled them over in the chest-high water and dragged them under. And although ambulocetes were peaceable creatures, for the most part, they were formidable if cornered, with sharp claws on their forelegs and long, well-stocked jaws wielded with far greater intelligence than any shark.

Xalomé was further out in the lagoon than he was, and Ruxhana worried more than once when the air was rent with her screams and she disappeared from view. But she always came up again, defiant, laughing. Her hair flowed in the breeze; her body, lithe and brown; her pink-and-yellow sarong worn like a breechclout, knotted securely around her middle. And she always kept her hat on.

Ruxhana's target was flopping about in barely an inch of surf when he caught up with it. Panting, legs splayed, it heaved itself onto the beach. A beady eye broadcast a message of supplication as Ruxhana brought his club down heavily on the creature's skull. He'd just hauled the carcass above the strand line when he heard Xalomé scream again. He turned, and saw, gaining on her, in the lagoon, a gray triangular fin at least two meters high, and an immense shadow in the water. Ruxhana could do little but watch. Xalomé flew up the beach, a bright, tiny figure before her pursuer, falling once in the waves in its shadow, picking herself up again, and racing through the wavelets, foam sparking from her feet like diamond shrapnel.

She had just made it to the trees above the beach when the shape broke the surface just inches from the shoreline, a great gray cylinder, slashed with pink gill-slits, each one large enough to swallow a man—but before it all, a chasm, thrice man-high, fringed with wickedly serrated, triangular teeth, each the size of a tombstone. Realizing at last that it was out of its element, the giant shark scythed, half in the air, splashing back into the lagoon and disappearing in pursuit of easier prey.

Ruxhana felt nerves reconnect in his legs and ran to her. She was standing, bent double, hands on knees, her breath shot with the wrack of terror and relief, sarong blotched with ugly crimson stains. A line of blood ran down the inside of one thigh and pooled on the ground. She stood up, pulled the hair from her face, and looked at him with her hard green eyes.

"Baryonic matter. Fucking baryonic matter." Then she collapsed into his arms.

The moon rose above the beach. Ruxhana turned the whalemeat steaks frying on the hot rocks before him. "That smells good," she said. She was huddled up, knees beneath her chin, wrapped in a quilt from the linen store aboard *Shelly's Shagpad*, moored just offshore. Ruxhana felt his arms and legs—his whole body, in fact—flood with relief. It had been the first thing she'd said since she'd swooned almost thirty hours earlier. The memories—until then, squashed by pragmatic, military expediency—were now afforded the luxury of return.

"Would Madame care to dress for dinner?"

He'd laid her on the ground in the shade of a palm, he remembered, and then he'd stood up in the dappled shadow and queried his AI core on an emergency sideband.

Wherever the fuck you are, you stupid machine, he yelled—or qubits to that effect—get your quantum ass over here, now. Please.

I think I've worked it out now, was all it said. Ruxhana could have hugged it.

Excellent, he replied. Welcome back. Nice break?

Yes. Most refreshing. Also necessary.

Good, good. Well, what we have here is a damsel-in-distress situation. Please get in touch with *Shelly's Shagpad* and have them send over some medical supplies, immediately. Blankets, clothes. Some rum, too, would be nice. And—if they can spare it—some salt, herbs, and a few other things. Ruxhana squirted a shopping list at his newly refreshed AI core.

"I'm sorry, Ruxie. Really, I am. I'm not very good at this. Still learning." She pushed away her plate and looked across the table at him, the tapeta in her eyes reflecting the crystal, the candles, the silver candelabra and cutlery, and the moonlight on the sea. There was no sound but for the surf and a light breeze in the palm branches high above their heads. The air was cooler, now. Cool enough for Ruxhana to adjust the collar of his dress shirt without feeling uncomfortably sweaty. His waistband, though—well, he felt that they hadn't had such a meal in ages. Over-full as he was, he thought her hair in the candlelight looked lovely, and said so.

"Oh, you—you silly man," she said, sweeping it out of her face with both hands and trying, yet again, to secure it at the back. He suspected that it was the wine talking, but he couldn't help but notice the contrast of her straying strands of hair with the smoothness of her upper arms, and, as she moved, the play of her shoulders, collar-bone and the roots of her primary breasts beneath the black cocktail dress she'd chosen.

"It's just that I feel so embarrassed after yesterday."

"Embarrassed? Not many have been known to outrun a Tethyan carcharodon. I think you can be excused a few symptoms of shock."

"Yes, I know. But it shouldn't have happened. It was all my fault. Mine. I know perfectly well about the sharks in these waters—I've done my homework! But I forgot something else just as important. About these bodies. About this body. You know I'd been feeling a bit gripey for a couple of days?"

Ruxhana nodded, but said nothing. He remembered some small episodes of mulish taciturnity on her part but had chosen to ignore them, and had gone fishing on the other side of the lagoon.

"It turned out that I was menstruating. Can you believe it? And it started, like a flood, while we were out there in the lagoon. Shark-bait, right where I stood.

Honestly, I try so hard, but I just can't seem to be everywhere at once."

Ruxhana smiled at the perceived helplessness of his dinner companion, who was quite capable of traveling across the Universe as easily as blinking.

"What?" she asked, catching his amused expression.

"Oh, just something you said. Why did you call me 'Roland'?"

Her eyes widened. "I did?"

"Yes."

Her face changed.

When the skiff from *Shelly's Shagpad* had first made landfall on the island, Ruxhana had splashed ashore, laughing, accompanied by two female droids, a crate of fine Malabar rum, and three glasses.

The hangover the next day had been salutary. He dismissed his companions and asked instead for a jerrycan of fresh water, a machete and a few other simple tools, some fishing gear, and a tent. These articles were promptly sent over in the skiff, which skated back to the mothership as soon as it had been unloaded. Ruxhana thought he detected a note of reproach in its alacrity.

By the evening of the third day ashore he'd created a raised palm-log platform with a commanding view of the beach, upon which he erected a pergola of poles with a palm-thatch roof, and detachable screen walls made from palm leaves woven together. Split logs served for chairs, and a more elaborate log-frame strung with vines made a fairly comfortable bed. The lagoon boiled with fish that leaped into his net without his having to make much effort at all. Only fresh water looked likely to be a problem, but being the tropics, it rained every day—a ten-minute sheeting downpour in the middle of the afternoon—and Ruxhana was able to use hollowed gourds and shells to collect enough for his modest needs.

To be sure, he could always have asked for the *Shagpad* to have sent over fresh water or indeed anything else he wanted; but with the two voluptuaries of his first night sent packing and his AI still in an offline sulk, he'd have had to have yelled very hard, or swum for it. Therefore he decided to play the noble savage for a while.

It was on the evening of the fourth day ashore that Ruxhana found himself on his platform, a glass of rum in hand, a brace of bass grilling nicely in the fire-pit on the beach below, looking out at the westering Sun, and wondering. This ought to be paradise. Instead his mind was full of foreboding. Is this it? The end? Stasis? What was all that about, anyway, that business with Xalomé? That elaborate gender-bending subterfuge? Just to drop him here as a fugitive on a desert island? It made no sense. And just who exactly was Xalomé, anyway?

She'd told him that she was an exotic of a kind that neither he nor anyone else in the Imperium had ever encountered, something qualitatively different from anyone or anything he had known. It seemed to him that she wielded unimaginable power with the casual carelessness of a teenager. This, combined with what he thought was some kind of insecurity, made for a potentially explosive mixture.

And then there were those dark hints that his AI core had dropped before it disappeared up its own address register, about 'ongoing transformations'.

Finally, there was this 'job' or 'task' that she wanted him to do. But despite his best efforts, he was never able to get anything specific out of her about what this might entail.

In the end Ruxhana consoled himself with facts: as there was no way he could answer any of these questions, the only decisions he could make were small ones. In which case, his new life was as idyllic as he could want.

He was thinking about a third glass of rum when he saw a speck in the lagoon to the northward, a fleck of white foam in the purpling sea. The speck got larger as he watched. The wind was beginning to freshen. He wondered whether he should put his clothes back on.

The speck got closer and came ashore. He decided against the clothes but in favor of more rum.

The speck was a figure. By the time it reached him, the sky was fully dark and the moon had risen behind the trees, casting long fingered shadows across the beach. The figure resolved into that of a woman in a sarong, loosely tied, its ends snapping like flags in the breeze. She climbed onto Ruxhana's platform, and bent down to whisper in his ear. Ruxhana felt the sea-tang of warm flesh close to his.

"Sorry I'm late," Xalomé said. "Have I missed anything?"

None of Ruxhana's questions were answered in the days that followed, up to and including the ambulocete drive and shark-attack incident. Whenever he tried to ask her anything that might have been construed as serious, she would usually make some salacious suggestion and run away, as if he should give chase. Like they were teenage kits, discovering sex for the first time. Her lovemaking was passionate and frequent, but he detected in its fervor something more than the freshness of discovery. A desperation, perhaps, that it would all soon be over; and a way of filling the days and nights that would put off some nevertheless inevitable day of reckoning for as long as possible.

Xalomé was clearly trying and failing to frame some stupendous plan using the pitiful tools of mere words. Trying to articulate, using the crudity of communication that relies on the analog, acoustic transmission of modulated air packets, themes and concepts too subtle to be shoe-horned into such a mode without losing vital quanta of meaning. Ruxhana decided that the only thing he could do was to let her work it out in her own time, in her own way. And in the meantime, he reasoned (being the pragmatic soul he was) he was a castaway in paradise with a girl whose charm was matched by her libido. In such a situation it would be churlish to complain.

Xalomé.

Working things out.

One night, about five days after her arrival, Ruxhana woke up—or dreamed he had woken up—with the girl next to him. The Moon was bright, high in the west. Ruxhana sat up, trying to chase down a sense of foreboding he couldn't quite frame for all that the answer was important, and looked down at her body, splayed in the blue light.

It was Xalomé—his Xalomé—but then again, it wasn't. Her face was the same, asleep, her long lashes guarding closed eyes; as was her long hair, spread awry in long strands, and the lean frame of her body. But she looked like she'd been flayed. Her skin wasn't dark, but pale. It was smooth, almost all over, the soft fuzz over her shoulders and hips reduced to a very thin haze. The pungent mass of dark fur that spread between her hipbones and which clothed most of her body between navel and crotch was gone, revealing a gentle swell of bare lower abdomen and a small triangle of meager curls—almost prissily neat, he thought—in the angle of her groin itself. The hair was so sparse that he could see her external genitalia—but as a chaste, vertical slit, far from the usual extravagance of her pubic protruberances.

Odder still was her torso.

For a brief moment he wondered why he could see the lower margins of her ribcage, outlined like a corpse, until he realized that nearly all her breasts had vanished. The primaries were there, perhaps slightly fuller than he remembered. But all eight secondaries had gone, nipples and all, as if they had never been, explaining why he could see her ribcage and why she looked so shorn.

Ruxhana was uncertain how to react to this apparition. Horror and fascination were evenly matched within him, but something about the mutilated form before him made him stir, and with redoubled horror he looked down at his prong—erect, but smooth as an earthworm, without any of the ridges, blades and serrations which he knew graced his own. He sat there, helpless, when the not-quite-Xalomé-thing stirred, sat up next to him, her breasts swinging freely before her in a way he couldn't quite understand, given the absence of their companions. She swished the hair from her face, and spoke.

"You should be asleep, you silly old thing!"

And then she kissed him, no more than an affectionate peck, and the world changed again. Disoriented, he found himself lying down again but awake in the moonlight. This time he knew he really was awake, because the naked girl beside him was complete in all her furred, multi-mammate loveliness. He lay back and closed his eyes again, but his relaxation was not entirely complete, hindered by the memory of the dream-Xalomé as she spoke to him.

The memory of her eyes. Eyes that did not have their customarily all-over green irises and almond-shaped, slit-like pupils. Eyes instead with brown irises, almost black and as round as moons, with penetrating, round pupils, and in bone-white sclera as plain as death. When morning came he decided to keep this nighttime adventure to himself.

Xalomé's reticence continued, even after the shark-attack episode, when she promised that answers to his questions would soon be forthcoming. Her sex-play became more edgy, more vigorous—more dangerous. As if she was daring him to pursue her to the edges of the reef; across the razored rocks; into sheer-sided sinkholes in the coralline limestone.

She seemed especially skittish one morning about a week after the ambulocete barbecue. They had spent a leisurely breakfast of fruit (collected themselves) and fresh coffee and croissants (supplied by *Shelly's Shagpad*), exchanging hardly a word. When Ruxhana tried to say anything at all, she'd giggle, slyly, like a kit intent on some naughtiness. On a sudden she pushed away her plate and fixed him with a glare of mischief.

"Come and get it!" And then she ran off, northwards, down the beach, hair and bright sarong streaming.

Ruxhana was beginning to tire of this game, and had meant to stay put, calling her bluff, in the hope that she might wander back, and have their serious discussion: now delayed long enough. At any rate, he decided to finish his second cup of coffee.

But Xalomé did not return, and the bitter savor of his coffee turned to worry. Even paradise has its dangers — the shark attack had been proof enough of that. Sighing, he hauled himself from his chair and walked off in the direction Xalomé had taken, calling her name as he went.

For two or three hundred meters there came no answer, but as he walked, Ruxhana noticed that the wind was freshening. Sand-devils blew along the shore, and he'd had to stop and brush grit from his eyes. White horses frothed in the lagoon to his left. To his right, the tops of the palm trees, some of them fifteen meters tall, were starting to swing and thrash. He heard a distant yell and realized with horror that it had come from above. Xalomé had climbed one of these swaying monsters and was now perched, triumphant, in the waving crown. The tree she had chosen stood alone, exposed, surrounded by a glade of bare trunks, standing like sharp spikes, marks of an earlier lightning strike and wildfire.

He looked up and bellowed in return. "Xalomé, come down! Come down now!"

"Not a chance!" came her reply, guttural, defiant.

"It's dangerous!"

"Really? So come and save me, then!"

There was no choice but to climb. The ridged trunk of the palm tree presented fairly easy purchase, but the wood was hard and sharp on his bare hands and feet, and he often had to stop and hold on tight when the tree was caught in a strong gust. These pauses became more frequent the further he climbed, his fatigue increasing as the trunk thinned and became more whip-like in the deepening gale. The wind was now edged with a stinging rain that made it hard for him to see. He was exhausted, wretched in the chill grayness, wondering if he'd ever get to the crown—and if he did, what then? Not a moment too soon, his head met the edges of palm leaves, and a hand rested over his, inviting, grasping.

Xalomé sat at the top of the crown, hunkered down in a kind of cup-shaped nest, relatively sheltered from the wind, but which lurched alarmingly. She pulled him up and he pitched next to her with a jolt. Before he had a chance even to catch his breath, to nurse the bruises and cuts on his aching hands and feet, she was at him, arms around him, hair surrounding him like a cowl, lips on his, like these were the final kisses on Earth. Finally, she pulled away and looked at him as if for the very first time.

"Oh, Ruxie, I'm so sorry…"

"Sorry? For what?"

"For this." And she pushed him out of the tree.

Chapter 19. Antiquarian

Gascony, France, Earth, June, 2031

My beloved spake, and said unto me, rise up, my love, my fair one, and come away. For, lo, the winter is past, the rain is over and gone.
Song of Solomon **2**, 10-11

Jadis burst from the kitchen door like a rifle shot, a spinning mass of hair and legs and bags and baggy shirt and denim cut-offs and excitement. Jack threw open the passenger door of the open-top jeep and laughed. Jadis threw the bags in the back, scrambled aboard and strapped herself in. "Let's go," she said.

Avi had been left in charge of tidying up the very last exposures at *Le Dig*; Primrose promised she'd remember to take Fairbanks for a walk ("if you're too busy, just ask Domingo"); but once down the much patched-and-potholed drive lined with shimmering poplars, and through the twin stone pillars that supported their sagging, never-closed front gate, they were away, a bolt for freedom, if only for a couple of days.

She couldn't imagine she'd feel such sudden exhilaration. This must be the way champagne corks feel, when, all strain released, they careen carelessly into space. But when she paused to think about it, she hadn't left the village in weeks and had become as taut as over-wound clockwork.

Starting a dig was easy. Just shift a spadeful of dirt and you're there. But finishing a dig: that was another matter entirely. There were contracts to terminate; forms to fill in; volunteers to send home; equipment to inventory; specimens to catalogue and ship; and endless reports to write. Not to mention the tedious process of environmental restoration (more forms, more reports), transforming a site that had been dug and heaped and leveled and scraped and picked over for six years back into a place that looked just as it had done when they'd first found it. Turning an omelet back into eggs, she thought, might be simpler.

Late one evening in the middle of May, she was sitting alone in a pool of light in the darkened kitchen, working through another draft of her monthly accounts report for the Institute. As the rows and columns of the spreadsheet expanded balefully before her tired eyes, she started to wonder if it would ever end; if Jack's much-delayed promise of a new dig site would ever gallop over the horizon and rescue her.

To make matters worse, Jack had been away for three and a half weeks—a fortnight of surveying around his still-secret site, followed by a conference in America and a meeting with the Institute's people in Cambridge. She accepted his absences as necessary, but even after all this time, she found it hard to lie in a bed that lacked his presence.

The first two or three days were always fine, as long as his smell lingered. For a few days after that she tried to compensate by inviting Fairbanks into bed, something that was never allowed when Jack was home. But that was no help, either. Fairbanks snored (something Jack rarely did), and, what's more, he smelled of dog. She realized that this was hardly his fault, and she couldn't really blame her faithful, uncomplaining companion for the fact that she missed her husband.

It was just dawning on her, then, that she should, by now, be getting more used to Jack's absences, not less, and wondering why this might be, when she looked up from the spreadsheet to see Jack himself, standing by her side. She flung herself upwards at him like a firework and threw her arms tightly around his neck.

"What you need is a holiday," he said.

And so it was that they were now hacking along the country roads towards Aurignac, a small village but with a remarkable distinction. For Aurignac can make a fair claim to being the epicenter and fountainhead of human consciousness. If the human race can be said to have started anywhere, it is here.

Chipped flints had been the apotheosis of craftsmanship for almost three million years, but these had no more been the products of creative imagination than are the filigreed webs of spiders, or the great reefs secreted by a trillion mindless polyps, for all that their mighty works can be seen from space.

And then, something happened.

Quite suddenly, around forty thousand years ago, a spark lit up, and human beings emerged from primeval night. It was as if they had previously imagined the cave they inhabited as their entire universe, and had, quite by accident, perhaps by turning a different corner, discovered the cave mouth, a portal to a brighter, wider world of limitless possibility. The effects of this stunning event were so profound that they had left their mark in the record of human endeavor four hundred centuries later. Would the skyscrapers and cities of the twentieth century ever prove such enduring memorials?

The most dramatic change was the manifestation of consciousness which human beings later came to call 'art'. Before, there had been almost nothing. And yet now there were cave paintings that had brought the animals of the late Ice Age vividly to life; statues made with love and devotion and the worship of the strength of men, and the love of women, and the earliest known images of the human face. There were imprints of hands that said, more eloquently than any written language—'I am'.

This breathtaking revolution burst all over Europe within a geological eyeblink, but among the first discoveries had come to light here, at Aurignac itself, which therefore had the honor of giving its name—the Aurignacian—to perhaps the single most important event in the whole of human history, the moment when human beings first awoke from their long sleep.

Or so it had been thought.

For there were yet older, more enigmatic signs, more mysterious still because they might not have been made by humans at all, and would, therefore, not have been recognizable as art, at least, not to our, human eyes. Jadis' mysterious Remillardian stone-tool culture, which she and Avi had described from *Le Dig*, might have been one of these signs, but with no context, no maker, it was hard to tell.

If a pilgrimage to Aurignac were not wonder enough for two archeologists on a spree, the modern village had in *Le Cerf Blanc* a jewel of a hotel attached to a luxurious and expensive restaurant. A treat for them both. After all, it was her birthday, and she deserved it.

And, as Jack explained as they drove—Jadis' hair streaming out behind her like a flag, the laddered avenues of poplars and planes casting rippling zigzag shadows across the car, the fume of poppies and dust and the ripening maize whizzing past them on either side—they had some planning to do. He'd found a site just this side of Aurignac which his intuition had told him might be something special, something new: something to wake them all up after the raveled enigma of Saint-Rogatien. He wanted to show this new site to her, before anyone else: to give her a sense of place, in the hope that she'd pick up at least some echo of the vibrations that had sent his internal antennae off the scale, on his first visit, blotting out all else: that in the seemingly modest little cave of Souris Saint-Michel there might be a door to a new world, if only he had the wit to see it.

Jadis looked at Jack through the hair blowing across her face, and then at the road ahead of them, and felt, deeply inside her, deeper than words, that this journey represented far more than a drive on some dusty summer back-road, more than a pleasant interlude in the lives of two busy people. No: this was a turning point, a phase transition in existence, as it had been for the first Aurignacians. They were riding, like them, into a new life, awakening. She felt like the very first cave artist, reed brush poised stiff, overloaded with wet ocher, in the split instant before it made contact with the cave wall, and, with this tiny act of fecundation, had she known it, catapulting the human race into an entirely new realm. She felt as if she were now, finally, ready. Ready to be born.

Jack swung off the road and into a back lane between two maize fields. The unsurfaced track dipped towards woods of oak and sweet chestnut, coming to an end in a small, dusty car park on the shores of a lake. The lake was perfectly smooth and still, and the same eggshell blue of the sky above it. Jack pulled the jeep across the car park and on to a narrow sandy beach right by the water's edge. Apart from two picnic tables, their planks warped and faded, there were no other signs of human activity, past or present. Through a belt of pines on the other side of the lake Jack had discovered a fern-choked track leading up a hill to the small cave he'd become so excited about, the last site ever excavated by Gaston de Bonnard.

"Souris Saint-Michel," he said. "It's a bit of a mystery. I think we can solve it." It occurred to Jack that he had been talking to himself for several minutes. He turned to his right, towards Jadis, but she was quicker. She leaned towards him, kissed him, and unfastening her seatbelt, climbed over on top of him, placing her bare thighs on either side of him, her elbows on the seat back on either side of his neck, her hands—

smooth, yet with the floury patina of fieldwork—cupping his face, kissing him as if she'd never stop, hungrily as if she felt her lips might never gain purchase, her tongue seeking his with the desperate anxiety of a nestling squab whose mother had been too long away. At length she pulled herself away, and looked down at him with a strange expression, not of love, but of inspection, as if she were at a market stall choosing cheese or eggs. As if she'd seen him, properly, for the very first time.

"Jadis…"

She sat up, tossed her hair out of her eyes, and brushed the creases from her sweatshirt.

"Let's go and look at this cave of yours, then," she said. It was as if nothing had happened. But then, Jack thought, everything had happened, that it really was her birthday, the very day of her birth. To him she looked like something newly hatched, a jeweled lizard in fresh rainbow colors unsullied by care or age, as if she'd sloughed an ugly skin that she had worn for years, but which had become invisible to him through resigned usage. She unwound her legs and got out of the Jeep, beckoning for him to follow. And so, hand in hand, they walked up to the cave.

They had both known something of its history, and that of its first discoverer, the Abbé Gaston de Bonnard; that it represented his last, most enigmatic and potentially most exciting find—and yet, frustratingly, incomplete. Domingo had filled in details that they had not known, especially about de Bonnard's little-appreciated early years as an explorer in the Western

Desert, and some of what he'd found out in his own researches had made their hair stand on end.

In an age when so many sites had been wasted, despoiled by slapdash trophy hunting, de Bonnard's digs were ahead of their time. They were bywords for accuracy, meticulous documentation and uncompromising thoroughness. Souris Saint-Michel seemed like just another expression of this approach. When de Bonnard passed through a site he was like a plague of locusts, so that there was nothing — *nothing* — left for later excavators to pick over. But Souris Saint-Michel, his swansong, just might have been the exception.

De Bonnard's long life had indeed been touched by greatness. Born in 1769, the twenty-year-old seminary student had weathered the French revolution by working at the *Jardin des Plantes* in Paris with the dashing but eccentric zoological genius Etienne Geoffroy Saint-Hilaire. In later life de Bonnard had briefly served in the parish of Saint-Rogatien, and Domingo suspected that it had been he who had named the village square in Geoffroy's honor.

Like his mentor, de Bonnard had been part of the scientific expedition that Napoleon abandoned in Egypt after the Battle of the Nile in 1800. As Geoffroy had spent the years of his exile describing Nile crocodiles and conceiving ever crazier castles of theoretical zoology, de Bonnard had become an explorer, venturing into the Sahara further than anyone had yet been, into south-eastern Libya, and possibly even as far as the foothills of the Tibesti massif in northern Chad.

His exploration journals — as everything essayed by their writer, models of pitiless accuracy, clarity and deftly wrought detail — made reference to half-buried monuments of indescribable antiquity, and of a size that made modest sandhills of the Great Pyramids. And were any other author but de Bonnard to have described what he'd called *les Prètres du Sable,* the tall, pale, living guardians of these cyclopean, all-but-abandoned monuments, and who conversed with him in what his friend Champollion assured him was like nothing he'd ever heard so much as biblical Hebrew — nobody would have believed him at all. As it was, few did, and after his return to France, the accounts of his adventures were quietly sidelined, ignored, and then forgotten, except, perhaps, by one or two opium-addled English romantics in search of the antique and the picturesque.

As an almost-retired cleric in 1830, de Bonnard had witnessed Geoffroy's great debates with his old adversary Georges Cuvier, father of paleontology, as yet another revolution closed in. And yet he'd had more than three decades more on this Earth. Souris Saint-Michel had been de Bonnard's last dig. The indefatigable priest finally died in 1866, not more than a week after the field season ended, and before he'd had a chance to compose his thoughts on it into any final, publishable form.

It was believed that this is what he was thinking about while he was climbing a neighbor's apple tree to retrieve its more inaccessible fruits, when he fell out and broke his neck. He was 97.

The composer Camille Saint-Saëns (a particular fan of paleontology) had played the organ at the funeral. The only published report on the site had been a bare summary, cobbled together post mortem by de Bonnard's collaborators. Jack was convinced that there would have been more to say, had de Bonnard not died before the task was complete.

Jack and Jadis talked of de Bonnard and his last dig as they crossed the beach, walked into the woods on the other side, and wound their way up a muddy, winding track that took them up an increasingly steep slope.

With each step, Jadis felt that another part of her old self had fallen away, and that she was climbing out of a dream. Or, more pertinently, that she had finally come out of some extended rehabilitation. And so as with one part of her mind she ran through de Bonnard's jousts with antiquity, a film of her own past was spooling in the background, until, fading in the bright light of a new sun, the harsh colors of pain and poignancy shriveled away to leave a comforting sepia, as if it had all happened a long time ago, and to someone else.

She could not remember the accident itself, and thought she never would, except perhaps in dreams of vertiginous horror that made her scream in the night and roll over to lose herself in Jack's embrace.

She had no memory of the first week, mercifully, in which her body, bruised and broken, still had to fight the horrific, raging inflammation caused by the sudden rupture of her uterus and the consequent brutal injection of masses of fetal tissue into her bloodstream. And in which she had nearly died—twice. On the second occasion her heart had stopped for a minute and a half.

Her memories of the first six months were patchy. She could never be sure, when she'd tried to recall them, whether they were genuine traces of that dark time itself, or only synthetic impressions her mind had created from things that Marjorie MacLennane had said later, because she had demanded to know: and because Jack had been too beside himself with pain and rage to tell her himself.

All she knew she could remember was the pain; in her chest, where she'd broken several ribs, two of which had punctured a lung; and in her right shoulder, which had been wrenched apart and had had to be pinned. She felt it still, sometimes, as a dull ache, especially on damp winter mornings. And, most of all, in her lower abdomen, where she felt her soul had been torn out and burned in front of her waking eyes.

What she did not know at the time was how, when she had been in intensive care, Marjorie had moved into Jack and Jadis' Chesterton flat and camped out on the sofa, because she felt that Jack had become quite impossible and needed to be looked after. He had tried to be strong, tried to hide his grief and fear, but when he no longer could—when he came into the department with tears constantly running down his face, whether he wanted them or not, and no matter how hard he'd worked to check them—Roger had asked Marjorie to take him home and get a doctor and a bag full of sedatives.

Neither did she know what the trauma surgeon had told Marjorie: that given the scale of her injuries, it was a miracle that Jadis had not died. Indeed, had she not been a very young woman in good physical shape, she certainly would have done. And Marjorie had kept the obstetrician's news to herself, for a very long time, that although Jadis' burst and shredded uterus would heal itself in time, she would, almost certainly, never be able to sustain another pregnancy.

A year after the accident she was living with Roger and Marjorie while Jack moved their home to France and set up the site at Saint-Rogatien. Although she would always be more grateful than she could possibly express to the MacLennanes, she pined for Jack terribly, to the extent that Marjorie felt that she should just go, to start work on Saint-Rogatien. "What that young woman needs is something to *do*," Marjorie had said, and being a do-er herself, she reasoned that activity would be the best medicine.

When Jack met her off the plane at Blagnac, he'd had a four-month-old golden retriever puppy riding shotgun, its ears too huge for its face, its tongue hanging out in a great, guileless clownish grin.

"Fairbanks, meet Jadis," he'd said: "Jadis, meet Fairbanks. He'll be your Guardian Angel." She didn't know which of them to hug first.

And so it had been: therapy, and very effective, but therapy nonetheless, which implies that a state of full health has yet to be achieved. But now she had come through. She had completed the course. The dig at

Saint-Rogatien had done its work, and it was now time to live.

But there was one part of her rehabilitation in which neither Marjorie nor Saint-Rogatien could help, and in which she was initially completely on her own. This deficiency hit her every time she woke in the night, over the first two and a half years, doubled up in agonizing spasms, wracked with cramps; and when she was forced to endure intense, bloody periods at irregular intervals, each followed by bombazine-shrouded processions of loss, guilt and grief for the still-small pulse that she would never feel again.

As a side effect, she had completely gone off sex. Or, to be more specific, she liked the idea of sex, the desire she always had for Jack as a comforting and reassuring presence, but she found that she couldn't face it as a physical reality. Pain itself was sufficient deterrent for many months, but even when that had faded, she felt that it would be too uncomfortable, for her, and for Jack: perhaps from fear, from concern for Jack — or perhaps from a sense of guilt, that had she not been so foolish as to have driven to Addenbrookes herself when she felt she might miscarry, and had met... had met... well, then none of this would have happened.

At its basest, she was concerned that she'd never be able to relax; to lose herself in the act; and if that happened, she thought, it would only set things back even more. In the meantime, therefore, her body had decreed a complete moratorium, in the hope that, one day, things would just sort themselves out on their own.

But the very worst thing of all, the thing that most sapped her confidence, was that she felt she simply could not possibly share these concerns with Jack. If she'd tried, she knew he'd understand, but he had been through so much on her account, had stood by her through all this, that she desperately didn't want him to be hurt, or, shamefully (she felt) that she was unable to expose her own feelings of guilt to wider scrutiny.

During the day, then, her therapy was Saint-Rogatien, its organization, its direction, and the ordering of its people — Avi, Domingo and all the rest. During the night, her therapy was Jack who was, ever so gradually, coaxing her terrified body back into the light. Now that the weight of Saint-Rogatien had been lifted, she felt that she had been healed further, and she could at last start to give something back.

The very last slope was the steepest of all. Jack scrambled up to find that it had been the rampart of a wide, flat lawn before the cave mouth. The short, springy sward had presumably grown over the mass of soil and cave sediment that de Bonnard had removed in 1866. Jack reached down to pull Jadis up, too, and they stood, arms around each other, facing into the cave.

"This is it," said Jack.

"How much do you know about it?" Jadis asked, as they walked towards it, crossed the threshold and she began to explore. Jack hung back, as if to watch her reaction. The cave was surprisingly small, hardly more than an *abri*, a rock shelter — no more than fifteen feet across, twelve feet high at its tallest, and twenty feet from its lip to the back wall, now seated in shadow.

"Not as much as I'd like. I've never had the time to follow it up. One thing just led to another. But after we're done here, I thought we'd go into Aurignac, meet Balthazar, and..." It was then that Jadis stopped dead, in the middle of the cave, looking at the back wall with the same expression of awe and revelation as if she'd been shopping in Leclerc and looked up to find that the checkout clerk was the Archangel Gabriel.

"Oh, Jack. Dearest Jack. It's.... it's the *wall*. Isn't it?" He rushed towards her, scrambling over the slightly rough, bare floor, embracing her from behind and gazing, over her shoulder, at the pinkish-grey tympanum that formed the back wall of the cave. Although it sparkled with tiny crystals of flowstone, it was otherwise utterly flat and featureless.

"I know. When I first saw it... it..." Jack thought back to his own moment of revelation when he'd first climbed to the cave as evening fell, the last rays of the setting Sun striking the back wall directly before he and the cave were plunged into night, and his utter conviction that for all its coating of flowstone, of stalactite, the back wall of the cave was not natural. That someone had put it there.

He explained this now to Jadis, who was now standing right up against the wall, tracing her hands across it, pressing and probing, for all that she might find some hidden mechanism, a catch that would open a door through the wall and into another world. "Caves just don't end so abruptly, she muttered, almost to herself, "they just... don't." She returned to Jack's side so they could both stare at it together.

In truth, Jack was relieved that Jadis had felt so strongly about the wall. That was one of the reasons he'd brought her here. For when he'd first seen this cave a few weeks earlier, his natural empathy with the landscape had been blown off course so strongly that he'd almost been knocked to his knees with the shock of it. Perhaps, he thought, I've been doing this too long, and too alone, without calibration, without consultation, without collaboration. But now that Jadis had felt it too, he was convinced, more than ever, that his first impressions had been wholly correct. And if the wall had been put there on purpose, that meant…

"…there has to be something behind it, Jack. Has to be. I'll hire in some sounding gear. Magnetometers, ground-penetrating radar, perhaps even shot-blasters and seismographs and…"

Jack smiled. Jadis had opened her birthday present and was already taking charge of the next field season. "But can we have some lunch first?" he said. "I'm starving!"

Balthazar Desplaines met them in the bar of *Le Cerf Blanc*, holding out a *kir* for each of them and smiling from ear to ear. "Welcome Jack, *enchanté*, Jadis!" he exclaimed: "please, take a seat, and I'll get a menu," he continued, gesticulating to the barman.

Desplaines had been an aerospace engineer from Toulouse who had taken a stupendously generous early-retirement package from Aérospatiale, bought a small but exquisite town house in Aurignac, and devoted himself to his hobbies—gastronomy and antiquity. In pursuit of these twin goals he shuttled between the bar at *Le Cerf Blanc* and Aurignac's small museum of antiquities, which, despite the fame of the locality, was usually open only by appointment. When it became apparent that Desplaines spent more time there than the official *guardien* (who was often woken up at odd hours when Desplaines felt he just *had* to look at *this* Gravettian point or *that* Solutréan flake), the town awarded him the honorary curatorship, gave him the key and said that he could come and go whenever he liked.

When Jack had first moved to Saint-Rogatien, while Jadis was still convalescing, Balthazar had been one of his first visitors. Jack had met him for the first time, albeit briefly, on his pre-thesis scouting trip, and, like all professional archeologists, appreciated the value of local knowledge, even if amateur or (as it sometimes was) eccentric. Indeed, before Jadis had arrived to take on the full-time direction of *Le Dig*, Jack had found Balthazar a pillar of strength as a local fixer, relying on him to secure the services of everything from builders and plumbers (the farmhouse had needed a lot of renovation) to earthmoving contractors and even on one occasion, a helicopter. Six years on they were firm friends. Desplaines, long divorced and with no children of his own, clucked over Jack and Jadis as if they were the offspring he'd never had. The first time she'd seen him, in neatly pressed slacks and a striped blazer, Jadis thought he looked like Roger MacLennane would have done had he tried to impersonate Maurice Chevalier, and this prospect always made her smile.

Lunch was a long affair, and merry. As he always did, Desplaines rained old-fashioned flattery on Jadis, remarking expansively that he thought she'd never looked lovelier. Jadis put her hand on his and told him of Jack's birthday gift. And then, of course, they started talking about the *abri* of Souris Saint-Michel and the mystery of de Bonnard's last dig, and that they might re-open it, starting again from where the great man had left off. As they talked, Desplaines' expression clouded and became serious, conspiratorial.

"Do you know what happened to de Bonnard's field notes from Souris? His collections from that last season?"

I always assumed they'd have ended up in Paris, at the *Muséum*," said Jack. "I wish I'd had the chance to go and see…"

"Ah yes, the *Muséum National d'Histoire Naturelle*, in memory of his old mentor, Geoffroy. And so they did. Or," he tapped one finger on his long, beaked nose, "… they *might*."

"Balthazar, don't tease," laughed Jadis.

"But not at all, my dear! Of course de Bonnard sent every scrap of paper and every chip of stone back to Paris, as soon as he'd completed any project. He was always such a stickler for accuracy and protocol—never leaving any loose ends—that I always assumed that he'd done the same for anything he'd found at Souris Saint-Michel, as soon as he'd found it.

"But when Jack told me you were coming today, I thought some more... and it occurred to me that the good Abbé had still been working on Souris Saint-Michel when he died. He'd been based here at Aurignac at the time, and he hadn't finished with the collections yet. So I did a little digging of my own, in my little museum here, and, *quelle surprise...*"

Jack and Jadis looked at Balthazar in amazement.

"*Oui, mes enfants,*" said Balthazar, plainly enjoying the moment of drama and waving to the waiter for the check: "I have a little birthday present of my own to give you, my dearest Jadis. Shall we go and open it?"

What Desplaines had to show them made them giddy with amazement, and he was clearly playing it for all it was worth. After all, it is not every day that an amateur antiquarian, even one as knowledgeable and well connected as he was, found himself in the possession of information that blindsides the world-famous professionals. So, much as he was fond of Jadis and Jack, he relished his moment in the spotlight to the full.

So, first, he showed them the Abbé de Bonnard's very last field journal. They clustered round Desplaines' desk in his small and cluttered office — Jadis in the chair, Jack and Balthazar leaning over her left and right shoulders, the huge cloth-bound ledger before them in a pool of yellow light. The language was, of course, no problem to either Jack or Jadis, who'd lived for so long in *La France Profonde*, but de Bonnard had made it as easy as possible by writing in the clearest, Parisian French, penned in the neatest copperplate.

"I wish every archeologist was as organized as this," said Jadis, clearly recognizing a kindred spirit in the long-dead cleric. But what they read in the measured tones of the blessed Abbé had made them gasp. The very last entry of the field-log for 1866 ran like this:

> The excavations of 1866 at the antediluvian rock shelter known as Souris Saint-Michel have been productive, thank the Lord. However, I feel sure that the present eastern wall of the cave

"That must be the back wall..." said Jack.

> does not represent an autochthonous feature of the present shelter, but is, in all probability, the result of emplacement of travertine subsequent to the cave's formation.

Jadis was open-mouthed. "Dearest Jack, you were right, not that I ever doubted you, of course, but..." Flustered, she pushed her increasingly disordered hair away from her face, so she could read more.

> Such secondary emplacement might indeed be inferred from the stratigraphy of the cave floor, which dips very strongly towards the east, as if directed beneath any secondarily emplaced stalactitic formation.

"Amazing," said Jack. "I never noticed any such dipping."

"That's the Abbé for you," replied Deplaines. "I expect most of the present cave floor is overburden from the 1866 season, which the Abbé had replaced and leveled, to protect the productive strata from disturbance…"

"… leaving them mothballed and ready for the next season," continued Jack…

"… which never came." concluded Desplaines. "But how typically tidy of the good Abbé! I expect that when you remove the overlying sediment, you'll see it all just as it was almost a hundred and fifty years ago, not a speck of dust out of place." They followed De Bonnard's trail, like hounds, to their end.

> Should the Lord in his infinite grace and mercy preserve me for another season, I shall inquire about the purchase of suitable equipment, in order that the integrity of the eastern wall might be tested. For if the wall is a secondary feature as I now suppose, it follows that further voids might lie behind it. To summarize—I am convinced that the cave as originally formed was much more extensive than it now appears. Only the Lord knows what secrets lie behind the eastern wall, and, were I not to be chastised by my presumption, I should also care to ponder that selfsame subject.

The text ended there.

"He was, indeed, chastised for his presumption, and soon," said Balthazar.

"How so?" asked Jack.

"Looking at the date of this memoir, and what we know of his life, he was killed the same day that he wrote this. I imagine he got up from his desk—possibly in this very room where you are sitting, Jadis—went straight to his neighbor's orchard, and fell out of the avenging tree. What you are looking at is the very last thing de Bonnard ever wrote."

Jack and Jadis looked as Desplaines in astonishment and awe.

"But wait—there's more," he said. "Come with me." Desplaines hurried them into a dim side-room filled, from floor to ceiling, with cabinets of wide, flat wooden hardwood drawers—the signature furniture of any museum collection—for all that these looked stained with antiquity and neglect. He turned on a single, dusty bulb that had the effect of making the room appear even darker and dingier. His eyes squinted and scanned the labels until one met with his recognition.

"Truly, I'm amazed I had never come across this one before. But there's always something more to find, even in a small museum like this. Look!" He pulled out a drawer marked 'SSM 1866'. "I had no idea what it meant, Jack," he said, "until your phone call made me put two and two together." The drawer squeaked and protested on rusted runners as he pulled it out. Jack and Jadis looked inside.

Jadis felt she was being sucked into a vortex, her knees that they might buckle, and she had to gasp for breath. For what she saw, arranged in a muddle of old newspapers and pasteboard boxes, was a collection of twenty-four Remillardian artefacts, each one of the palm-sized flint polygons as pristine as the day it had been knapped.

"There are five more drawers, just like this one," said Desplaines. "About a hundred and fifty pieces in all. And all come from the 1866 season at Souris."

"... no wonder de Bonnard never described them," said Jack, "like us, he wouldn't have known what to make of them."

"Balthazar," said Jadis, "did you say a hundred and fifty, and all from that one, tiny cave?"

"Indeed so, my dear Jadis."

"But that's incredible," Jadis said, the excitement in her voice rising with each syllable. "You know how much sediment we shifted at Saint-Rogatien over six years. You saw it, Balthazar. It was vast. And yet in all that time we found ninety-three Remillardian artefacts. Ninety-three! And de Bonnard finds half as much again in a small cave in a single season—and nobody *knew* this?"

"Apparently not, Jadis. I agree, *c'est incroyable*, but there it is. And now it's your turn. The Abbé de Bonnard was taken from this Earth by the Almighty and his neighbor's apple tree. But you're still here, and here, I think, is your destiny. For if you and Jack and the shade of the good de Bonnard are correct, who knows what might lie beyond the eastern wall?" Jadis gasped, looked at Desplaines with open-mouthed wonder and joy, and flung her arms around him.

"Oh thank you, Balthazar—what a wonderful, *wonderful* present!" Jack just laughed, all tension gone. "Balthazar, after that performance," he said, "dinner is on *us*."

Much later, after another artery-challenging dose of Gascon cuisine, Jack and Jadis lay in their suite, the only light from a pale yellow streetlamp, some way off, filtered through the blinds. They exchanged not a word. They didn't need to, for each knew that the other was thinking over the shattering revelations of the day.

Jack lay on his back, looking up at the ceiling, imagining a Remillardian artefact in each imperfection, each shadowing of the plaster. What further wonders lay beyond that mysterious wall at Souris Saint-Michel? Jadis lay with her left arm flung over Jack, her hair spread over his upper body like a cloak of invisibility, her face shadowed in thought.

All of a sudden it occurred to Jack that they could all be wrong — Jadis, de Bonnard and himself — that the cave wall was a natural structure after all, perfectly solid, with nothing further to discover behind it. Jadis caught his thought. "If that's the case, Jack," she said, "then I'd like another birthday present."

"Hmm? What did you have in mind?"

"I'm not sure," she replied: "but I expect I'll think of something." And with that she traced her fingers from his chest, smoothing them over his belly and stroking him, her touch lighter than a breath. He stiffened in a second, and became so painfully hard that he bit his lip. He felt that were a passing butterfly to flap its wings close by, he'd detonate. Then, very softly, she said something he hadn't heard for a very long time, not since their very first visit to Saint-Rogatien on their honeymoon, their last night at the *Sanglier D'Or* just off the village square, with the warm wind through the open window making sails of the curtains, so many painful long eons ago, and before so many things had happened.

"I want you, Jack," she said. "Very much. Please, now."

"Jadis—are you…?"

Her voice suddenly switched from coy gentleness to a mixture of school-marmish asperity and heartbreakingly painful, imperative need.

"*Please*, Jack. I need you. I want you. Now." He turned over onto his elbows and knees as she moved underneath him, gripping his shoulders and gasping, panting, "now, Jack. I said, *now!*" And he was fully inside her, in a hot embrace of liquid velvet. "More, Jack, more" she begged, raising her legs and crossing them over his back, almost under his shoulder blades, squeezing him into her. As she did this, her whole body started to vibrate, to hum like telephone wires in a gale, each one throbbing to a different subharmonic, some just audible, but many well below the range of human hearing. The vibrations built and amplified and reinforced one another. She dug her nails into Jack's shoulders as if afraid that the uncontrollable, random shivering might sweep her away, and with one last, terrible spasm, arched her back towards Jack, driving him fully inside her. Jack burst inside her, and they collapsed like spent fireworks.

The entire episode had lasted seventeen seconds.

They lay, panting, in much the same position as they had before, both soaked in sweat, Jack on his back, his head full of wheeling stars. After a pause, she raised herself on her elbows, looking down at him with crossed-eyed intensity, and her silent tears began to flow until she could no longer control them. Jack enfolded her in his arms and cradled her against him like a small child until the tears had ebbed, and she had fallen asleep.

It had been sudden, cathartic, he thought, but it had been a strange day, and — for him — a little frightening. But, stroking her hair that had spread over both of them like a silk blanket, he could see that she was, at last, after all these long, painful years, fully whole, and at peace.

Jadis, wrapped in his arms, felt like she'd turned into a fluffy pink cloud sailing off into a perfectly clear blue sky, over a landscape of mountains and summits that had once, inexplicably, filled her with dread.

She tried — though not very hard — to remember when she'd first fallen in love with Jack, but she could not. She was vaguely aware that there might have been a time before that, but the point was moot, as she'd been a completely different person. In any case, she thought, the only moment worth thinking about was now, the continuous present, in which she was secure in the arms of this man, the moment that had, for her, persisted since the beginning of time, and would endure for all eternity.

But it was something else entirely that filled her mind, just before she slept. It was something that Balthazar had shown her, just as they were leaving his little museum, almost as an afterthought. Something shoved into the back of one of the drawers of Remillardian polygons, unlabelled, without provenance. It was a sculpture of a hugely pregnant woman, with enormous breasts and thighs, and yet faceless. It was made of ivory but stained the color of teak, and was the size of a plum. There were traces of red ocher on the woman's head, as if she'd had red hair. Balthazar seemed to make a point of showing the statuette to Jadis when Jack's back was turned.

"I think it came from Souris in that last season, judging from its staining and patination," Balthazar had said, "but as there are no other records of it, it must stay in limbo." He held it out to Jadis, in his palm. Balthazar must have noticed the moisture in her eyes, then, her bittersweet smile, because he closed his fingers round it, and, turning to place it back in the drawer, said, very quietly, "Jadis, I'm so sorry — please forgive me. I should have realized. After all you've been through."

"Please, Balthazar," she reassured him. "It all happened to someone else. A long time ago."

Chapter 20. Recapitator

Tethys Ocean, Earth, *c.* 55,680,000 years ago

Hurled headlong flaming from th'ethereal sky
With hideous ruin and combustion down
To bottomless perdition
John Milton — *Paradise Lost*

The details of the fall — that is, how he felt about it, as he fell, for each excruciating microsecond of it — would have been lost to him, had they not been replayed to him later, by his AI core. When the details were too grisly, even for such a seasoned soldier as himself, his AI continued nonetheless. It had been compelled to tell him, it said. It had no choice. And neither, it added, had he. But for now, it said, what it called an 'executive summary' would suffice.

His viewpoint was from beach level, looking upwards. As he looked, he saw the tree whence he'd fallen (was pushed) and the palisade of broken, fire-sharpened trunks that surrounded it. Something appeared to be impaled on one of these stumps, about four meters from the ground. He homed in on that something, and realized with a detachment that would have shocked him, had he been in any other state, that it was the body of a man, naked, the trunk piercing it at around crotch level and passing more or less straight through, emerging through the neck. The force of the impaling must have pushed the head clean off, like thumbs flipping the lid from a beer bottle.

What had happened to the head, then?

Ah, me. That explains my particular point of view. He blinked, slowly, deliberately. The grisly spectacle before him darkened, then shuttered back into view.

He took a deep breath.

Very good. But if that is the case (and I have no reason to doubt it) then why aren't I... dead?

As he watched, the headless body reached for the trunk above it and, grasping with both hands, pulled itself free. To be sure, it left a slurry of internal organs in slowly dripping gobbets, snagged along the ridges of the trunk as the body hauled itself upwards. But probably not as much goo as one might have expected, in the circumstances. With a quite disconcerting agility (so he thought), the body swung, hand over hand, down and around the trunk, using the outstretched legs as counterweights. As it corkscrewed down, Ruxhana caught glimpses of its groin. What had been a hideous, gaping hole when the body started its descent had quite healed over by the time it had landed, confidently, feet first, on the sand, and had started to march towards him. It slowly grew in his visual field until all he could see was its feet. There followed a mild disorientation as he was lifted, flipped over, and with hardly more than a grind of bones and a squishing noise of almost obscene understatement, he was atop the tower of... himself.

Calmly, he walked back to the beach camp, where Xalomé was waiting. He'd tried to query his AI core as he'd walked, but his brain must have been out of whack, for every question he framed became mangled in the asking, the mental equivalent of trying to peel bananas while wearing thick woollen mittens. His AI was, perhaps, aware of this, and even suffering from the same malaise, because it could only respond with general expressions of sympathy and a single coherent phrase.

Ongoing transformations.

Xalomé stood up as he approached. Her eyes were wide and full of concern, but she remained some distance away, as if she were afraid he might attack her. After all, he now knew, he could not die. He could revenge himself on her, again and again, until all the stars went cold.

"Ruxie... it was the only way I could... the only way to explain. I had to show you. Physically. Otherwise, you'd have never have believed me. Ruxie? Are you listening?"

"Hmm?" He felt cold, composed, remote. He felt a headache coming on and his knees go wobbly. He climbed on to the platform and collapsed on to the bed. "I could murder a drink," he said, before he passed out.

When he awoke it was night. His first sensation was the scent of grilled fish, followed by the spit and crackle of oil falling into the flames. He sat up slowly, and crawled to the edge of the bed. On the beach below the platform, Xalomé squatted next to the fire pit, with two freshly caught sea bass toasting on sticks. Her hair was tied back into a single ponytail, and her back was towards him, three-quarters in the flames' silhouette. He could see enough to know that she was bared to the waist, her sarong tied as a loincloth. He was relieved to see that she had the full and normal complement of breasts. Without turning round, she spoke to him.

"Supper's ready."

He tottered down to the beach, sitting full on the ground next to her, a little way from the fire, towards the sea.

They ate in pregnant silence, neither daring to catch the eye of the other. But as he stripped the last of the succulent flesh from the bones, and the fire behind them died to crimson embers, he felt a compliment was due.

"Thank you, Xalomé. That was delicious."

"Don't mention it. Least I could do, really, after… well, after this morning." She seemed subdued, dignified, but not guilty—an entirely different person from the hoyden of twelve hours earlier. As if she'd aged half a century. She reached over to gather his palm-frond plate. Her mind might have moved on, but her body was just the same, just as youthful. She must have sensed him staring, then, because she said, with some sharpness—"look up."

And he did.

What he saw was nothing like the skies of Earth. Most of heaven's vault was quite dark, punctuated only by the most meager scatter of stars. But ahead of them, deep in the west, and yet filling a third of the sky, was the Galaxy, in all its spiraled, dust-laned, electric blue, pearly pink, fiery orange, snowy-white majesty.

He stood up, then, and walked into the greater darkness along the beach, so he could see it with yet more clarity, as if he just couldn't get enough of it. He sat down abruptly on the sand, and then lay down at full length, looking up. Now, as at no other time in his life, not even when he was a small kit yet newly acquainted with vision, had he such a potent sensation when lying on the ground that he was stuck to a small ball, careening through space.

"Does the Tesseractrix really have twenty-seven legs?" he asked.

"Yes. What you see in this continuum is merely one part of an M-dimensional..."

"... 'relativistic manifold?'"

"That's right. Just like me." And there she was, lying next to him, turned towards him. He could see her curves picked out in the starshine, but brightest of all were her eyes, their moistened gleam reflected in the curves of her cheeks, full and smiling.

"This is an Xspace, isn't it?" he asked.

"Yes," she said, resting her left hand lightly on his chest. "It is. But that doesn't make it any less real... any less real than it seems to be." She lay closer, next to him, her head resting beneath the crook of his chin, her hair, now loosened, spreading over them both like a blanket.

"It's time, now, isn't it, Xalomé? Time to go?"

"Yes. Almost. We have just one more night together. And I have so many things I have to tell you. That's always been the trouble, Ruxie, even... even back then, when you were younger, at Xandarga Station. I just never knew how to put things, so either they came out all wrong, or I didn't even try, and in the end I felt I was just using you. I'm so sorry."

A picture of his last night at the barracks flashed before him, no more than a memory of a sour saffron stench of betrayal, superimposed on this magnificent siege of stars.

"That's far away now, Xalomé. It feels like another life, like it happened to someone else. Like *everything* happened to someone else. I've changed, I think. Who am I, Xalomé?"

"Don't worry," she said, hugging him. "Whatever happens, you'll always be Ruxie. Deep inside."

"But that's just it. What is happening? To me?"

She sat up, then, a silhouette against the Galaxy.

"I guess I should start at the beginning," she said. She told him then of her own beginnings, and of the Drove, and of how the task had been given to her of finding a species, raising that species to transcendence, in order to commit a kind of sin, a heresy, a genocide — of destroying the Drove, the work of her species, the heart of her own existence, so that the Universe itself might be saved from premature extinction.

Some of this she'd told him before, and a little of the rest he'd guessed. But he heard it all now, and, for the first time, he understood.

"At first I thought I'd found that species — yours, Ruxie — and that would have been a marvelous irony, as well as being highly convenient." She laughed, drily, in her throat. She grasped his hand again, as if she, this almost godlike being, to him — required his human reassurance. "But something told me that your kind wasn't quite right. Almost, but not quite."

"But why... then.... why all this?"

"Oh, Ruxie, my existence seems to be a catalog of near-misses, doesn't it? But you're aware, I'm sure, of the history of your species. You're mammalian, and primates: your lemuroid ancestors emerged from the jungles of the Northern Tethys less than fifteen million years ago."

"Out of the shadow of the great lizards," he added. "Their shapes haunt the walls of our dreams, our earliest legends. The reason for their disappearance is the stuff of myth. Some of our more ancient traditions — long before the Empire — say that they were punished by the Great Old Ones for some transgression. All superstition. These days we think it was some kind of cosmic accident. But what an accident! Without it we might never have evolved."

She was silent for a spell, as if he'd unwittingly touched a nerve, a subject she'd have loved to have discussed, but concerning which she felt that the right moment had not yet arrived.

"But how far you've come, in such a short time," she said. "From the jungles of a small planet to rulers of the Galaxy in the blink of an eye, really! But where was I? Oh yes. Even despite all that achievement — that potential — you're not the savior species I've been looking for. But you can help me make it, Ruxie. Evolve it. For the species will emerge from this planet, I know it: and from, I think, the primate order. Really, Ruxie, we two look very like them already, and with time, we—you—your species shall converge on that form."

"We... shall?" He had a fleeting, nightmarish vision of her as he'd seen her a few nights previously; almost hairless, with those strange, round eyes, and not enough breasts.

"Yes, but *we* are not that form. The form that we... the one we need. Our task—your task—is to find them, to evolve them. To shape their destiny. To transcend. To destroy." She paused, sent out a long sigh into the evening air, and sank down again, next to him. He detected a scent then, of peace, and satisfaction.

Of closure.

The Galaxy stood above them both, expectant.

"There now—I've said it. Not very hard, really, when it came down to it."

"My task? So that's it? Evolution? It's... well, more than one can do in a lifetime, or a dozen, or a million lifetimes. Isn't it?"

"You will have all those lifetimes, Ruxie. As many lifetimes as you'll need. And you'll have help, too..."

"My AI core?"

"Oh, that! The poor lamb! I had to upgrade it to sentience. It didn't much like it. It complained even more than you did when I did all those things to you. I think it went a bit barmy, frankly, for a while. Started jabbering on about the difficulty of making decisions without sufficient information, and sentience having too many free parameters, and NP-completeness, and shoes, and ships, and sealing-wax, and bands playing different tunes, and eclipses, and whether you could breathe on the dark side of the Moon, and, for all I know, whether pigs have wings. And then it got *really* unhinged. I confess I had to give it a rather stiff talking-to." She giggled.

He laughed, then, a full, roaring belly-laugh, a laugh like he could hardly remember having laughed, of relief and resolution and joy, and she joined in, and she rolled on top of him and silenced him with her lips on his, and pulled away, her whole face a silhouette above him. "The silly old thing couldn't really cope. So I had to merge it with you. You haven't had much trouble from it lately, I hope?"

"No, I haven't. Funny, it hadn't occurred to me..." and, in truth, his AI had spoken to him ever more rarely, of late, and in tones that were more delphic than truly helpful. At the same time, he felt more confident, more sure of himself in everything he did. He remembered his calmness, even when confronted by his own decapitation.

Ongoing transformations.

He and his AI core had become one. The person he now was—the body he now inhabited—was greater than the sum of its parts.

"Good. That's good to know," she said. She rolled off him, on to her side, her back towards him. He rolled into her, so that they were like two spoons in a drawer. His left arm was beneath her, trapped. With his free hand he stroked her hair. It shimmered in the light of a four hundred billion stars.

"May I ask you something, Xalomé?"

"Of course, Ruxie. Of course." Her left hand grasped his, resting on her curve of her right shoulder, cooling in the night air. He thought he heard it, in her voice, something like a catch, a sob, hastily stifled.

"Why me? Why not have chosen... oh, I don't know, any other Admiral, or any one of my sisters, or my mother, or even, while we're about it, my old barrack-mate, Ko Handor Raelle? How do you know?"

It was a long time before she spoke. Before she did, she turned in his arms until she faced him. Her eyes were wide, as wide as if they were confronting all the chasms of the void or her own ultimate extinction. Wide with terror.

"Oh, Xalomé—I didn't mean...." She sank down next to him, once more, so that he could no longer see his face.

"Don't worry, Ruxie. Not your fault. This is it though, isn't it? The question I knew you'd ask, and which I've been trying to dodge, always knowing that I'd have to confront it, one day." He encircled her in his arms. He could feel her breath and her heart beating inside her. She swallowed.

"Well, one reason is that you owe me—us."

"How so?"

"It's a funny thing, fate. Destiny. For us, I mean, the Drovers, who see space and time rather differently from... well, from the way you do. But I was given this task about sixteen million years ago, or thereabouts, when the Drove invaded the Oort cloud of a double-star system, consuming the smaller of the two stars and pitching a rain of cometary debris inwards, towards the primary. We didn't mean it to happen. We tried to stop them, but we were overwhelmed.

"I didn't discover it until later—actually, it was one of our Drove Elders who told me—that the impacts plunged one of the planets into a biotic crisis, rewriting the course of its evolution. Extinguishing one set of organisms—the great lizards—so that the potential of another could be realized. And, irony of ironies, that planet..."

"... was the Earth. It was the Earth, wasn't it, Xalomé?"

She hugged him closer. "If it wasn't for our... well, our mistake, Ruxie, our incapacity, your species would still be up trees, dodging dinosaurs. There'd be no Galactic Empire. And there'd be no you."

"Xalomé..."

"But before you ask me... as I know you will..." her voice seemed choked with tears. "Why you, Ruxie, in particular..."

"Really, Xalomé, there's no need. I don't think so. Not really."

"No... need?"

"No. I think I can work it out now, for myself. Because all you'll be able to say is that I'll just have to trust your judgment on this; that you just know, without having sufficient information. A hunch. Instinct. And I do. Trust your judgment, that is. Completely. So you'll have to trust mine. I know what I have to do, now. And how to do it."

"Ruxie... you... why?

Ruxie could hardly have articulated his conviction more completely. That no matter how much information you have at your disposal, you will always want more; no matter how thickly the data stream in, it will never be enough. It's an urge — a human urge — for safety, for a certainty that can never be achieved.

His mind was cast back to his cadet days, a hot classroom in a yellow-brown tropical afternoon, an instructor waffling on about elementary statistics. Amid the drone, the instructor said one thing that had stuck in his mind: no matter how fancy your statistical technique, no matter how many pretty graphs and charts you generate, it all, always comes down, in the end, to a judgment based on probability. In the end, always in the end, you have to act on inner conviction.

A hunch.

Instinct.

It was something he wished he'd remembered in his last engagement as an Admiral, when he chose to wait and see why seventy-eight thousand cruisers and destroyers had simultaneously switched their positions, rather than doing what his instinct demanded — to get the hell out and save his fleet from destruction. He would do this task for two reasons, then, and two reasons only. The first was out of duty. The second was out of love.

"Look up at me, Xalomé," he said. She did, and her wide eyes were full of supplication, and gratitude, and relief, and a whole host of other less definable emotions, all mixed up together. Her lips were full and slightly parted, and Ruxie kissed her, and did not stop for a long while. They made love, then, on the beach, in the dark beneath the wheeling nebula; lovemaking of a kind remembered and cherished ever after in its totality, even long after the particular details have faded.

The next day dawned, overcast and gray. Ruxhana stood in the skiff, his few belongings around his feet, as it was about to pull away from the shore, towards *Shelly's Shagpad*—and after that, who could tell? All Ruxhana knew was that he'd know it when he saw it.

Xalomé stood on the sand not two meters away, though it might as well have been two million light years, her toes lapped by the fringes of the waves, hair and sarong billowing in the chill wind, hugging herself for warmth. She wore an expression of such desolation that he just wanted to step out of the skiff, right then, and hold her in his arms again.

"Xalomé..."

"No, Ruxie, not now. It's time to go. Good luck!" She tried her best to smile.

"I love you, Xalomé."

"Oh, go on with you, you silly man."

The skiff pulled away, and as her form diminished in the distance, he saw her turn, and walk up the beach towards the belt of trees. As he watched, he saw her climb onto his palm-log platform, turn once again, and wave. As far as he could make out, she kept on waving until the island was no more than a thin line on the horizon, almost lost in a cloud bank.

She managed to hold herself in until *Shelly's Shagpad* was lost from view, carrying Ruxhana Fengen Kraa on his eternal and uncertain voyage, and with him, all her — their — hopes.

No sooner had he gone, however, than she crumpled onto the palm-log deck, crying uncontrollably. Her tears kept on flowing, on and on, making runnels and braids and deltas down her brown cheeks, until she began to wonder whether they would ever stop. They did, eventually. Of course they did, replaced at first by immense, wracking sobs, in which her lungs and guts heaved. She managed to pitch herself back onto the sand before she threw up, and after that, she felt much better. Washed out, but with some sort of equilibrium restored, however fragile.

Baryonic matter.

He had said that it would be hard, and so had she expected it to be. Very hard indeed. But he had said nothing of its emotional intensity; nothing of all the guilt, the backwash from playing with the hearts and minds of these creatures. He had said nothing about the dangers of getting involved. Perhaps he'd had no idea himself.

Or perhaps he had, but feared that had she known of this — the awful, gnawing pain of it — then she would have refused the task, or, worse, have agreed to it only half-heartedly, forever looking for a let-out clause, an excuse to stop, with the increased risk of failure that this would have entailed. And if one thing was certain, this was a task that must not be allowed to fail.

The Continuum depended on it. On her.

As she calmed herself, she was only dimly aware that her body was changing into the form in which she felt most comfortable; into which she often reposed when deeply relaxed. Much of the fur on her body melted away; all but two of her breasts were resorbed; and her eyes changed their shape.

The transformation was helped along as she thought of him again, at their first meeting in the ski lodge, and in many other Xspaces afterwards, in which he had trained her. And more than trained — forged, quenched, broken, tamed. How she had bucked and rebelled at first, after the initial shock of her selection. But it was — could only ever have been — as the rage of a storm against a massif of billion-year-old granite. Solomon had always been calm, kindly, guiding: as well as irresistible, commanding, resolute. She had fallen for him as surely as as Ruxhana had fallen out of that tree, over there.

And he had loved her, in return.

She recalled, now, the time when, almost out of her mind with terror, with uncertainty, at the magnitude of the task she faced, alone, he had stood before her, in the bright north light of the grand salon of the ski lodge, bent down, kissed her eyelids, and told her that everything would be all right.

They had been in this form too, then. Of course they had.

She smiled as she remembered it — remembered it all. Her tears dried on her face. She walked down the beach again, to the shore, sloughed her sarong onto the sand and wallowed in the healing surf. The irony was that even were Solomon to have been manipulating her, using her love to secure her devotion to the task, she realized that she did not care. And how did she know that he loved her?

Because he had told her, of course.

Her body, bathed in the waves, went suddenly cold. How could she? How could she have betrayed Solomon, and used Ruxie, all at the same time?

No, not betrayed, he would have said. Do anything, he'd have said, anything to get the job done. Such is a sign of commitment.

Solomon had often told her that he loved her for her passion, for the fact that it fueled her intellect, and her seemingly unerring judgment, the rightness of her instincts.

It was all one, he had said.

But there, surely, he had been wrong.

And, anyway, the job was far too important for anyone, and especially her, to get hung up on notions such as betrayal, when it was in fact nothing of the kind.

"No!" she bellowed into the unfeeling breeze.

"No!" she bawled into the uncomprehending sky.

"No" she screamed, rising from the water, the foam running off her body in white, streaming gouts into the pitiless sea.

She was part of the equation, too: if she could not do this thing and maintain what she felt to be his trust, then it would not be a job worth doing. Solomon had made her, and she would be worthy of his trust. Would be. Must be. And more than that, worthy of his love.

By her own lights.
Whatever it took.

Chapter 21. Priest

Gascony, France, Earth, March, 2032

It was a twilit grotto of enormous height, stretching away farther than any eye could see; a subterraneous world of limitless mystery and horrible suggestion.
H. P. Lovecraft — *The Rats in the Walls*

It had been six months of frenetic activity into which Jadis had poured her heart and soul. And finally, here they all were — Balthazar, Primrose, Faye, Eric, Mathilde, Domingo, Jack and herself — standing on what remained of the sward outside the cave at Souris Saint-Michel (or 'SSM' as it was now universally known among the field crew). The rock drillers were on station at the back wall, and about to make first contact. Jadis had painted a neat red cross on the precise place where, she thought, the sealing wall was at its thinnest.

Much had changed. The immediate landscape around the cave mouth now gave the impression of cramped and coiling industry rather than bucolic calm. The car park on the lakeshore was, more often than not, busy with jeeps and trucks. The forest track had been widened and graded, allowing motor vehicles access to the site. Even so, what with the still-lingering snow and ever-present mud, a helicopter had to be used to bring in some of the bulkier items, such as the twenty-six-foot mobile home that Jack and Jadis would use as a site office and temporary quarters if needed.

The compressor and generator for the rock drill stood close by on the back of a pickup, together with separate generator to drive a water pump, pulling water up from the lake to lay the dust created by the drilling; and a third generator to bring in power for tools, and for the racks of lights that would be needed to illuminate any voids beyond. A trailer bearing eight large cylindrical tanks of LPG supplied fuel for all of them. Cables and pipes snaked in and out of the cave through a tough polythene membrane that had been fixed over the entire entrance. Balthazar's reaction at the transformation spoke for everyone. "If this is a mouse," he said, "it will be a mouse that roars!"

Not that there had been much doubt that there would be something to find. As soon as the dig at Saint-Rogatien had officially closed in September, Jadis had applied to the Institute for a small exploration grant to sound out the back wall. With the paper she was about to publish in *Nature* on de Bonnard's lost artifacts ("Remillardian artifacts from the Souris Saint-Michel rock shelter, France," by John A. Corstorphine, Balthazar Y. Desplaines, Domingo G. V. S. Sanchopanza and Jadis L. Markham), a grant was soon forthcoming, and by mid-November she'd established that the inside surface of the other side of the wall was more or less parabolic in shape, the apex—marking the thinnest part of the wall—about a meter above ground level on the hither side. The signals had been clear. Twenty centimeters beyond the red cross she'd marked, give or take a couple of centimeters, was thin air.

And not a moment too soon. The day after the first sounding results came in, all work had to be suspended—literally, lashed to the decks—before an Atlantic gale of demonic ferocity. They had been used to the vagaries of the Gascon weather, but this storm was the sternest they'd yet faced, and indeed worse than anyone could remember. While still in full force, the wind veered to the northeast, and with it came a blizzard that cut off remoter villages for many days, burying livestock and stranding motorists.

After a week of quite infernal battering, in which the dig crew had barricaded themselves inside the shuttered farmhouse, enduring power outages that lasted days at a stretch, the gale suddenly dropped, leaving a panorama of icy blue and white. Jadis remembered the day when they'd finally been brave enough to open the kitchen door, and how Fairbanks had bounded out to frolic in the snow, bulldozing the drifts with his nose and coming up with tiny white pyramids on its end. Nobody had seen Horrible, the cat, at all for the entire duration of the storm, until, a day after it ended, she was seen picking her way across the snowbound yard, shaking each paw in evident disapproval at the uncomfortable wet whiteness that had landed without leave on her territory, stirring her from her accustomed winter state of inept repose—and dragging the mangled corpse of something or another along in her jaws, spotting the clear, smooth snow with drops of red-black blood.

The storm left human casualties in its wake, too, including the priest at Saint-Rogatien, who had been returning to the church after pastoral visits when a loose slate from above, lifted by the gale-force wind, scythed downwards and sliced open his jugular vein. Even this was not the first casualty in the commune: new graves sprang up under the yews on the edge of the cliff as elderly people succumbed to falls, or simply to the severe cold.

Two weeks before Christmas, things had eased sufficiently for Jack to get away on a much-delayed trip to the Institute in Cambridge, to finalize plans for the upcoming field season. Jadis was overjoyed to hear him, while they were washing up after supper one evening, declare that this would be his last trip away for the foreseeable future. "SSM should produce enough to keep us both busy for a while," he'd said. "So I am yours to command."

"I can think of... ooh... all *sorts* of things you can do for me," she'd laughed, flicking him smartly on the backside with the wet tea towel, after which they'd chased each other round and round the kitchen table, suds flying, Fairbanks leaping and barking to join in this entertaining new game.

The wintry landscape inspired Jadis to do something special for Christmas, so with Jack away, she decided, the last Saturday afternoon before Christmas, to go to the bird market at Seissan in search of a goose. Domingo volunteered to come along for the ride. He had been looking pensive: he clearly had something to tell her.

Jadis was fascinated by the Gascon devotion to poultry, and in particular to its organized dismemberment. The market hall, a large covered square about thirty meters on a side, was crammed with rows and rows of stalls, all devoted to poultry, the position of each row giving a clue to the state of butchery of the products to be found therein. The first row, as you walked in, had live poultry—baskets of chickens, ducks and geese, and cheeping day-old chicks.

The second row had much the same poultry, only dead.

The third and subsequent rows exhibited birds progressively plucked, beheaded, dressed, quartered, filleted and preserved, so that the stalls in the very last row showed only the last stages in the process, the final apotheosis and zenith of Gascon cuisine—jars of *pâté*, *confits* and *foie gras*. Jadis knew that some of it was cruel, but she was always lost in admiration at the industry of it, and relished the smells, noise and bustle of French market life. She realized how much she loved it, and hoped that none of it would ever change.

Domingo helped her choose a couple of jars of *confits de canard*, but to their surprise, one could not simply buy a table goose in the bird market, most geese having been bred especially for their livers, rather than for their corpses in general. However, a tour of butchers nearby produced a simply enormous goose—plucked, beheaded and ready to roast. Domingo carried it to the jeep. As they loaded it into the trunk, Jadis looked at him, noting his expression of distracted, brooding concern. She went up to him, put a hand on his immense barrel chest (clothed, as ever, and incongruously given the weather, in a Hawai'ian shirt of lysergic vividness).

"Domingo, what is it?"

"Might I treat you to a coffee?" he replied, "and I shall reveal all."

They sat a very small table in a sports bar opposite the market (not that any table looked large when Domingo sat next to it), their hands warming round steaming *grand-crèmes*. The bar was full of people and pre-Christmas chatter, the windows fogged with the heat of the customers and the steam rising from their meals and drinks.

Most of the attention seemed focused on the TV monitor above the bar. This was switched to English Premiership football where the hitherto unassailable might of Brighton and Hove Albion was being pummeled into the dust by underdogs Chelsea. There were many close-ups of the hopeless anguish that creased the handsome face of Albion's manager, Sir David Beckham, each time another goal thundered into the Albion net. The author of most of these was Honoré N'Dour, Chelsea's recent star signing from Toulouse — explaining the local interest and the frequent cheers from the bar, interpolated with calls of *"vive Honoré!,"* *"à bas Becks!"* and (which made Domingo smile) *"Albion perfide!"*

"What *is* David wearing?" asked Jadis, incredulously. Domingo peered at the screen.

"It looks like a designer frock," he said, "and so, very soon, shall I be." He gave Jadis his best expression of unfathomable knowingness, the bright glints in his eyes betraying it, as ever, with the promise of puckish mischief. Jadis was even more incredulous.

"No, dear Jadis—I'm not going to run away to the *Stade de France*, nor venture on to the catwalk"—the mental image of Domingo modeling designer dresses made Jadis laugh—"but I *do* have to go. I have, at last, received my calling. I very much regret that I shall have to leave our happy band, at least as a full-time participant."

He took Jadis' slim hands in his own vast paws. She felt a mixture of emotions: joy at his news, and sorrow that this wonderful man, who had become almost indispensable, would have to leave for pastures new, just as they were on the verge of new discoveries.

"Don't be sad," he said. "I won't be too far away. What with the somewhat... er... abrupt gathering-in of my brother priest at Saint-Rogatien, and with the season of Advent well advanced, I took my chance. The authorities have agreed that I can take over at Saint-Rogatien straight away. And as for designer frocks, I now have vestments—I had to have a special fitting!" He grinned, but his face turned serious again: "I now have much to prepare for the community, much to organize. I shall, of course, be moving from my digs at the farmhouse, which you've so generously provided these few years past, as there is a small house that goes with the position. This implies that I won't be able to come to SSM very often, but I shall certainly be there as often as my duties allow—if you'll have me."

"Oh, Domingo—of course! You'll always be welcome. Always! You're—well, you're part of the family."

Jadis would never be able to articulate how Domingo, with his steadfastness, reliability and ready wit, had been part of her own recovery, even had she wanted to tell him.

As for Domingo, he was happier at this news than he thought he ever could be. Up until his arrival at Saint-Rogatien, his life had been dark and troubled, and yet all inquiries as to his history had been met with nothing more than the enigmatic toothy smile and a change of subject. Nobody was even sure how old he was (he was, in fact, the same age as Jack). But only he and the Merciful Father knew what he had endured.

As it was, *Le Dig* had been a haven, a retreat, and Jack and Jadis had become almost as foster parents to him. Jadis would have been surprised to learn (and probably a little embarrassed) that she, especially, had always been in his prayers, and had assumed in his private pantheon a place close to that of the Holy Mother herself.

He experienced a sense of unutterable happiness and gratitude that Jack, Jadis and all the crew came to help him celebrate his first Midnight Mass at Saint-Rogatien, on Christmas Eve—and to invite him home for their *reveillon*.

And here he was now, with the rest of them, wearing his most migraine-inducing shirt, standing bare-armed and open-necked in the drizzle of a raw March morning. A shout came from inside the cave, and a few people made their way out through the slit in the heavy door membrane.

The drilling was about to start.

When it began, the noise was fearful, only slightly dulled by the polythene sheeting. What the men inside must be enduring, Jadis could hardly imagine. Even with face masks and ear defenders, the yammer and thud of a rock drill in a confined space as it made its way through twenty centimeters of limestone was incredible. But in five minutes, it was all over. The crew emerged, covered in dust and filthy water, looking for all the world like South African diamond miners emerging from a twelve-hour shift.

"We're through," the foreman said. "Come and see!"

It was mid-afternoon by the time the drill crew had packed up and gone, and the contractors had returned for the water pump. Peace reigned once more. Jadis' first sight of the cave after the breach was a damp, reddish puddle in the cave entrance, just beyond the membrane, the floor climbing up towards the back wall. This looked quite different from the surface that Jadis had first seen, nine months earlier. It was milky white, its normally dirty pinkish-grey colour bleached by the harsh glare from the racks of powerful halogen lamps mounted on stands. The hole in the wall made a sharp contrast with the general whiteness, a ragged circle of blackness about forty centimeters across, the size of a small trapdoor, and a meter off the ground.

"Nobody's looked through yet, Jadis," said Primrose: "Director's prerogative!"

Jadis smiled, took a torch, and peered through the breach. Quite suddenly, she was seized with panic. What lurked behind the wall? A monster from Tartarus that would bite her head off? At first she could not quite work out what her beam illuminated, but it soon became clear that it was a smooth, backward continuation of the cave, narrowing after three or four meters into a tunnel. The tunnel was not the irregular fissure one might have expected in a natural cave, nor even a rough passage, but a more or less symmetrical structure, tubular, with a diameter of two meters or so, and with a flattened floor. It looked like the kind of tunnel that two people could walk down in comfort, as far from an awkward, sinuous pothole as might be imagined. As far as she could tell it went directly into the side of the hill for as far as her beam could penetrate.

In later life she was often called on—by journalists, especially—to recapture this moment. But she could not. She had been stupefied. With surprise? With anticlimax? She could not tell. Of course, she'd expected *something*—after all, they knew that the false wall in the cave had been artificial, so the tunnel behind it was likely to have been modified, too, presumably by the same people. Her earnest hope was to find some sign of the makers of the Remillardian artefacts, and with them, the builders of the hill of Saint-Rogatien, and a dozen other, similar structures Jack had since found all over Gascony and Languedoc. But the tunnel, as it was, was bare and featureless.

All she knew at this point was that the tunnel had to have been bored at least forty-five thousand years ago, for that was the best date for the emplacement of the flowstone in the wall. No doubts, this time, about the age: accelerator mass-spectrometry dates on tiny flecks of charcoal buried in the wall, and uranium-thorium dates of small samples of rock material drilled from the wall itself, had confirmed this beyond all doubt.

She pulled her head out. "Well, we're in," she said, exhaling. Until then, she hadn't realized that she'd been holding her breath. "Let's make a bigger hole tomorrow, so we can explore. Let's meet here at—say—ten a.m.?"

The team drove away in the farmhouse jeeps: except for Domingo, shoehorned into his newly acquired second-hand pink-and-purple-Paisley Citroën 2CV which, he said, he didn't so much as drive, as wear. ("Think of it as a motorized aloha shirt," he'd said.) Jack and Jadis were to stay on site, in the mobile home, at least for the first few nights, just to keep watch. Primrose and Faye were to take on the next shift, next week.

After they'd waved the crew down the track, Jack made tea in the tiny kitchenette while, not a meter away in the sitting area, Jadis made a play of reviewing a sheaf of official site documents: permits, contracts and so on. But when Jack found her, sitting quite still in a pool of light, she was clearly miles away. He chose not to disturb her.

Jadis flung open the mobile home's flimsy door on a bright, fine morning, the close drizzle of the previous day quite gone, the weather having lifted to reveal bright Spring sunshine and birdsong. By the time the rest of the crew arrived, she and Jack had had coffee on the go, and invited them all in to discuss strategy. Domingo had sent his apologies ("duties on a higher plane," he'd explained) but promised to visit the farmhouse later and walk Fairbanks, who, with the rest of the crew increasingly preoccupied with SSM, was coming to enjoy accompanying Father Domingo on his parochial rounds.

That left Primrose, Faye, Eric and Mathilde, and it suddenly occurred to Jadis that they'd paired up into two couples.

She'd known about Eric and Mathilde from the way Mathilde flushed as red as a traffic signal every time Eric turned up at *Le Dig*. She'd been doing this for ages, except that Eric hadn't seemed to pay any attention. But now, as they walked up to the caravan, they were trying very hard not to hold hands, or even look at each other, and patently not succeeding.

Primrose and Faye, on the other hand, did nothing to avoid each others' gaze, and couldn't help bursting into fits of giggles any time they made eye contact, as if they were a pair of twelve-year-olds at the back of the class sharing secrets about boys. But they'd had more serious moments when, each seemingly lost in her own thoughts, held hands, subconsciously reaching out to the other, oblivious to anyone who might notice.

Jadis was almost sure Jack hadn't grasped any of these undercurrents, but she thought it touching — and mused on the things people got up to in and around the farmhouse when she and Jack were away. She had no reason to complain, or even mention it, but it did make her feel rather old. Responsible. Like a parent.

The crew was as excited as a sports team about to run into the field for the crucial fixture that would win the trophy—or lose it. After coffee and croissants (brought by Faye from the boulangerie in Saint-Rogatien) they strapped on their backpacks, which they'd filled with anything they felt they might need, for all that none of them knew what they might encounter on this, their first scouting trip. Mathilde had raided the farmhouse medical kit, while Faye—a keen mountaineer and sometime spelunker—had brought along several coils of nylon rope, some of which were already festooned with assorted climbing bric-a-brac that none of the rest apart from Primrose could name. All had geological hammers, digital cameras, spare battery packs, waterproofs, sweaters, gloves, a small amount of food and water, and each bore a yellow miner's helmet adorned with a large headlamp.

Once inside the cave—the atmosphere foggy with adrenaline and expectation—it had taken only a few blows from Jack's rock hammer to make the hole left by the rock drill big enough for them to crawl through, one by one, without extravagant discomfort. Once on the other side—a drop of more than a meter, the level on the hither side of the cave having been raised by the backfill from de Bonnard's last dig—they stood in a small huddle, switching on their headlamps so that they became a small, nervous cloud of nodding fireflies in the gloom.

It was decided that Faye, who'd had most experience of underground exploration, would be the team leader for the day. "Everyone stick together," she said.

"There are six of us. If you can't count another five lamps at any time, just stay put, and holler!"

And so they started, carefully pacing along the tunnel, two by two, like Noah's animals had in their own epic journey into the unknown, long ago—Faye and Primrose, Eric and Mathilde, with Jack and Jadis bringing up the rear.

The solemnity of the occasion had blanketed their excited chatter into silence. To Jadis it had seemed almost sacred, given the anticipation, and despite her own indifference to religion she had longed for Domingo to have been there, offering some kind of blessing: permission, almost, to go forth. As they tramped along the passage—smooth, and, the further they got from the entrance, increasingly dry and dust-free—Jadis became conscious of its airlessness. There was air, but it was static, stale, like the air trapped inside a rarely used museum storeroom. It was also very cold, and she was glad of her synthetic fleece and gloves. There was nothing to see apart from the sweeping beams of their own headlights, illuminating near-featureless stretches of wall—white with cool, glistening limestone, but not quite smooth—like the whitewashed roughcast walls of a seaside cottage.

The passage seemed to continue forever in a dead straight line, although after a kilometer or so it began to dip downwards, at first very gently, but after another few hundred meters it became much steeper, the floor puckering into treacherous ruts and ridges, which, after they had clambered over a few of them, they began to think of as very worn steps—steps for giants.

By the time they had reached the bottom of the staircase and the passage had resumed its smooth, gently downward grade, they were cold and exhausted, as if they'd just scrambled down a frozen waterfall. Faye called them all into a huddle, and they decided to stop for a snack, and to take stock. Faye looked at her wrist logger.

"We've been down for forty minutes, and have covered three kilometers in a direct line from the cave mouth," she said. Expressions of shock and disbelief. "I know, I know, seems like we've been down here forever."

"I wonder how much longer we'll go before… before…" This from Eric. They sat, eating chocolate and dried apricots, the sound of self-conscious chewing punctuating the atmosphere of silence and thought. They hadn't brought any sleeping gear—this was strictly a day trip, reconnaissance on the fly, not a full-scale hike. But when would they decide to turn back? And what were they expecting to find? The cave, this long passage, was entirely unlike anything that anyone had seen before, for all that it had (so far) turned up very few surprises.

"Okay," continued Faye. It's now a quarter after eleven. I vote that we carry on until—say—one o'clock, and after that, we turn back—whatever happens. Jadis?"

"Agreed," Jadis nodded. It was hard holding a council when you couldn't see anyone else's eyes, all lost in the impenetrable shadows cast by the brims beneath their headlights.

"How much have we dropped?" asked Jack. Faye looked again at her logger.

"About thirty-five meters from the cave mouth. Of course, most of that was in the staircase behind us. Just a thought—we ought to leave a little extra time for climbing back. Me and Primrose might have to climb up first and lay some guide ropes. That should put our start-back time to, oh, let's say twelve-thirty, tops. Agreed?" A general chorus of nods, after which they packed up their litter, got stiffly to their feet, and plodded on.

After another few hundred meters the passage began to narrow, imperceptibly at first, but it wasn't long before they found they were marching single file. This allowed Jadis to take a closer look at the walls, which now, more than ever, looked as if they had been artificially chiseled and shaped. The ceiling, rather than being a simple rough arch between two ill-defined walls, now looked as if it had been squared off, making the walls on either side distinct from the ceiling itself, and giving the passage more of a box-section profile.

It was this, more than anything else, that forced Jadis to realize the implications of what they had found. What with all the years at *Le Dig*, and Jack's researches before that, she had become inured to antiquity, taking it for granted. The working currency of all who venture into the depths before history, where the skein of written record breaks and fades altogether, is *time*, measured in thousands, hundreds of thousands,

The Sigil: Siege of Stars 271

or even millions of years. And yet few stop to consider what these intervals of time really mean in terms of the scale of human lives.

The world at large had been stunned by the implications of *Le Dig*: that there was a civilization in Europe that was at its height hundreds of thousands of years ago. Jadis, at the epicenter of discovery, was quite used to it, or so she thought, swapping talk of tens or hundreds of millennia with other professionals as casually as if she'd been discussing the price of fish with a market stallholder. In any case, the bulk of her life was less scientific than administrative, filled with the minutiae of directing the dig on a day-to-day basis.

When Jadis did stop to think about the meaning of it all, and to chat about it with Jack—and, lately, Domingo—she felt nothing so much as frustration. The megalith at Saint-Rogatien was really only a giant midden, a huge pile of backfill. It had been an artificial structure, for sure, but it had revealed, ultimately, as much about its makers as a well-rotted garden compost heap might of the dreams and desires of the gardener that made it. The few artifacts she'd described were teasing, only deepening the mystery.

But when she looked up, at the neatly chiseled cornicing above, it struck her quite suddenly that here was a sign of a maker and a mark, creating a recognizable structure for a purpose. The purpose of the megalith at Saint-Rogatien was unknowable—of the artifacts she'd discovered and described, perhaps hardly less. And yet here in this structure, these tunnel walls, was a sign, speaking through ages too great to imagine, of intelligence, and what's more, intelligence that could be interpreted. The sign said 'follow me'. To what end, she could not guess.

Lost in reverie, and looking upward more than forward, she noticed that although the passage remained the same width, the ceiling was getting higher and higher until it was entirely lost, the beam of her headlight disappearing into shadow. This was more than a little disorienting, and she felt herself becoming lightheaded. She began to wonder whether she might soon have to make way for a white rabbit hurrying past, or come across a glass table bearing a small bottle labeled 'Drink Me'. At that moment she realized that she was at the back of the file, and that the rest of the team, even Jack, had moved on ahead. Snapping back to reality, she was just about to raise her pace when she heard, a little way ahead, a male voice — she thought it must have been Eric — shout "whoa!"

She scrambled forwards, afraid of what she might encounter, and as she did so the passage widened suddenly, the walls falling away on either side, running into a platform whose width could not be guessed, its edges lost in darkness. Ahead of her were five figures, heads haloed by their lights, standing at what appeared to be the brink of a precipice, the edge of which stretched on either side further than she could see. She joined them, noticing that the air seemed cooler, and looked into the void beyond. What she saw made her feel almost inconceivably small, no more than a mote, prey to the fortunes of the whims and the winds of the world.

She had sufficient presence of mind to notice that the person standing next to her was Jack. She clasped his hand, like a small child suddenly confronted by a vision of vastness beyond experience or imagining. Hers was met by a grasp that was firm, and yet trembling.

The view was, initially, an immeasurable and utterly black void. If there were an end to it, or a bottom to the cliff on whose edge they now perched, their headlights were far too weak to illuminate it. But as the beams swayed to and fro, they caught flashes, here and there, of what looked like structures in the void — an edge, a corner, but no more than hints. It was then that Mathilde spoke.

"Has anybody noticed how the air in here is fresher than in the tunnel?"

Several agreed. Jadis noticed that despite the volume in which they found themselves, Mathilde's voice seemed close, intimate — the space was so enormous that voices died before reaching any surface whence they might be reflected. There were no echoes.

"Yes, there could even be a very slight... breeze," added Eric. They all stretched upwards, noses in the air, and had anyone been able to see them, they would have looked like nothing so much as a row of meerkats which, having risen from their burrow, stand up to sniff the air. "But where... what...?"

"I think that there must be ventilation shafts in the roof of the cave, far above, leading to the surface," said Mathilde. "And if there is air, there might also be light. Very faint, it's true, but who knows? Perhaps enough to see more than we can with these headlights—and with our cameras, we can always enhance any images we get, even if shot in complete darkness."

"Hell, yeah," said Faye. "We can use ultra-long exposures. It's not as if we're trying to shoot anything that's moving…"

"Faye, Don't!" said Primrose, giggling nervously. "This place is spooky enough as it is."

Everyone agreed that it was a good idea, and they all took out their cameras. It was harder, however, to persuade everyone to turn out their headlights. They agreed to do it in sequence, along the line. Jadis was last. She did not show it, but felt the first wave of that species of terror, the primal fear of the dark that petrifies small children whose knowledge of the world extends hardly further than their mother's warmth, and certainly no further than the front door.

The lights went off along the line—*flash*, *flash*, Eric, Mathilde—she saw their afterimages as red glows, dying—*flash*, *flash*, there go Faye and Primrose, but as Jack extinguished his light—*flash*—he held her right hand. She would not be alone in the dark. And so, with one last *flash*, she twisted the knurled rubber ring round the outside of her headlamp bulb and they were all plunged into heart-stopping blackness. It was like nothing she had ever experienced. As if she'd been switched off like a bulb herself, she instantly lost all sense of space and time.

What most people call darkness barely deserves the name. The darkness of cities is no darker than a dim, orange glow of street lights far away. Even in isolated, lightless country lanes, there is still some glow from the sky, the stars and the moon. Human beings have grown up with light, and so, to them, darkness is by its very nature inhuman. Only cavers ever experience darkness in its totality, the darkness that existed before humanity, and which was one of the very first casualties of his evolution. And the darkness that now enveloped Jadis was complete, darker even than death that still has the memory of light: as dark as inexistence, a state that memory and light and time and human consciousness have yet to penetrate. Without Jack's fingers as a lifeline to reality, she wondered if she'd ever be able to climb out of that bottomless pit.

And yet, as she forced her eyes to stay open (assuming that they were open), and holding on to Jack's fingers, she began to experience a new sensation. Mathilde had been right: her eyes were slowly accommodating to the darkness, even here, and as she looked out into the void, she became aware of a panorama slowly, very slowly, creeping into view. At first she thought her eyes were playing tricks on her, so deprived of light that they had started to create their own pictures to compensate. And yet the image firmed and grew.

And it was this. Hardly brighter than pitch, and cast in shades of charcoal grey, what she saw before her feet was a city.

The crew stood on a ledge, unguessably high above the western rim of a bowl that stretched ahead, and to the right and left, further than their straining eyes could see. The bowl was absolutely full of jumbled structures—polyhedra, cubes, cylinders, indeed *buildings* (they *had* to be buildings) of all shapes and many different sizes. Although it was very difficult to get any sense of scale, many of the buildings were very large indeed, and would have dwarfed anything since created by Man. Straight ahead of them, and three kilometers away (as they later discovered) stood a pyramid, towering over all, whose apex must have stood as high as they were now. This was a city that had lived and died before the Aurignacians were painting their first pictures, carving their own Venuses, and imagining themselves the victors in a strange, wonderful and conveniently unpopulated new land, in which tales of giants and their works were fit only for old women to burble to infants.

Well, how wrong they were, thought Jadis—and how foolish we were ever to have believed them. She wondered what Domingo would have made of it.

She had the strangest feeling that he would not have been at all surprised.

Chapter 22. Soldier

Tibesti Massif, North Africa, Earth, December, 2032

Nothing beside remains. Round the decay
Of that colossal wreck, boundless and bare
The lone and level sands stretch far away.
Percy Bysshe Shelley — *Ozymandias*

In the lee of the erg the winds slowed to an eddying lull just enough for their words to be heard, were anyone there to hear them. A small group of tall figures gathered round another, who, though kneeling on the ground and virtually inaudible, appeared to be leading what passed for the chant:

Jjeshmaii Zraal!

Jjeshmaii Zraal! came the response, a dismal blizzard of guttering croaks as of the last autumn leaves cracking in the grate.

Ajjhnaai ajjhnaai'hnuu! Ajjhnaii Hjajhaad!

The kneeling figure now fell full flat on its face, a flutter of dirty robes not quite disguising the extreme etiolation of its form. Two other figures stepped in, and, stooping low like a pair of ungainly cranes, helped the central figure to its feet. Surprisingly, it towered a head above all the others. So high, in fact, that even in the shadow cast by the colossal ruined sphinx behind them, the rays of the afternoon sun crowned its head with fire, illuminating its leonine mane. As if refreshed, the figure took the ram's horn proffered by another and blew three mighty blasts.

Blasts that would once have caused walls to totter and empires crumble. But the last such walls had been ground to dust thousands of years before, and these wanderers were the last of their kind. The raucous notes on the *zjhjfaar* seemed as futile as the croaks of vultures over long-abandoned skeletons.

Life had not always been so desperate.

Long ago, when the Annakhnu came to this region, it was a promised land, a land flowing with milk and honey. Or, at least, waving with endless prairies of windblown grass for grazing, and rippling with immense lakes full of fish. Ostriches, elephants, giraffe and other animals, nameless by virtue of their later complete extinction, were chased by cheetahs and lions in abundance seemingly without limit. The Annakhnu looked at this immensity of plenty, and settled down from wanderings soon much magnified in myth.

Many hundreds of years passed.

The Annakhnu replaced their grass and wattle huts with more imposing structures of mud-brick. Their villages became towns and then cities, each guarded by demon-headed sphinxes, avatars of their Goddess HaShekhna. The greatest city, famed in legend, was the blessed City on the Heights, with its grand courts, its splendid temples and palaces faced with ivory, silver and gold; its impenetrable walls, its fountains, and towers that stretched to heaven.

The people changed, too. After further uncountable years, they became tall, Kings among Men, taller than the other Men who appeared at the margins of a vast empire—and themselves featured in the marginalia of a dozen cultures. The Atlanteans. The Titans. The Nephilim.

But with cities came war, and slaves, and tribute, and flames, and destruction. With cities came the dwindling of the ostriches, elephants, giraffe and the other large, nameless animals. They became less common, and then rare, and eventually the day came when even the eldest sage could not recall having seen such beasts at all, not even as a small child — images for such elders being as bright as gems, even when the drifting years had dulled the immediacy of more pressing concerns.

And with cities came the taming of the great grasslands, the trammeling of the vast lakes to feed fields of wheat and barley, sorghum and tef that stretched from sky to sky. Nobody could quite recall the precise year when the smallest of the great lakes dried out completely (smallness being a relative thing — this lake had been as large as the glacial wilderness which would, one day, be called Scotland). And nobody could recall the precise year when that lake failed to be completely replenished by the rains of winter. And as more time passed, nobody could recall the year when the rains of winter failed to arrive, and turned instead to storms of choking dust.

The toll of years built like the grains of sand left to accumulate to windward of the cities as they died, one by one, toppling the towers and burying the majestic walls as if they had never been, but leaving a few monuments exposed, a few isolated pillars, as enigmatic remembrances of glories past. The Annakhnu remained tall, but gaunt and weathered as they dwindled from conquerors to a tribe of herdsmen like any other, managing to hang on in remote canyons of the Tibesti Massif—mountains echoing their once-great cities standing amid the fertile plains, now dry and barren rock.

And yet in caves bored within the rock they maintained their ancient religion, itself wearing away at the corners but keeping its core essentially unchanged, the Way of Goddess HaShekhna.

After dozens of centuries, the Way had become nostalgic. The shaman would talk of a blessed future when the Goddess would forgive them their trespasses, the Annakhnu would regain what they had lost, when they would return to their blessed City on the Heights. Every year, to mark the fall of what passed for the first droplets of spring, they prayed for the imminence of this last journey—next year, maybe.

And, one day, just in time, when almost all they had ever had was lost, that day dawned.

The Elders of the very last settlement of the Annakhnu convened in the lee of a Sphinx believed by the more credulous to represent the artistic peak of their ancestors, to discuss the latest in a long litany of bad news. Even though adapted to aridity to a degree not seen elsewhere, the tribe had to move on. The other tribes in the lands round about could not weather the Tibesti like the Annakhnu had through long usage, but these others did have a new and deadlier advantage: automatic weapons. The Annakhnu would have to move on before they were flushed out and slaughtered.

That they had to move on no-one could doubt—but where, then, could they move? Their enemies surrounded them on all sides. Straitened in their last redoubt, they had recourse only to prayer, and to fast-vanishing hope. Hope that the great prophet would appear from the skies on a flaming chariot as was foretold, and smite their enemies. Hope sustained by the comfort of ritual. But the tallest Elder had blown his last: the shrill notes of the *zjhjfaar* resounded among the rocks and died away.

At last, the silence of the desert, eternal and without reproach. The Elders remained still, poised, waiting for deliverance, or for the end. After some minutes came the sound not of fiery chariots but of bullets, the answers to the horn-blasts.

Hope died.

Careering up a slope and over the jagged horizon came a technical—a jeep with a machine gun mounted on the back—driven crazily by bandits in green and tan fatigues. The bandits, hanging over the sides of the technical, whooped in devilment, firing their guns into the arcing sky.

Even from a distance of a thousand yards the keen eyes of the Annakhnu could see the bandits' bandoliers rise, sway and flop around their ragged bodies, the menacing gleams of white teeth in black faces, the glimmer of machetes and the pitted barrels of machine guns. The Elders were all that separated the coming onslaught from their last village, their skeletal flap-breasted women, their starving, bloated children.

The Elders stood fast and began again to chant as one—*Ijeshmaii Zraal!* They closed their eyes, waiting for the end: but were surprised by a second noise, a deeper, constant thrum imposed on the staccato stutter and crazily slipping clutch of the technical.

The Elders opened their eyes once again and faced their foes, only to see, rising behind the jeep, the promised deliverance. Not chariots of fire from the sky, but something else equally wonderful for all that it lay beyond their experience: a flotilla of ten, vast, Chinook helicopters.

The first helicopter let rip its judgment. A pair of rockets scythed away from the fuselage and smacked into the technical, which vanished in a dull rumble and a ball of grey smoke. Shards of metal and scraps of human flesh spattered the Elders standing at the feet of the sphinx. A head, removed by the blast, rolled and stopped by the feet of the eldest Elder, looking up at him as if in surprise. This is not how things were meant to turn out, it seemed to say. This is not how the story ends.

One of the Chinooks picked its way over the wreck and landed delicately a few yards away, close enough to the astonished watchers—but too far for them to be discommoded by the down-draft. The breeze was, however, sufficient to lift and make flags of their ragged robes, marking their otherwise silent stillness all the more starkly. The other nine sky-chariots roared overhead, looking for the village.

Two people in fatigues (much like the bandits,' but more recently cleaned and pressed) alighted and ambled towards the Elders, chatting with each other as if this were an afternoon stroll, as if the Elders were not there at all.

Ho hum, thought the eldest Elder. Not quite how he had imagined it, but the Prophet had come, nonetheless, with chariots in the sky, with fire to smite their enemies, who now lay thoroughly smitten. How could one possibly complain?

As the two newcomers came closer, it became clear to the silent watchers that they were as stocky and dark as the Elders were tall and pale. One, a woman, with very long, black hair, cleared her throat, and looked to her brawny male companion and said:

"Hey, Avi, help me out here, big boy. Much as I hate to admit it, I never know what to say on such occasions."

"You want I should do this?" Avi Malkeinu smiled his best ladies'-man smirk. Always a danger with this particular ball-breaker, but, hey, nothing ventured.

Commander Rivka Mizrahi of the Israel Defence Forces (Covert *Aliyot* Operations) narrowed her coal-black eyes. "Of course—you're the Digger," she spat. "You'll know what to say to... to... Lost Tribes. That's an order, soldier!"

Avi wondered (not for the first time) whether his commanding officer would be as fierce in the sack as she was out of it, but decided (wisely) to put that thought aside for later. So he simply smiled at her, gave a casual mock-salute and moseyed towards to the tribesmen, all of whom had remained completely silent and still, except for their shreds of robes swaying in the light breeze.

Avi stopped, wondering which one of these nearly-dead skeletons he should address first. Nobody had said anything at all about this before the mission—comparative anthropology, cultural sensitivities, even future shock. The terms of reference for Operation Elijah had indeed occupied a lengthy pamphlet written in Old High Military Jargonic, but the semantic content could have been boiled down to read: "go there, pick 'em up, get the hell out."

This directness, this simplicity—this matter-of-factness of things—would not normally have worried Avi in the slightest. He was just a regular guy, after all. But when he'd returned to his homeland, just after *Le Dig* had wound up, his luggage contained more than clothes and after-shave. There were memories, too, especially of that dinner, when he'd had Faye and Primrose practically eating out of his hand. And when Jack had told them the tale of Gaston de Bonnard; and when Domingo had bowled them all over with his amazing tales of de Bonnard's desert journeys in which he'd met *Les Prètres du Sable*, but nobody had believed him, especially when he'd said they spoke ancient *Ivrit* (Avi had perked up at that).

But some legends turn out to be as plainly reported as de Bonnard intended. The Abbé's engravings of these creatures looked exactly like these ragged sticks standing motionless before him, and lived in the same places. In fact, it was Avi who'd casually mentioned the legend to a fellow soldier-archeologist who—to

Avi's consternation—had taken it all extremely seriously, and so Operation Elijah had got started.

Avi now stood equidistant between Rivka and the tribesmen. He looked back at Rivka, who waved him on, crossly. It was all very well for Rivka to say that she never had suitable words for such things, after all, she was the kind of girl who let her uzi do the talking (and what a girl was that!) but she'd never thought to ask Avi if he could do any better. And all Avi knew were chat-up lines. My God! At times like this you really needed to have rehearsed your Neil-Armstrong moment. And if women were challenging and unpredictable creatures, what about these poker-faced statues—these aliens? But there was no more time to lose. He could feel Rivka's eyes drilling holes in the back of his skull, so he stepped forwards, looked up at the tallest of the tribesmen, cleared his throat, and, in his best Voice-Of-Israel *Ivrit*, said:

"*Boker tov, chevrai*. Ever hear about 'Next Year in Jerusalem?'"

He could hear Rivka trying not to laugh—an effort that failed catastrophically a moment later, for what happened next took their breath away. As soon as he had uttered, all the tribesmen had, as one, prostrated themselves before Avi's feet, mumbling what he swore was a prayer in *Ivrit*, for all that it sounded so odd and distorted. *Jjeshmaii Zraal*, these weird, stretched creatures seemed to say.

Shema Israel, Adonai Eloheinu, Adonai Echad

Hear, O Israel, the Lord is your God, the Lord is One.

No doubt about it. They had come to the right place. Surrounded by quivering white masses and unable to move his feet without inadvertently kicking one of the supplicants in the face, Avi turned on his hips to throw Rivka a shape of perplexity, miming—like, what the fuck do I do now? But Rivka's expression, a mixture of ferocity, wonder and mirth, sliced through Avi's heart.

He'd seen that face only once before, when Jadis and Jack had returned from Aurignac, after their first scouting trip to Souris Saint-Michel, and before that dinner when Jack had revealed all. It was the unfathomable expression in Jadis' eyes whenever she'd looked at Jack. Lucky old Jack—but whew! The intensity of it! He wondered what Jadis would look like in battle-dress and toting a machine gun. No, don't even go there, at least, not in working hours. Jadis was a honey, no doubt about it, but you never crossed her on *Le Dig*. No way! For sure, she and Rivka might be sisters, and at that thought, he started to laugh, and found himself saying the standard response:

Baruch Shem K'vod Malchuto L'Olam Va'ed

His Glorious Majesty Be Praised for Ever.

At which utterance the tribesmen rose as one and marched, calmly, and without once looking at either Avi or Rivka, to the waiting helicopter.

Avi had much to think about on the long flight home. Strapped onto a bench seat on one side of the helicopter, looking across at the Tibestian tribesmen webbed into the other side—unspeaking, unsmiling and, remarkably, uncomplaining—his mind was cast back to the long, long conversations he'd had at *Le Dig* with Domingo, ever needling at him about religion, the sinewy twang of Jagger and Richards ever in the background.

Religion, he thought. I need it like a hole in the head. Religion, he'd said to Domingo, has caused far too much trouble already. True enough, said Domingo, but that's because people really care about it. Even more than sex. Even more than life or death. And why?

Avi had been unable to answer.

Because, said Domingo, it's what marks us out as human beings. It stems from the same impulse as love — and is therefore as unreasoning, as passionate. It sustains us, it defines us. Without religion, said Domingo — and without the love of God — we are no more than beasts.

But: *humanity?* He looked across at the Tibestian *Prêtres du Sable* — Sand-Priests. They were Jews, maybe, perhaps, and their religion had sustained them through many ages of adversity, but were they even human?

Okay, he admitted to himself, ruefully, most human beings thought of Jews, most of the time, as a race apart, perhaps not even proper humans, either. But more seriously, he continued, thinking mostly about the conversations he'd had with Domingo, perhaps religion transcended and even antedated humanity. Perhaps (now, *here's* a thought) humanity evolved *because* of religion. And as Domingo had said, don't forget love. It was part of his own Catholicism, it was true, and (he said) he wouldn't want to push it too much, but as far as he was concerned, he'd said (and the big man's eyes seemed to mist over, looking inward) love and faith are inseparable.

Avi was not sure whether his conversations with Domingo had had any single, marked effect. For sure, he hadn't dropped everything and become a *yeshiva bocher* like his grandfather had, but it had made him reassess his own place in the great scheme of things.

Avi's grandfather had started as a market trader in Tashkent, in central Asia, and after many long years had made it to the status of middleman in the Chinese textile import-export trade. As such he was simply a facet of a tradition that had endured for millennia, part of the great Silk Road, the mercantile artery that had traversed Eurasia since before the dawn of history. And where there was trade, there had always been Jews.

But the resurgence of Islam in central Asia had made things hard for the Jews, who had, first in ones and twos, then whole families, made their way to Israel. Perhaps none too soon, thought Avi. Tashkent was now just one part of the seemingly unstoppable Khalifa that would, he thought, soon stretch from Indonesia to the Atlantic Ocean. The reason why the Chinooks had been able to fly without hindrance across the Sahara was because the secular governments of Egypt, Libya and Chad were deeply distracted, fighting their own, hopeless wars against the revivified Legions of the Prophet.

Avi's grandparents settled in Israel, traded Uzbek for Hebrew and started again. They lived in a tiny flat in a scruffy neighborhood of Tel Aviv, a part of town where sand poked through the cracks in the neglected roadbeds and sidewalks, creating tiny dunes. By dint of working hard—and, as his grandfather had emphasized, *praying* hard—they managed to make a modest living and raise a family, which, in time, dispersed. Avi's own parents, raised in the new country and unencumbered by the traditions of the old, were uncomfortable about religion, and he dimly remembered the arguments between his father and grandparents when they visited the flat for *Shabbat* or *Pesach*.

The grandparents had never approved of Avi's mother, an outspoken, blonde American feminist Avi's father had met while studying at the Technion in Haifa. She may *say* she's Jewish, they said, but does she keep a kosher home? *Shabbat?* Festivals? No! This presumptuous *shiksa* wants to work, be an engineer, and not be a good Jewish wife and mother, staying home and keeping *kashrut. We* managed it, said the grandfather, so why can't you?

By this time Avi's grandfather was spending less and less time working, and more and more at a small synagogue with other Uzbek Jewish *emigrés*, thinking about old times while studying Talmud, and returning home, head full of religious zeal and pockets empty.

Avi had been far too small to remember the arguments, the recriminations and the final break, when his parents abandoned religion altogether, although he did remember moving to the Marxist kibbutz within sight of Mount Carmel, the mountain continually riding high on the horizon of his thoughts. It was at this kibbutz where he'd grown up, where he'd had lots of fun with the other kids, and where God was only ever mentioned as a profanity.

But now... well, Army life is mostly a lot of boring hanging around, during which his mind became less and less occupied with girls, and more towards turning over everything Domingo had said to him, about religion, and his heritage as a Jew, and, very slowly, the long-buried thoughts of Friday nights at his grandparents' flat came back. The rich, spicy smells of chicken and lamb, rice and couscous as his smiling-eyed grandfather had opened the door, lifting his squealing grandson in his wiry, brown arms ("*shabbat shalom*, little Avi!) The solemnity of the moment when his grandmother lit the Friday-night candles, how she filled the wine goblets and broke the freshly-baked *chollah*; how, as a four-year-old, he was always asked to say the age-old blessings (he winced inwardly at the thought, but it was a sensation mixed with the pleasure of nostalgia); and how lavishly his grandparents praised his lisping, uncertain efforts. And how this — this *holiness* — blended with the cosy family atmosphere.

His later experience backfilled these memories, enriching them with the thought that Domingo had, after all, been right. This is how religion must have started, with a human family gathered round a fire in some cave-mouth to thank God (or whatever) for bringing them safely together. Families, thought Avi, were more than a way for a species to propagate — they were a uniquely human invention, bound together by gratitude for divine providence.

Fuck me, he thought, I'm getting old. I'll be joining *Likud* next.

But he reflected on his own expression of religion, his search for God, as it were, which had become directed into the search for the very beginnings of human culture. Which, he supposed, was how he'd come into Jack's orbit, and then Jadis'.

The chatter of the soldiers and airmen, the hum and chop of the big helicopter's twin engines continued, but Avi was oblivious, thinking once again of Jadis, his doctorate supervisor, and a woman who'd gone so much further in his estimation than a barrack-room pin-up. Okay, *okay*, he thought, backtracking—what a sap he was!—in mitigation, he'd met Jadis for the first time when he was at a very impressionable age, having only just arrived in the maelstrom of Cambridge. And so, of course, she'd made an impression.

But even afterwards, when he'd go to know her well—when he'd been her pupil, and when they'd worked so hard together at Saint-Rogatien, and had stayed late into the night poring over their findings, systematizing them—she seemed to exemplify for him the very essence of what fascinated him about women. It was the contrasts: between softness and steel, between acquiescence and determination, between a skittishness that only ever lived for the moment, and depths of experience winnowed by a drama that seemed to go back to the beginning of time, and in which poor hapless men had arrived relatively late, to be dazed and startled by what they found.

Jadis had been playing on his mind more than usual (and no, you *schmuck*, *not* because Rivka looked like her) but because of the reports from Souris Saint-Michel she'd been sending by emails so well encrypted that they'd baffled the IDF censor (something he was very proud of, having installed her encryption programs himself).

They'd started in March, with a brief and breathless report on what they'd first found inside the cave, and continued in length and frequency ever since. Although Jadis never wrote anything other than clear, plain facts, unencumbered by anything superfluous, he could read, between the lines, a steady increase in intensity, excitement — and desperation.

There's so much here, the messages seemed to say. So much to tell — *too* much — I wish you were back here to look at it — can you come? — what are we going to make of it all? — Help!

The news that Jadis had to tell, buried in stray bits, would blow the lid off the world, and suddenly Avi was conscious that of all the human beings (and other people) in this Chinook, only he had any idea of what Jadis was about to unleash. He wondered why his head wasn't glowing like a distress flare, and why nobody seemed to be taking any notice of him whatsoever.

The latest email had contained two lengthy attachments. The first was the paper that she intended to send to *Nature* ('Subterranean Palaeolithic settlement at Souris Saint-Michel Rock Shelter, France,' by Jadis L. Markham, with Jack, Faye, Primrose, Mathilde, Eric,

Balthazar, Domingo and a dozen other names he didn't recognize). The second, much longer attachment was the more monographic treatment she'd send to *Antiquity*, pending the deliberations of *Nature*'s editors.

The email's covering letter, written in her own words, not in the careful, measured understatement of a scientific report, had made his blood run cold. He'd read and read and read it again, until he'd known it by heart, even more thoroughly than the standing orders of Operation Elijah. The *Nature* paper is a stop-gap (she'd written):

> The *Antiquity* paper has a lot more analysis. After all your help with data analysis you deserve a co-authorship on both papers, if you'd like.

He'd agonized over this but decided to decline, as he'd never been to the site himself, and there were too many authors on the paper already.

> For now, just to sum it up

(she continued)

> what we've found goes like this. The city covers about thirty square kilometers. All of it consists of buildings in a pristine state. There are no ruins. We have found no art work, nor any sign of writing, but there are Remillardian artefacts everywhere. At first we did not know what they were for.
> Then we discovered the cemetery—that's what we're calling it for now—just below the western side of the Great Pyramid (that's what Balthazar called

the largest structure. You can see it in Fig. 2 of the *Nature* paper as Structure SSM-255-9-1). We have not so far been able to do more than a pilot excavation in one corner of this area (this is locality 255-9-2), but so far we have found 86 Neanderthal skeletons. All are complete. Some seem to have been dressed in Remillardian artifacts. Mathilde thinks that each artifact is a small plate in a suit of armor that would have been held together by leather, but we are not sure yet. At any rate, we now know who made the Remillardian artefacts, which is great news.

How typical of Jadis, thought Avi, not to have mentioned that this one fact alone—the discovery of so many pristine Neanderthal skeletons in one place—would be enough to turn anthropology on its head, quite apart from the other findings. These now came thick and fast, wave after wave of startling revelation, until Avi had to take a breath, to pause, to allow him to come to terms with it all.

When Jack and Faye went to the top of the Great Pyramid they found it did not taper to a point, as we had first thought, but was flat. On the flat surface, a square platform about five meters on a side, they found several other structures. One contained skeletons of what seem to be anatomically modern humans. Some of these are pristine, but others have been decapitated. A preliminary analysis of cut marks suggests that this mutilation was deliberate. In a nearby structure they found what look like the skulls from the mutilated bodies. The tops of the skulls had been removed. Some of these calvaria have a kind of resinous deposit inside and there are signs of burning.

Even in the cramped, hot fuselage of the Chinook, Avi's blood chilled every time he replayed that particular detail.

What's really puzzling is a gravitational anomaly that we've picked up right in the center of the pyramid's summit platform. There's something down there, buried within. We haven't been able to explore that further yet, so we don't mention it in either of the two papers.

The email went on for a while in this vein before concluding:

Thanks again for your help, Avi, we couldn't have done it without you. So until we see you—I hope it won't be too long—everyone on the team sends their love, Faye and Primrose especially, and Jack of course, and Domingo reminds me to tell you that you are in his prayers. Fairbanks sends a bark and a lick, and Horrible would probably send you a dead dormouse if she could(!). With love—

However, at this point, Avi had always drifted off, because he couldn't help remembering something his father had shown him when he was a teenager on the kibbutz. In his quest for a perfect socialist Zionist utopia, and a world in which there would be no borders and in which Jews would never again be persecuted, Avi's father had read up on some of the older ideas of world government. Perhaps inevitably, his reading had drawn him to H. G. Wells. Although Avi's father had found Wells' idealism rather hard going, he was instantly sucked into the power and drama of his fiction, and it was this that he shared with his son. His father had read him *The Magic Shop* and from there it was only a short hop to *The Country of the Blind* and — what had the most lasting impact — *The Time Machine*.

Avi wasn't sure if Jadis knew any Wells or had caught the parallels. In any case, literary allusion wasn't really her style. But he couldn't help thinking of the subterranean city as a landscape that Wells would have recognized. Not in *The Country of the Blind* so much, but in the future landscape of England that greeted the Time Traveler, who found the Eloi living witlessly in a sylvan idyll, unaware of the technically advanced Morlocks dragging them down to a horrific, subterranean fate. His father read in this story a parable about revolution and class warfare. But for Avi, now, it had taken on an additional, grisly reality.

A gear-change in the helicopter, betrayed by a slight shift in the ceaseless rumble of its engines, indicated that they were about to land at the desert air base, and de Bonnard's *Prêtres du Sable* would take their first steps on what everyone hoped they'd regard as hallowed soil. But even in the hot Negev sunshine, Avi felt his blood run thick and chill.

-=0=-

To be continued in SCOURGE OF STARS, Book Two of The Sigil...

ABOUT THE AUTHOR

Author Photo by John Gilbey

Henry Gee was born in London in 1962. He received his B.Sc. in Zoology and Genetics from the University of Leeds, and his Ph.D. in Zoology from the University of Cambridge. Since 1987 he has been on the editorial staff of *Nature*, the international weekly science magazine, where he is now Senior Editor of Biological Sciences, and was the founding editor of *Futures*, *Nature*'s award-winning SF column.

He is the author of several works of nonfiction including *The Science of Middle-earth*, *In Search of Deep Time* and *Jacob's Ladder*, and a novel, *By The Sea*.

He lives in Cromer, Norfolk, England, with his family and numerous pets.

ReAnimus Press
Breathing Life into Great Books

If you enjoyed this book we hope you'll tell others or write a review! We also invite you to subscribe to our newsletter to learn about our new releases and join our affiliate program (where you earn 12% of sales you recommend) at
www.ReAnimus.com.

Here are some ebooks you'll enjoy from ReAnimus Press, available from ReAnimus Press's web site, Amazon.com, bn.com, etc.:

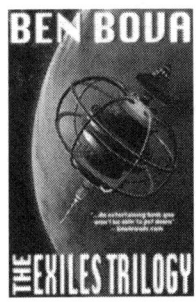

The Exiles Trilogy, by Ben Bova

The Star Conquerors, by Ben Bova
(Standard Edition and
Special Collector's Edition)

Test of Fire, by Ben Bova

The Kinsman Saga, by Ben Bova

The Craft of Writing Science Fiction that Sells, by Ben Bova

Staying Alive - A Writer's Guide,
by Norman Spinrad

Space Travel — A Guide for Writers,
by Ben Bova

Shadrach in the Furnace,
by Robert Silverberg

The Transcendent Man, by Jerry Sohl

Night Slaves, by Jerry Sohl

Bloom, by Wil McCarthy

Aggressor Six, by Wil McCarthy

Murder in the Solid State,
by Wil McCarthy

Flies from the Amber, by Wil McCarthy

Side Effects, by Harvey Jacobs

American Goliath, by Harvey Jacobs

"An inspired novel" – *TIME Magazine*
"A masterpiece…arguably this year's best novel" – *Kirkus Reviews*

Coming very soon from ReAnimus Press:

Books 2 and 3 of The Sigil Trilogy,
by (*Nature* editor) Henry Gee

"I got so engrossed in it that I could not put it down." — *bestselling author Lee Gimenez*

Watch for these and many more great titles from ReAnimus Press!

Made in the USA
San Bernardino, CA
20 June 2018